To James,
with

THE
FALKLANDS
INTERCEPT

a novel

Crispin Black

Crispin Black
Nov 2012

GIBSON SQUARE

First edition published in the UK by Gibson Square

info@gibsonsquare.com
www.gibsonsquare.com
Tel: +44 (0)20 7096 1100 (UK)
Tel: +1 646 216 9813 (USA)
Tel: +353 (0)1 657 1057 (Eire)

ISBN   9781908096388

Printed and bound by CPI Group (UK) Ltd, Croydon, CR0 4YY

For my mother and father,
with love

I

The blood-red balls, symbols of the Medici, shone against the gilt background of the candle-filled sconces, the only source of light in the Fellows' Combination Room of St James'. They had been a gift from James I to commemorate the engagement of his ill-fated son Charles to Henrietta Maria of France. The French ambassador had arrived with the assent of Louis XIII while the court was lodged at the college. The sconces bore the arms of the college, the scallop shell of St James impaled on those of Henrietta Maria, the Fleur de Lys of the Capets and the six blood-red balls of her Medici ancestors against a gold background. A High Anglican foundation in a city of Puritans, the sconces had been hidden from Cromwell's men. At the Restoration Henrietta Maria had lavished money and property on the college. The High Anglicanism remained with choir services of glorious musicality. But so did the secrecy, intrigue and devotion to worldly pleasures. It was appropriate that the arms of a Medici princess whose father was assassinated, whose husband was beheaded and whose mother was widely suspected of poisoning and sorcery should adorn the college's walls and stained glass.

General Sir Christopher Verney drank off his glass of champagne ice cold and popped a small piece of rye bread into his mouth – it was deliciously covered with smoked salmon and a little soured cream. He thought what a splendid way to begin a meal. Recently promoted full general and appointed Chief of Defence Intelligence, chosen personally by the prime minister over strong competition from the navy and air force, his life was going through that period of achieved sweetness so similar for many to its earlier more vigorous counterpart – the sweetness of youth. Already professionally successful, tonight marked a personal fulfilment as well for Verney. He was in Cambridge to give the biennial St James lecture. Endowed by Charles II to please his mother it was designed for a distinguished individual to tell of his work and travels in far-off lands. Verney had come to lecture on Scott's 1912 expedition to the South Pole.

While serving as a staff officer in the Falklands War thirty years previously the region had cast its spell on him as on so many Englishmen before. Curiously, the Falklands are the same distance from the South Pole as London is from the North Pole. But the call of the South was strong. Standing as a young man on the windswept hills outside Stanley, overlooking the stormy Drake Passage, it seemed to him as if Antarctica was only a few steps away. Since then Verney had eschewed the normal pleasures of an ambitious army officer like polo and rugby and devoted his spare time to the history of Antarctic exploration, Captain Scott especially. Every detail of both of Scott's expeditions fascinated him. The details of Scott's arrival at the South Pole – the navigation, the equipment, the food and most of all the personalities were almost an obsession.

The caressing shadows of the candles and silver on the

long highly polished oak table framed the general's face. He looked what he was – a highly intelligent, experienced and decisive military man, current guardian of the British military's innermost secrets and instigator of its clandestine operations. He was chain-smoking as usual. But the clouds of smoke could not hide the restlessness and wariness behind the almost Roman exterior. He looked every inch the part, but not as though he was among friends. A tall figure in a scarlet tailcoat emblazoned with flat silver buttons approached Verney with a tray.

'Calvados, please.' Verney wasn't good at dealing with servants. A basic insecurity prevented him from being anything other than off-hand. But this was the Fellows' Butler – most senior servant of a very rich college. In scarlet college livery and wearing his campaign medals – the South Atlantic Medal in pride of place. Verney had visited Cambridge a good deal over the last few years but he belonged to a different, less grand college. This was only the second time he had dined at St James'. The first time had been a quiet weekend supper to which his research assistant Charlotte Pirbright who was a fellow of the college had invited him. It had been fun and the food and wine delicious but not quite on the scale of this feast, and the Fellows' Butler had not been in attendance – he would have noticed the medal. They had both been part of *Operation Corporate,* the codename for the operation to recapture the Falklands, and Verney felt a strong bond with his fellow veterans. The general smiled. 'I see you are a Falklands Veteran.'

'Yes, General. Colour Sergeant Jones 74, Celtic Guards.'

Like all soldiers called Jones or Williams in regiments with large numbers of Welshmen Mr Jones was often addressed by the last two digits of his army number. The practice was surrounded by a difficult and nuanced etiquette. Young officers rarely addressed even their own non-commissioned officers with their numbers unless they were asked to. It was a weird Welsh form of the French process of "tutoyer". For Jones to introduce himself to a general officer in this way was a sign of great respect.

A large, taciturn but cheery Welshman "74" smiled and poured out a glass of Calvados from the college's own estate in Normandy. General Verney smiled in response, almost as if he were a priest bestowing a blessing, and drank. Mr Jones smiled back, nodded his head slightly and moved to the next guest. He had a low opinion of many senior officers but this one was a Falklands veteran and deserved his respect. Jones still bore the physical scars of the conflict – small pieces of shrapnel from the Exocet missile detonated on the crowded decks of the landing ship they had found themselves on. He had been lucky not to lose a leg and on the coldest, dampest days of the bleak Cambridge winters when his old wounds played up he could be seen limping through the frosty courts of the college.

And sometimes still, at Christmas and on the Falklands anniversaries his brother's voice would come in the night. His brother Bryn. His younger brother. Mam had been so proud when he too had joined the army. There wasn't much money and Mam was strict and religious – but she loved them. As the band played Auld Lang Syne on the quayside at Southampton he had promised her he would look after Bryn. And Bryn had laughed. The golden laugh of a boy going off to war – confident in himself and his friends – and his cause. In the care of his older brother. And sometimes still, Bryn's screams would come. No one dies quickly burning to death in the bowels of a landing ship. They could not get to him and the others. The heat was too intense and the stacked mortar ammunition was "cooking off" in the fire. But they could hear them dying – screaming for help. And he heard Bryn, screaming for him in Welsh. Just behind a twisted and jammed steel door. The left side of Jones' body showed more scars – in a final frenzy of effort he had tried to force the jammed door open. Every ounce of maddened strength hammering on the red-hot door with his broad shoulders. Bryn was inches away. But they had to go or die themselves. Jones had his own men to rescue. And there was shame in it.

The terrible irony was that Bryn shouldn't even have been on the ship. He had been despatched the previous day on a tractor and trailer carrying mortars and ammunition, but some useless officer had turned them back. It would have been a bumpy and unpleasant ride over the hills surrounding the landing beaches but better, far better than the death sentence of sitting on ammunition boxes in the bowels of a landing ship. Even if Argentine aircraft had attacked the ramshackle convoy at least Bryn would have had a chance. At the very least he would have died in the open. Jones brought his mind back to the present.

The next guest was a young lady don – Charlotte Pirbright. Jones smiled again. He took a strong interest in the younger fellows of the college. Pirbright was the proverbial English rose – an Antarctic historian by profession, originally from Oxford. If you took messages or parcels to her rooms as

Jones occasionally did you could hardly miss the dark Oxford blue dominating the decoration. She was one of the prettiest girls ever to grace the college. The candlelight and the cloak-like effect of her black Oxford Master's gown made her look magnificent. Jones liked her and admired her looks – as did many of the sets of eyes in the room, both male and female, that flickered in her direction from time to time. In others she aroused stronger feelings. Jones had heard that she did most of the work for General Verney although his sources suggested that they were not 'stepping out' or 'courting' as these things were still referred to in parts of Wales.

There can be few more glorious and worldly pleasures than dining at the high table of a wealthy Cambridge college. The night before the St James lecture was by tradition a feast with all manner of food and drink brought in from the college's estates across Europe. Vintage champagne – the dons of St James' liked it a degree or two above freezing – and the setting of Cambridge normally set off a crackling atmosphere as distinguished guests mixed with the stars of the academic firmament.

But not tonight. Mouths smiled but many eyes barely concealed nervousness and distrust. The great and the good of the Western intelligence elite were all gathered in one place. In addition to the heads of the London Stations of the major Western agencies – a number of senior officials from both the CIA and Mossad had flown in for the occasion. Security ministers from the British government were also in attendance accompanied by "C", the head of MI6, and the Director Generals of MI5 and GCHQ. Armed security was tight. They should have been able to relax. Men and women with nerves strong enough to order assassinations and look a Doomsday scenario in the eye without flinching seemed nervous. Most of them knew General Verney professionally. Most knew that he was to speak on some sensational new research about Captain Scott. So far, so good. They knew also that in the morning he would make some remarks about the state of the Western intelligence effort in Iran. On this they were less sure. It was a Monday night away from the office – time to relax. The next day would be the 100th anniversary of Scott's arrival at the Pole. But the senior British officials would be hard at work back in Whitehall as soon as the lecture had finished in the morning. The prime minister had called a conference on Iran for the Thursday and there was work to do. It would rely heavily on an intelligence assessment currently before the Joint Intelligence Committee. In the usual Whitehall way the intelligence picture had been massaged so that the prime minister would be given the feeling that he was being presented with options. To the military and the intelligence establishment there was only one option – to stick with the Americans all the way.

'General.'

'Master?' Verney was alert.

'We wait with bated breath to hear your views on Captain Scott – although to be frank I am surprised that there is much new to say.'

'Master I mustn't give too much away but I think I am right in saying that no one with an intelligence background has ever tested the various accounts of the expedition, or Amundsen's for that matter.'

'What do you mean?'

'Well, Scott's account quickly passed into legend. There has been some debunking of Scott as a heroic figure. Chippy most of it. And his critics have tended to build up Shackleton at his expense, famously making him a role model for pre-credit crunch Wall Street if you remember. Amundsen benefited from this as well. Amundsen the Norwegian hero from a humble background versus Scott, pillar of the Edwardian establishment. Amundsen a hero and the consummate professional. Scott an incompetent amateur. The modern explorer Ranulph Fiennes tried a rehab job in his great biography but the debunkers are back in time for the hundredth anniversary.'

'But this is really a cultural and literary matter – not hard science.'

'Well up to a point I would agree.' Verney lit another cigarette. 'But it is more than that. No one has ever carried out a close reading of Amundsen's diaries in a hardheaded historical way. This is what he was saying about an individual, say, or the weather on this particular day and then comparing it with what we know from other sources. Tricky I know on a small expedition but nevertheless it has never been done. Even more importantly, no one has ever tested Amundsen's navigational calculations. He and Scott appear to have gone to the same place but it wasn't like Everest – you know you are at the top because there is nothing else above you. And you can photograph yourself with other peaks in the background which prove that you made it. Both Amundsen and Scott thought they had made it but how do we know?'

'Yes, I see what you mean. Interesting stuff Verney and I am sure the audience will be fascinated tomorrow.'

'General, long time no see.' A tall and dapper American

leaned across the table to address Verney.

'Well, Mr. Dixwell, indeed. Master, this is Mr. John Dixwell the head of the CIA's London Station.'

'Oh yes, very good to meet you. You are always welcome in this college Mr. Dixwell if you are a spy. Sixty years ago Bletchley Park and St James' College were practically the same thing – although I do hope our food was better than theirs, even in wartime. When I arrived here as a young don in the 1960s there were senior members trying to recruit me every night into the intelligence services. I have to say though that we are proud that none of the so-called "Cambridge Spies" came from this college. We prefer to call them the "Trinity Spies" after our large next door neighbour that educated most of them.'

A ripple of polite laughter went up the table in response to the master's anti-Trinity quip. Learned heads were thrown back and sips of wine taken. The effect was like an elegant and donnish Mexican wave.

Dixwell smiled. 'You were optimists then, Master. The guys at Bletchley had a can-do attitude. I hope it's the same these days. What do you think General?'

Verney smiled back in the candlelight. Their man in London was trying to wind him up. 'Well, Mr. Dixwell and Master it is no secret that my views on dealing with an Iranian nuclear weapon have begun to diverge from Washington's. I suppose not being the people in charge means we have the privilege of being able to change our minds.'

'But not if you want to keep the Special Relationship going', Dixwell shot back. 'Sorry, I meant the Essential Relationship. It would be easy. A couple of big bangs and the mullahs would be without their bomb for a few more years. We've got the intelligence and we've got the weapons.'

It was a good-natured exchange fuelled by the college's extraordinarily good claret. The Master looked indulgently on. This kind of debate was what a college's high table was for.

'I think that's slightly unfair', Verney retorted, 'perhaps you are too easily influenced by some of your other allies.'

Dixwell turned to the Master. 'The problem with the good general is that he likes to pretend that things can't work when they can.'

Mr. Jones hovered nearby, refilled both their glasses and began to move away.

Dixwell looked directly at Verney. 'Under the fancy coats of arms that you Brits like to indulge in you have mottos in Latin. Maybe General Verney's should be on the lines of "It does work but why don't we just make it look as if the thing has broken down."' Dixwell laughed.

Jones was still within earshot just. He stood absolutely still. The head turned slowly and he looked back at the general. As the head turned Jones' smile was gone. The usually kindly face wore an expression of hatred, pure full-on, outraged high-octane hatred – sharp and strong at first but then with a moment of confusion. The eyes blazed in barely controlled fury. Luckily no one could see Jones – it was frightening, as if he was having a fit. Then the face reposed once again, like a clown changing expressions, as he served the next guest.

Verney laughed too. The Master laughed but felt uncomfortable, although he could not work out why. The jibe was perfectly within the bounds of civilised conversation, even if Dixwell's aura of triumph, "Gotcha" he believed the Americans called it, did seem over the top. Verney reached for his glass. His hand was shaking.

'Rather a lot of Americans here tonight don't you think? Time I think for some port.' With that the Master pushed back his chair.

The Jamesian dons and their guests took their cue from the Master. They got up together gowns flapping and processed to the other end of the college's Combination Room to drink port.

II

The prime minister's morning intelligence report was due with the duty private secretary by eight o'clock. It was not yet dawn. But behind Gibbs's 18th-century façade at 70 Whitehall and the guarded, bulletproof entrance, the second floor of the Cabinet Office was already busy. Colonel Daniel Jacot had been working half the night to make sense of over 100 separate intercepts and intelligence reports on the situation in Iran. The scarlet Cabinet Office folders bulged. But he had reduced the thousands of words to a side and a half. Really, couldn't these politicians follow a complex story? Jacot was a soldier on secondment to the senior civil service. His passion for accuracy, attention to detail and critical judgment made him the ideal intelligence analyst. Immaculately turned out as was expected of a Guards officer, he wore plain and severely cut suits always in dark blue or dark grey. His highly polished black shoes made his colleagues feel underdressed.

Jacot also wore gloves – all the time. They covered his hands badly burned thirty years before during the Falklands War. The skin grafts taken from his thighs had worked well over the years but had a different tone and texture from the remaining original skin on his hands. The tips of some of the fingers were missing – burned through. Jacot had never minded their gnarled and blotchy appearance but as he grew older the skin scratched easily and the fingers ached after hours typing at a computer. The cool silk of the gloves soothed and protected. Usually black but occasionally, for fun, Jacot would wear brighter patterns and colours often given to him by friends and relatives. At least he never got socks for Christmas.

The pale blue eyes had a steadiness and clarity that many found reassuring. Towards the end of the day Jacot sometimes had an air of melancholy softening his brisk and military manner. The vulnerability this revealed was attractive to women – not that Jacot understood this for a moment.

He pressed the speed dial key on his secure phone connecting him with the duty CIA desk in the complex below the White House. Although the middle of the night in Washington his American colleagues, some he counted as friends, would be working on the PDB, The President's Daily Briefing. Most of the intelligence on the Middle East was shared – by official diktat. Slightly unfairly in Jacot's view since much of it was actually acquired by the British in the first place. But he for the most part liked and admired his American colleagues. All of them were highly patriotic. Most of them believed in a 'Higher power called Washington'.

'Wendy. How are you? It's Daniel. You sound exhausted.'

'Yeah. These presidential briefings can be a pain.'

'But I thought you liked Obama. And at least you get to see him. We are kept away.'

'It's not the President. It's the Veep, Biden. He goes to the eight o' clock briefing in the White House but we have to brief him on his own at 0630hrs and then one of us goes with him in the car in case of last minute developments. He's a nicer man one to one than you might believe but I can't brief him in a dressing gown. And the full Stepford-Wife-look that the White House prefers is costing me a fortune. Still, only a month to go and I think he rates me so it will be good for the future.'

'Any developments in Iran?' asked Jacot.

'Nope. Not in the last 48 hours. Satellites not showing much. NSA not picking up anything other than routine messages but Iranian communications security is good. So all we will have is political developments.'

Jacot could not resist. 'Wendy I am not sure that's quite right. We reckon there might be some Revolutionary Guards on the move.'

'Daniel. Don't mess around, the whole region is close to meltdown.'

It was always fun teasing the all-knowing American intelligence people. 'Easy Wendy. It's just that for the first time since the mullahs took over the Revolutionary Guards have cancelled their annual party. No booze, no pretty girls but still a big shindig.'

'Dan, for goodness sake. Our billion dollar satellites and eavesdroppers are telling us that at least for the next twenty four hours no major units of the Revolutionary Guards are likely to be on the move – so that's it. What's that Brit saying you taught me, "Brains of an Archbishop"? Yeah. It doesn't take the brains of an archbishop to work out that the intelligence might of Uncle Sam is heavily focused currently on the guys with beards who guard what may or may not be their nukes. What is it with you people?'

'Wendy, I'm not saying that our bearded chums are moving to a launch position or anything like that. Maybe they are up to something defensive. Their boss did after all get blown up a couple of months back in what the official news agency called 'an unfortunate ammunition accident.' All I am saying is that they have cancelled a feast. It's like the Irish cancelling St Patrick's Day. Therefore, it seems likely that these guys have something going down. Never mind that your billion dollar gizmos are suggesting all is well.'

'A cancelled feast! Daniel, get real.'

Satellites and eavesdropping were one thing. But even with those you had to look for the clues. Iranian signals discipline was good. It was difficult to break into their command and control systems and even if you got in the messages were highly encrypted. If you couldn't break into the centre you had to prowl the periphery – like finding out someone had cancelled a party.

'Well there you go Wendy. And yes, you can call Mossad. You were going to anyway.'

Wendy rang off. The intelligence was reliable and would certainly enhance Wendy's status with the Vice President. Jacot would send a written version to Langley later with the source details well disguised. You scratch my back. I'll scratch yours.

Jacot typed the last line, gathered up the key supporting documents and marched along the corridor connecting the Cabinet Office to Number 10. He was heading for the National Security Adviser's office. A senior civil servant, she was the official who delivered the daily intelligence briefing to the prime minister. She never took anyone with her.

Held firmly in his hand was a Cabinet Office scarlet leather folder. It was a beautiful thing. Embossed with the royal arms and the classification in gold – Top Secret Cabinet Joint Intelligence Committee. It contained the fruits of Jacot's overnight labours entitled: "Immediate Assessment – Middle East overnight." The National Security Adviser, Lady Nevinson, would brief the prime minister in a few minutes. On her return she would make a few changes and then instruct Jacot to issue it. Emissaries from ministerial private offices across Whitehall and the intelligence agencies would then pick up their paper copies.

'Come in Jacot. Sit down.'

Celia Nevinson was the classic English diplomat. Understated, beautifully turned out, with a dry sense of humour and a formidable brain. She had been brought in to restore credibility to the centralized government intelligence machinery after the intelligence fiascos of the middle Blair years. Contrary to expectations, she had proved a grand success managing to clean up the system without putting too many noses out of joint. When the Coalition Government limped into power she became the first National Security Adviser. Jacot was privately amazed that she had managed to last as long as she had, but she exploited the insecurities of the new government to imprint her personality and methods on the collection, analysis and dissemination of intelligence.

She was more of a sceptic than the spies were used to, and openly boasted in the presence of senior spies of various types that she had never seen a Bond film or watched what she called 'That ridiculous television programme, *Spooks*'. For a woman in her early 60s this seemed unlikely. Rather healthily, she regarded spying as a below stairs activity and assessed intelligence as a useful guide rather than holy writ. It wasn't clear where she stood on politicians. But whereas her predecessors had returned from their morning meetings in the prime minister's 'den' charmed, stimulated and exalted by their closeness to power, Nevinson usually looked as if she could do with a stiff drink. She conceded that the public school manners of the Coalition Government were an improvement on the blokeish paranoia of the previous regime but you could tell that she did not really like professional politicians. While she believed passionately that she should serve whatever ministers had been put in place by the electoral process it did not mean she had to admire them. If you came to see her late in the evening she would often have a glass of whisky on her desk and sometimes offered her subordinates one if something that day had especially pleased or amused her. It was rather good whisky Jacot reckoned – smokey and peaty. He always accepted a glass if she offered but he preferred white burgundy or gin.

She looked just a little bit harassed, if not hungover. She barely glanced at the briefing on the Middle East. But then she had been reading intelligence reports for over thirty years. 'OK, so no major developments on this front but a question mark over some especially unsavoury group of the Iranian Revolutionary Guards. A seedy and unattractive looking bunch those Iranian leaders. No doubt the PM is ordering what is left of the RAF into the air as we speak. Come to think of it, it's the deputy prime minister this morning. Do you know some of his advisers really do wear shoes shaped like Cornish pasties? What a treat. But don't go. I have a late breakfast at the Travellers' Club. My guess is the security people would agree to me being walked across the park by a Guards officer and I'll buy you coffee.'

The voice remained casual but the pale green eyes focused on Jacot and were deadly serious.

'Yes, of course, Lady Nevinson. I'll meet you at the back door after your briefing.'

Forty-five minutes later they met at the back door of the Cabinet Office and walked along Downing Street towards Horse Guards Parade. Something generations of Londoners had been allowed to do until the IRA security alerts of the early Nineties. The armed policemen at the door of number 10 acknowledged Nevinson as she passed and went down the steps just by Lord Mountbatten's statue. It was a cold morning. The threat of rain meant fewer tourists and it was still early. Nevinson did not speak. In the middle of St James' Park she looked around as if nervous of being followed.

'What does the word Magenta mean to you?'

'Nothing really. Ask me one on sport or pass are the appropriate answers.' Jacot could not see her face but sensed that she was not smiling.

'I have had complaints about you.'

'Really?'

'Yes. From the US Embassy and from the deputy head of the CIA.'

'But I get on well with our American friends and...'

'Yes. I know. You are friendly with a number of their analysts. James there isn't much I don't know about you.'

'It's not that I dislike Americans at all – I have American relatives. But what I cannot stand is this idea that their interests are the same as our interests. And while I enjoy socializing with the CIA I cannot bear the endless kowtowing that seems to have to go on with them. It's all right at our level. But the higher up you go the more obvious and ridiculous it gets. That JIC meeting last week with "C" getting hysterical because you chopped out some precious piece of US intelligence from a paper on the Middle East. The CIA had gracefully passed to us what appeared to be the views of someone close to the Iranian leadership but it had Mossad all over it. Doesn't mean it was wrong but shall we say "Designed to influence as well as inform". And the meetings on Afghanistan make me weep. We have got soldiers dying there. Do we get any credit for that?'

'Daniel calm down. I am not walking across the park with you to give you a dressing down. I know how you and some others feel. I need your help.'

'You can get a grip of the Joint Intelligence Organisation for a start.'

'Come on Daniel. It's not that simple. Listen, I need your help. As I said before what does the word Magenta mean to you?'

'Nothing. No, I tell a lie. I think the sporting colours of my house at school were magenta and silver. We were rather successful I remember.'

Nevinson laughed. 'Some Englishmen never become old boys of their schools. It's as if they are stuck there forever.' Her smile faded. 'This is not schoolboy stuff Jacot I am afraid. Magenta is the codeword we use for a small group of people within the intelligence establishment who, shall we say, have secrets to keep from the Americans. It also applies to the special communications arrangements those people have to use.'

'You're joking of course?'

'No. And I want you to be part of the group. It's small for now anyway but all of us are absolutely on side.'

'Who else?'

'Never mind. Not yet. We are not big enough. Well here we are at the Travellers'. I don't think there's time for coffee. I will give you a cup in my office when I get back.' She turned and walked up the steps into the Travellers' Club.

Jacot was stunned as he made his way back to the office across the park and busied himself with reading a Foreign Office report on the ins and outs of Shia Islam, particularly as it affected Iranian politics. It was a long document, profusely and beautifully illustrated. The ranks, views and factions of the Shia clergy in Iran were fascinating. It was a shame Anthony Trollope's clerical novels had been confined to Barchester. But the Foreign Office had made a good effort. Background reading was essential in the intelligence business and Jacot was absorbed for nearly an hour and a half. His mind was far away in the Middle East listening to the Muezzin's call and the gentle clacking of prayer beads when the intercom on his desk buzzed. His presence was required by Lady Nevinson – probably a few routine details needed changing in the morning report.

She looked up at him as he went into her office. 'The Chief of Defence Intelligence, General Verney is dead.'

'You're joking.'

'No. Found early this morning in a guest room at St James' College, Cambridge. Looks like a heart attack. News embargo for now but it will become public soon.'

'How awful.' Jacot was genuinely shocked. But after nearly a month working on the Middle East 18 hours a day he was looking forward to going on leave that afternoon.

'I was due to go up to Cambridge today for his lecture. The car is ready outside. I last saw him at the Joint Intelligence Committee meeting last Wednesday. He was grumpy and agitated. He emailed me yesterday asking for a private chat on a matter of some urgency – using a private and unbreakable cipher. And now he's dead.'

'Well, Lady Nevinson. Maybe it was his heart making him uncomfortable. He never stopped smoking.'

'I need you go to Cambridge. Now, this morning. St James' is your old college isn't it? I have rung the Master.' Celia Nevinson was used to ordering men around. Most took it fairly well. Jacot never had a problem with her. She was clever, charming (when she wanted to be) and attractive in an English house-master's wife sort of way. But there was something strange. Her eyes contained only authority and the voice sounded confident. The hands drummed on the scarlet folder on the desk. Usually a sign of impatience, something about the rhythm suggested fear.

'Get down there or up there or whatever it is these days, Jacot. Find out what happened. I am convinced it was a heart attack but we need to be sure. Anyway he wasn't in a bag or anything like that. Thank God. Poor man. I have already issued some instructions as you might expect. The Cambridge Police are handling the investigation. Because of who Verney was there will also be a Military Police detachment in attendance. There will be no, I repeat no, intelligence people there.

None of the agencies and no military intelligence, except for you. We have had enough trouble recently, with code-breakers being found in suspicious circumstances, and then the cloak and dagger adolescents muddying the waters. If you see anyone you don't like the look of get the Cambridge Police to arrest them and let me know. Anyone under military discipline deal with yourself and hand over to the Military Police. Is that clear Colonel?'

'Yes, Lady Nevinson.' Jacot felt a surge of excitement. She was clearly on a roll. It would mean foregoing a bit of his leave but it would be refreshing to get involved in something practical. Analysing secret intelligence had its own intellectual satisfactions, but even in a crisis-ridden world it was a bit like playing chess all day, every day. Ferreting around Cambridge as the National Security Adviser's emissary would be interesting.

'I'll expect you back here whenever you have anything to report. The trains only take fifty minutes these days and my driver will pick you up at King's Cross. If you need to discuss anything sensitive in a hurry, ring me on your encrypted mobile phone. I will issue you with the Magenta bits and pieces in the car. If you run into trouble there's an emergency number to ring just in case. You are not to discuss this matter with anyone else – no one. Do you understand? I will brief the prime minister if necessary. Come on I will come with you to King's Cross Station.' She smiled wearily.

The staccato bureaucratic clarity softened the instruction and its implications. But the thrust was clear. Jacot was essentially to investigate the death of the most senior military intelligence official in the country and report on any developments personally – not to the police, not even to the heads of the UK's Intelligence services, not to Number 10 but to the National Security Adviser only. He was on his own.

III

St James' College, Cambridge
— Tuesday 17th January 2012

Jacot got off the train at Cambridge station. Arriving in the university town always lifted his spirits and he cheerily hailed a taxi to St James'. It was an extraordinary place. As the taxi moved through the cold and rainy streets he mused on what had been discovered in this small damp Fenland town. Within a hundred yards or so, the length of an obscure street called Free School Lane, most of the key discoveries of the modern world had been made. At one end of the lane stood the Cavendish Laboratory where Lord Rutherford and his team had first split the atom. Half way down, the building blocks of life, DNA, had been discovered by Watson and Crick, in of all places a pub – The Eagle much beloved during the war by American bomber crews based nearby who came into town to let off steam after their daring daylight raids over Germany. Given the almost fifty per cent casualty rate they deserved a good time. Some even signed up for courses at the university and a few managed to stay on at the end of the war.

At the bottom of the lane was the entrance to King's College where a young don, Alan Turing, later to become a brilliant cryptologist at Bletchley Park, had written his famous paper *On Computable Numbers*, laying the theoretical ground-work for the entire computer age and more immediately the defeat of Nazi Germany. It was a source of great pride to the university and of chagrin to its rival which lay somewhere to the west of London. And of course the Americans were so put out by these extraordinary achievements that they cheerfully pretended they were their own. But that was enough pleasurable musing. He might find time for a pint in The Eagle at some point but he was here on business – an unexplained death of the head of British military intelligence.

He looked up at the glorious gateway of the college with its huge gilded scallop shell, symbol of St James, glistening in the sunlight. A friendly porter in a dark blue bowler hat emerged, explained to Jacot where he would be staying and grabbed his suitcase. Jacot would settle himself in later. First, he had a body to attend to. He walked through the First Court towards Medici Court which lay next to the river. Verney's rooms were just to the left of the Bridge of Sorrows which straddled the river Cam connecting the two sides of the college. At first sight it could have been the scene of any suspicious death, much rarer in the ancient English university towns than the television would have us believe – except that alongside the blue and the curiously comforting roman hats of the Cambridgeshire Constabulary were, as promised by Lady Nevinson, the scarlet slashed peak caps of the Royal Military Police. One of the British Army's most senior officers had died very suddenly in unexplained circumstances. It was only right that they should be there.

He recognised a major from the Special Investigations Branch of the RMP, the people who investigated real crimes, rather than the more run of the mill pub brawls that characterised most modern garrison towns.

The military police major looked hassled. 'Redcaps', as the

rank and file knew them, were never quite comfortable being questioned about their activities. Disliked by most of the junior ranks in the army they had a thankless task. Most soldiers had had a run in with them at some point in their career. Jacot remembered being arrested by a detachment on Cyprus. He and some friends were enthusiastically attending a wine festival officially "Out of Bounds to Troops". He shouldn't have been there and it was fair enough that the Cypriots did not want their festivals overwhelmed by refreshed British soldiers, even young Foot Guards officers. But the military policemen who had rounded them up and returned them to their base, and extended periods of extra-duties as a result, seemed a little officious. This time round Jacot was certainly pleased to see them. To a man they were trained in observation skills and more importantly for his present purposes to brief succinctly.

'I am Colonel Jacot from the National Security Adviser's office.' He flashed his military identity card. 'What happened?'

'Found about eight o' clock this morning. Both doors to his rooms locked from the inside and a small chock inserted beneath the inner door. Standard security at night for someone like that I suppose. Somebody called the Fellows' Butler, whatever that is, took him up his breakfast just after eight. No reply to the knocking. Door appeared to be locked and bolted. In the end this butler type and the head porter broke down the door. And there he was, lying dead in his bed. No blood. No signs of a struggle. No cyanide fumes. No gas. No poisonous snake slithering into the pantry. No weird stuff either – wigs or high heels like that case in London a couple of years back. Thank God. All the windows of the set of rooms overlook the river. No way in. No way out. Not formally identified yet but almost certainly General Verney the current Chief of Defence Intelligence. Body about to be taken away for a post mortem. I was despatched down here by the Provost Marshal no less, who also told me to expect you sir. Seems to be a big flap on – more than just about a dead general I would say. That's all I can tell you Colonel. We await the post mortem.'

'Has anyone been inside?'

'I doubt it. Only the people that found the body and the local police. The nearest Provost detachment is in Wisbech and we had a car here just a few minutes after the Cambridge Police. And the Provost Marshal's orders were absolutely specific about keeping people out.'

'Can I see the body? I used to know him.'

It was Verney all right. Lying under a duvet drawn taught as if for an inspection at Sandhurst. It looked as though he had died in his sleep. The set of the face itself was peaceful, like someone's grandfather dying at the end of a long life in a rather nice room overlooking the River Cam. Jacot moved on from the body inspecting the room itself. He glanced around for a quick first impression and then divided the room into segments in his mind and inspected each one in turn, in detail. He began with the windows overlooking the river – mullioned, as you would expect. They might even have been the originals when this part of the college was built in 1560. Like those dark and tragic chambers at the Tower of London there were letters scratched into the glass. Jacot could see a number of scallop shells scratched into the central window and, as was well-known to just about everyone in the college over the years, the initials "WS" in 17th-century script. No one knew who WS might have been and despite the best efforts of some very clever History and English dons there was no record of a William Shakespeare ever being put up in the college, let alone matriculating there. What a prize that would have been if the great poet and dramatist William Shakespeare himself had been a Jamesian. The truth of it was that these were casual graffiti – the equivalent of "Kilroy woz here" or "Chris fancies Carol" rather than cryptic messages from the past.

One window was open but the set of rooms was on the second floor overlooking the river. Access to the windows from below would have been challenging for a Himalayan climber and impossible to accomplish without equipment or without being seen. The façade of this bit of the college was floodlit till quite late. In theory someone could have abseiled down from the roof. Again difficult to do without being seen but Jacot decided he would go up on the roof later. Dangling ropes digging into 17th-century brickwork would surely leave behind some kind of trace, but it was a long shot.

Jacot stood for several minutes looking at the room wall by wall, his head turning slowly. He repeated the process a second time, the head moving slowly and methodically and his gloved hands flexing and un-flexing as he reached a peak of concentration. At the end he stood perfectly still for a moment and then walked through to the sitting room. Painted in white and gold – and hung with pictures of 18th-century Cambridge – it was a beautiful room befitting a distinguished and honoured guest. The bookshelves were stacked with standard editions of the great works bound in striking scarlet leather. The rooms were a kind of Don's dream – the ideal space in which to study, entertain and hold forth – the essence of the Cambridge spirit. A devout man, at least a man devout in the Jamesian style could study and devote himself to God in such a set of rooms. And live well too. Wasn't an elegant and civilised life a compliment to the Creator? A sceptic would find the rooms a validation of cool rationality and a comfortable setting in which to undertake academic investigation before the darkness closed in forever. Jacot doubted whether Verney had been a religious man. Like his hero Captain Scott maybe he just took things as they came and sought what comfort there was in a contingent universe by relying on himself. Perhaps his religion was himself and his career – it seemed a popular if ultimately depressing philosophy these days. Somewhere in that glittering career there must be something, thought Jacot, that could explain Verney's sudden death – even if it was only the smoking.

Jacot returned to the bottom of the staircase and the military police who were already becoming convinced that the whole thing was due to natural causes – middle aged men died suddenly in their beds with great regularity despite modern medicine and diagnostics. They also died at moments that could be very convenient for some of those left behind. John Smith and Robin Cook sprung to mind but no one would suggest that in a modern country like Britain there could have been anything untoward. Indeed not. And Jacot would be very surprised if the post mortem showed anything unusual or remotely suspicious.

But something wasn't quite right. The college wasn't full of shifty characters straight out of central casting who would not look him in the eye. At first sight the most likely explanation seemed to be the most innocent. But the atmosphere was somehow wrong. It was as if the walls themselves of these beautiful Elizabethan and Jacobean buildings had suspicions. It was hard to put your finger on but he had seen and felt it before. On the Falls Road in West Belfast many years before, when just after a soldier had been shot by the IRA everyone was polite and a little wary as you might expect. But no one had seen anything. Just as in a Hammer Horror film when everyone but the luckless late arrival at the Transylvanian inn knows that it's not a good idea to go up to the castle late at night during a full moon, but no one dares say anything or even wants to.

But we should be grateful at least, thought Jacot, for some small mercies. Individuals important to the state and/or privy to its secrets had on occasion died suddenly in more embarrassing and distressing ways than this. At least Verney hadn't keeled over in a brothel or in the arms of a young girlfriend. Such circumstances were difficult to manage in the modern world. It should be possible to establish what exactly happened away from the public eye – less stressful for Verney's family and friends and much less stressful for the secret parts of the British state.

The military policeman was hovering. 'But what if I may ask is a gentleman like you doing down here and why the flap? He was in his late fifties – it's a peak time for middle-aged men.'

Jacot smiled. 'We shall see.' He turned away and walked north across the court to the rooms he would be staying in. He had acquired all the information he needed, for now. The body had been positively identified. The military police were unsuspicious. Nevertheless, it was clear from Lady Nevinson's briefing that she suspected foul play. She hadn't spelled it out but he had not been sent down here as a "Sherpa" to assist and gently oversee a routine investigation. She expected him to find out what exactly had been going on. He would spend the morning ferreting around. If he needed to brief her he could get a late train back to London.

He had better get on with interviewing the various people involved. The American officials had been allowed to go back to London and Washington. They were apparently above suspicion. But, if necessary, Jacot could easily get access to them later – and he would. He was unpopular with certain parts of the embassy. He invariably called it the American High Commission and enjoyed making some of the more militant and neo-con members of the CIA station feel uncomfortable. But others at Grosvenor Square respected him for his judgement, sense of humour and obvious patriotism. Inside the DNA of every American was a verse or two of The Star-Spangled Banner and the most educated and civilised understood that others too loved their own countries just as much as they did theirs. But they were getting fewer on the ground.

There was another sickness abroad in the intelligence machine on both sides of the Atlantic which Jacot and many others were trying to stand against with limited success. Intelligence was meant to be an honest effort to find out what was going on in the world, an intellectual quest to understand and make sense of an increasingly complex world without fear or favour. The process was like trying to put together a complex jigsaw puzzle. But, crucially, in the style of the purist 1930s jigsaw enthusiasts who tried to solve the puzzle without the benefit of a picture on the front of the box. Jacot did not mind so much what those in charge of his or any other country chose to do about the various pressing and alarming issues that sometimes intelligence helped to illuminate. That was a decision for those set above him in the machine. But he did mind very much about the process of intelligence analysis. It could never be free of the usual human frailties of ignorance, pride or sheer wrong-headedness but it was becoming on both sides of the Atlantic more and more a vehicle for ambition or political partiality. Verney had had many qualities but the one he was particularly known for was his uncritical almost unconditional admiration of Uncle Sam. Not that there were any dissenting voices. To get ahead in the British army these days you had to have a high opinion of Uncle Sam or at least fake one. In a way the US armed forces were like a dealer to our own. They supplied the conflicts which the military junkies craved but which we were too small to undertake off our own bat.

IV

Jacot climbed the wooden staircase to a set of rooms fifty yards or so away from the scene of Verney's death. He entered a small hall with a tiny kitchen running off it with a small mullioned window looking out onto the roof at the back. To the left was a bedroom of the usual Cambridge Spartan appearance with a tiny loo and shower room somehow squeezed in. For some reason the set came with the added amenity of a four-poster bed – a luxury in years gone by and still a useful antidote to the bitter Cambridge winters. His suitcase was on a chair to the side. To the right the sitting room was plainly but pleasingly decorated in white and gold, with prints of scenes from the frankly rather sad life of Marie De Medici, including one of her standing with her arch-enemy and nemesis Cardinal Richelieu portrayed almost as a pantomime villain. Two large sash windows overlooked the Cam – this part of the college appeared to have been reworked in the eighteenth century. It was a rich college and rather like staying in a smart but slightly old fashioned hotel in Venice.

Jacot locked both the outer and inner doors. The closing of the outer door indicated that he did not wish to be disturbed – in the slang of the University his "oak" was "sported". A raw and freezing Cambridge evening, the mist was rising from the Cam almost to the windows of the room. It was time to start ferreting around the life of the college so that he under-stood its personalities and routine. There might be something significant. He settled down in front of the gas fire (but it looked real) to compose his thoughts.

There was a knock at the door which Jacot opened to the Fellows' Butler immaculate in a dark black suit.

'I'm sorry to bother you Colonel, but I just thought I'd check that you had everything you need.'

' '74 good to see you.' They both smiled broadly but did not go on to shake hands, despite having been in the same platoon years before. Instead, they held each other's shoulders briefly like a couple of middle-aged French generals at a Liberation Day Parade. They had both been burned on the *Oliver Cromwell*. Everyone's hands had been just too painful for many months for the usual act of human greeting. Even after they were all recovered the habit stuck.

'Come and have a drink and tell me how you are getting on. Golly, it's thirty years ago this year since we were all blown to kingdom come and more than five or so since my fellowship here.'

'Very good sir. I've got half an hour before I have to get High Table organised.'

Jacot fetched a newly opened bottle of Veuve Clicquot and poured two glasses.

Jones laughed. 'Do you remember that we would bring Veuve Clicquot to your room in Germany? Five pounds a bottle in those days.'

They talked of this and that – regimental gossip, the lives and achievements or otherwise of those they had served with both in the Falklands and the Rhine Army. Their opinions on

most people seemed to coincide and both were appalled that
one of their least favourite creatures had gone on to become
a general.

Jones said 'Total charisma bypass as I remember but
became a top general. No discernible personality at all most of
the time. Nasty piece of back-stabbing work and not much
good down South either.'

The glint in Jones's eye reminded Jacot that Jones held
unforgiving views about on those he felt were not up to scratch.
He had been on glittering form during the Falklands and
selected highlights emerged from deep inside Jacot's memory.
His summing up of Mrs Thatcher after one of her sub-
Churchillian orations broadcast by the BBC World Service was
a Swiftian masterpiece of character assassination. His views on
the Americans and US Secretary of State Al Haig's efforts to
broker a deal with the Argentine military junta were unprintable.
It was as if the United States of America, far from being the
shining beacon on a hill of post war legend, was responsible for
most of the ills of the world. But Sergeant Jones reserved his
real slashing hatred for the BBC World Service.

As they sailed south on the QE2, the 50,000 tonne Cunard
liner more used to cruising the Caribbean, initially Jones'
mood had been genial. Like everyone else in the regiment he
wanted to go to war. People had been returning from all over
the world in an effort to go south. It didn't seem to matter
whether you were flying a desk in Hong Kong or trudging the
streets of West Belfast undercover with raincoat and revolver,
everyone wanted to be part of it. But as he listened each night
to the BBC's take on the Falklands crisis, sitting on his backpack and sipping sweet tea, Jones' mood darkened. He could

not understand that the BBC, in whatever guise, appeared to treat the British task force in the same way as it treated our opponents. The tone of the newscasters was neutral. The progress of Her Majesty's armed forces was described and then the activities of the occupying forces of the fascist Argentine junta were described. It sounded like the commentary on a particularly dull football match with the commentators entirely indifferent to the eventual outcome. Jones was appalled and cursed them in colourful terms. It was more than soldiers' black humour. It was a revolt by a rough but simple spirit against what he saw as treason. Jacot could not explain it to him. He was as puzzled as Jones himself.

'Worse than the IRA. At least they don't want to be British. It's as if these bastards actually don't mind if the Argies win.' And then Jones would crack obscene jokes about the imagined and highly irregular sexual proclivities of the various newscasters he had seen on television back home. But as the voyage South continued he stopped cursing them in English. The offence was too great. He reverted to his native Welsh which Jacot did not understand. The curses and expletives were so strong that they seemed to shock the Welsh-speaking guardsmen. Everyone knows that Welsh is a good language to love or sing in. It is also good for hating – Jones invoked the curses of the Druids, apparently learned at his mother's breast – in thunderous contempt for what we had allowed our world to become. It was simple for Sergeant Jones and indeed for everyone except the BBC – the Falklanders were kith and kin. Jones was particularly offended that he had to pay the licence fee to fund what he described as 'treasonous crap'. He had proudly shown Jacot a paragraph at the end of a letter home instructing his wife not to renew their television licence – a big step. Llanbedr, the remote village in Snowdonia that he came from may have been poor but it was still god-fearing and law-abiding.

Jacot laughed a lot. It was, as always, good to see Jones. The bonds between them forged in the Falklands remained strong. They had led a platoon together in difficult circumstances. Jacot was acutely conscious that Jones had pretty much saved his life. Gratitude was a positive emotion. But he also felt guilt. If he had agreed to Jones' perfectly sensible suggestion to get the men on deck a few minutes before the missile hit every-thing would have been different – at least for their own platoon.

Once, while they were recovering in hospital he had begun both to apologise and to thank him, but Jones turned quickly away his eyes signalling both embarrassment and anger. Some things were better left unsaid. Nevertheless, a great unspoken military intimacy still existed between them. They laughed and chatted and drank their champagne.

'I need some answers 74. I need you to help me. You vol-unteered for special duties in the 1980s and you know the kind of world I currently operate in. I can rely on you not to blab.'

'No worries, Colonel.' Jones grinned and took a long sip of his champagne.

'OK let's start with the basics. Did you see anything unusual when you took Verney up his breakfast?'

'Well, no. The door was locked. Odd in a private house but not in a hotel or a Cambridge college. I banged on the door for a while and when there was no reply I got worried very quickly. The general had asked me specifically to wake him and bring him breakfast. The St James', or more properly the

Charles the Second Lecturer, is a big deal so of course I was happy to help out but breakfast in bed is not normally something we would do. General Verney knew that so it was strange that he didn't come to the door. I am a big bloke, as you know. I tried pushing quite hard but it was clear the door was locked and bolted so I had to get the head porter to help.'

'You went to the porters' lodge to get him?'

'No, I called him on my mobile. It's a lot easier in these big colleges. So, yes I was outside the room from that time until the head porter arrived.'

'Could anyone have got into General Verney's room unseen?'

'I doubt it very much. You never know in these colleges. I suspect girlfriends were smuggled in using some imagination about the routes until all that was swept away in the 1960s. But there are no secret passages as far as I know. Tunnels would be difficult this close to the river anyway. There is also a great tradition of night climbing in the university. Dates back to the Thirties I believe. I have on occasion seen young male undergraduates scaling walls and gates that would make me nervous. But actually getting into a double locked set of rooms directly overlooking the river – well nigh impossible I would say. And remember too we are a tourist attraction. The Bridge of Sorrows is the second most visited sight in Cambridge. It's lit up at night, all night. Oh and there's a live webcam. Fanatical Jamesians have it set as their home screen on their computers – and they have it too at the porters' lodge.'

They had half finished the bottle by now.

'What about someone sneaking upstairs with Verney after the feast?'

'Colonel, you've clearly remembered what I was doing before the Falklands. I wangled my way back to the battalion from special duties in Northern Ireland. You know what that means?'

'Yes, of course – 14 Company', said Jacot. 'Or more properly 14 Intelligence and Security Company. Now I think called the Special Reconnaissance Regiment.'

'Precisely. A year's training in 1980 and nearly a year out there – noticing things. That's what we did. Can't say I was particularly sharp at the surveillance and my size was always a problem. I wasn't even so beefy then. So normally I was the guy in the car, although I got quite good at covert entry techniques. Do you remember how basic the army was thirty years ago?'

'I think the world was more basic full stop. No computers. Either not enough or far too much central heating.' Jacot laughed and re-filled their glasses.

'Nissen huts. I remember being taught about locks in a Nissen hut in North Wales. You walked into the room and there were lots of army desks covered in army blankets. And on top of each one six different types of lock. Every day for a month as the rain pissed down outside. The nearest pint was about ten miles away and no one had a car. Not even the officers.' Jones laughed and his eyes lit up at the memory. 'By the end of the month most of us could pick a lock in seconds. It got quite competitive between the lads. And the IRA never worked it out. They had all sorts of precautions. You know bits of hair on the door like in a James Bond film. Useless Paddies. But the point of my story is that I notice things and I understand locks. I just can't see how anyone could have got into General Verney's room, killed him and then got out again locking and chocking the door and closing the windows. Can't be done.'

'All right, all right. Let me move on. What about Dr Pirbright, General Verney's academic assistant and a fellow of this college?'

'Yes sir.' There was a trace of wariness in Jones' voice.

'What sort of a person is she?' asked Jacot.

'Well what you see is what you get really. Very good looking and very clever young lady. Very good looking.'

'How good looking?'

'Well sir. You know what I mean, and no doubt you will be meeting her this evening or tomorrow morning.'

'Good looking enough for it to cause trouble.'

Jones smiled. He was basically an honest soldier. 'Exactly sir. She's a nice girl. Always polite and considerate to the college servants. But looks like that…'

'Who is or has been after her?'

'Well in the college everyone likes her. I am not aware she is stepping out with anyone just now. Although she is said to be something of a "femme fatale", I think the phrase is.'

Jacot knew well the effect of a very beautiful girl within a closed community. 'Anyone else?'

'I don't think so. But some of our young men are prone to take a strong fancy to her. She has only been with us eighteen months.'

'Look 74, I'll cut to the chase…'

'Don't worry Colonel. I'll find out everything you need to know about her love life and her researches with General Verney, if you like. There have been some strong rumours that they were on to something interesting about Captain Scott. You know the explorer.'

'Good man. And anything else I might need to know about. Come on let's finish the bottle.'

'How are things back in Wales?'

'Mam soldiers on. Luckily for her as you know we were a large family. But I don't think she has ever got over Bryn's death. He was her favourite. Not in a bad way. He was the youngest and it seemed natural to the rest of us. My brother Bryn and all those men. I was there the other side of the door. I could hear him dying. We couldn't get through. You were there and I bet those hands still hurt in the winter.'

Jacot said nothing.

'It still comes back to me sometimes in the night.' Jones was shaking a little now as if he was shivering. He moved towards the window overlooking the Bridge of Sorrows. 'What about you sir?'

'Well, the Veuve Clicquot all those years ago helped. Yes, sometimes. Like you, it's mainly in the night. The screaming is what comes back but not so often now. Sometimes during the day it's the smell of paint. Do you remember all those ships smelled of paint? And blood and burning flesh. Sometimes I can even smell my hands burning all over again. But that's life. The only really difficult thing is confined spaces. I hate those small lifts more than anything else. They tell me therapy would help.'

Jones laughed. 'Therapy my arse. I can't get into lifts. It's life. What was it the boys used to say when things went wrong or got tough? Tel Aviv, Tel Aviv.'

Jacot laughed too. 'Yes it was the Welsh version of "C'est

la vie". A useful phrase. On really bad days some of them would say "Tel Af...ingviv." Always good for morale that one.'

Jacot had one further question he should put to Jones. 'Had you met Verney before?'

'No I don't think so. It was getting dark. It is getting dark rather. I like that view of the Bridge of Sorrows just as it's getting dark. There is something about the water surging under the bridge all day every day that cheers me up.' He turned full towards Jacot his massive frame almost blocking out the setting sun. The glory and calm of a sharp January evening in Cambridge reasserted themselves. The raw sorrows and resentments of long ago were gone. 'You are right. It's funny, over the years I had got over it. I am not nursing a grudge from thirty years ago. Mam may never have got over Bryn's death but to be honest I had forgotten him, except for every now and then. Life is for the living as they say. I had better go. The dons will be gathering in the Combination Room soon.' Jones smiled. 'Thanks for the champagne. Let me know if there is anything you need. I'll bring it up myself or if I'm busy send one of my team.' His body was no longer shaking.

'Hang on 74, what's that noise? It's as if I can hear voices in the room. Must be the champagne.'

'Oh that. What staircase are we on now?' Jones listened. He could hear what sounded like the dispatcher of a taxi firm talking to one of his taxis. He smiled. 'I think that's the baby alarm in the room above you on the staircase. Occasionally, very occasionally the radio frequencies of local taxi firms interfere with it. Sometimes it's stuff on other electronic equipment like films streaming onto a computer – something to do with the atmospheric conditions. It's probably coming from Hildegard Von Schoenberg's rooms, a German PhD student from Tubingen. Theology if I remember. Just here for the year. Her husband stayed behind in Germany and she brought her boy with her. Nearly one I think the little chap is and never makes much noise so you won't be disturbed. He's got a wonderful German name, Odo. Some evenings she goes to the library on the other side of the court and takes the other bit of the baby alarm with her.'

'I must make sure I say hallo to Hildegard and Odo', said Jacot.

They touched shoulders again and Jones was gone. Jacot went to the window and looked out at the Bridge of Sorrows. There was indeed something solid and comforting about the bridge and the water flowing beneath it. It was sad about Bryn. He had been one of a small group of guardsmen who had been trapped behind a steel door that had warped in the heat. The door itself had saved them from the effects of the blast, in particular the searing flash burns caused by the initial detonation of military high explosives. They must have felt lucky for a few seconds, but the extreme heat jammed the steel door into its hinges. There was no other way out... Jones looked cheery enough, sounded cheery enough, but Jacot very much doubted if he had forgotten his much loved younger brother in the way he suggested. His eyes gave it away as he talked about him – a kind of blankness and puzzlement that could only be a sign of fresh ongoing grief. And something he said about Verney could not be quite right...

V

St James' College, Cambridge

Dinner at the St James' High Table was a supremely civilised experience, even in the aftermath of a sudden and unexplained death. A string quartet played light-hearted baroque music in the body of the hall. Jones made sure Jacot's glass was re-filled frequently with wine from the College's cellar of the type that Jacot could not usually afford. It was a relaxed and contented Colonel Jacot who returned to his rooms just after midnight. He had almost forgotten why he had been despatched to Cambridge. Round and round in his head went thoughts not of murder, but of a delightful dance tune that the student quartet had finished with. Maddeningly, he could not identify it although he was sure he had heard it before. Jones had left a half bottle of the college's addictive Calvados on top of the fireplace and Jacot thought he would finish off the evening with a large slug.

Opening the window he breathed in the cold January air. It was good to see Jones again. They had been close thirty years before. Jacot enjoyed being a platoon commander and Jones had been an excellent platoon sergeant. They had got on famously, mainly Jacot suspected, because he let Jones more or less run the platoon – which he did well. He hadn't thought much about the Falklands for a while, suppressing frightening and unpleasant memories. But the memories came back to him strongly as he gazed at the floodlit Bridge of Sorrows. It wasn't a nightmare like the ones he and others had experienced in hospital or like the ones that very occasionally revisited him with a vengeance in the night. It wasn't a daytime flashback that came unwished for and inconveniently – set off mainly these days by smells. It was a stream of memory of a particular episode in his life when he was young – grim but not all bad as his conversation with Jones earlier had reminded him. He sipped his Calvados. It was time to relax and remember thirty years on.

…They were right. Barbecuing pork. Human flesh cooking smells like barbecuing pork. The missionaries in the South Seas were right. Except it wasn't human flesh in a history book – it was his own flesh in the here and now. His hands were cooking. And like pork they were dripping warm fat. Jesus Christ, he was on fire. Flames and thick smoke were everywhere. For a second, only Jacot's sense of smell worked – nothing else. And all he could smell was his own flesh cooking. Then suddenly he could hear. The sound had come back on. And all he could hear was screaming. Desperate, animal screams from men in his regiment close by. Ten parts pain as exposed skin shrivelled and burnt. Ninety parts despair – they knew they were going to die.

Minutes earlier Second Lieutenant Daniel Jacot of the Celtic Guards had been sitting on his backpack smoking yet another cigarette. Tense and angry at the repeated delays, he wanted to get out of the tank deck and off the ship taking his soldiers with him. 'On the bus, off the bus' as the guardsmen repeated mantra-like, all the time rolling their eyes with a combination of irritation and mute acceptance. Clausewitz, the great philosopher of war, called it 'friction' – how the simplest things in war become immeasurably hard because of both enemy action and the complexity of circumstances. That was why orders had to be obeyed unquestioningly and immediately. Any relaxation of rigid discipline, any chink in the system and chaos burst through. Yeah, right. But there was one problem, a really big problem that Clausewitz never really addressed. What if the people in charge were just useless?

Now at last they were about to 'get off the bus' the loading ramp at the back of the ship was jammed tightly shut. There was nothing in Clausewitz about "Murphy's Law". The more senior officers were starting to shout and swear, never a good sign. Stuff it, he would go up onto the open decks and see what was happening for himself. It had been light for some hours. Lifting the heavy bergan onto his back he started to climb the steep steel stairs.

'I am just going up to check what is going on', he said to his platoon sergeant – a grizzled and ironic veteran of Aden and more tours of Northern Ireland than he cared to count.

'Very good, sir. Shall I bring the men up on deck now? They could do with a breath of fresh air and we must be about to get off.' Sergeant Jones grinned hopefully.

'No better stay down here for a few minutes otherwise there might be a scene, I think, with our superiors.'

The strange alchemy that allowed experienced Welsh soldiers to be led by wet-behind-the-ears English public schoolboys certainly worked between Jacot and Jones. Jacot's job was to read the map and represent the interests of his men up the chain of command. Whatever the system, and whoever was in charge, Jacot did not like the idea of his men sitting around on a lightly armed, unescorted ship.

He reached the top of the companionway and squeezed himself through the door onto the deck. There did not seem to be much going on. Leaning over the side he grabbed a big breath of fresh sea air. A large motorised float was taking on board ammunition and supplies. Better get back to his men before he got into trouble.

Come to think of it he did not even know the name of the ship. They had been on so many in the last few days. Most still had names that would have been familiar to Nelson's captains. But they had got on this one in a hurry, in the middle of a windy and rough night, and he hadn't quite caught the name. No one in his platoon had heard it either and he was too embarrassed to ask in case he got shouted at. Turning to go back to his men he saw a large diamond shaped shield in gold. It was beautiful and glistened in the sunlight. At its centre was a portrait, just the face, with a Latin motto underneath, nothing else. A tough looking man in his early forties maybe, not handsome but certainly not hideous. The motto read *Pax Quaeritur Bello* – Peace is sought through war. Rather appropriate thought Jacot. Beneath it the name of the ship in gold lettering – Royal Fleet Auxiliary *Oliver Cromwell*. It was an odd name for a fleet auxiliary, ships mainly involved in supply and transportation rather than fighting. *Oliver Cromwell* would be a better name for a warship but it was hardly one the admiralty would choose. It was odd, thought Jacot, that there was a ship at all in the service of the crown that commemorated this great man. It was odd too that here he was in the middle of a war when just a couple of years before he had been a schoolboy.

He looked at the face again. There was something about the heraldic design that was unsettling. It wasn't derived from the famous "warts and all" portrait so the face itself was pleasing enough, but the way the thing had been painted brought to mind the dead Cromwell more than the living – the head looked as though it had been recently severed from the body. As indeed it had been after the Restoration, when Cromwell's body was disinterred and his head stuck on a spike above Westminster Hall. The head, if Jacot remembered rightly from his recent school history lessons, had fallen down in a storm a few years later eventually ending up, after many adventures, being buried at Cromwell's old Cambridge college sometime in the 1960s. Jacot shuddered. Suddenly he felt vulnerable and far from home.

He was sore in need of another cigarette already, and cheering up by Sergeant Jones whose pithy, apposite and obscene commentary on unfolding military events was invariably a refreshing tonic.

It was Jones' voice that somehow reached him in the midst of the smoke and the flames. 'This way. This way lads. I am in the doorway. On me lads. Follow my voice.' He must have been shouting with all his might but the tone was even – it was a command not an outburst of panic. It was this voice faintly heard through the smoke that brought Jacot back from the brink of hysteria. He had assumed that staying calm in a crisis would come naturally, that he was born to lead. But he had not reckoned with being trapped on a burning ship – indeed he was burning himself. But then the voice was lost in the noise.

Jacot had to get up and get out. Thick black smoke meant he could see little. He could hear men screaming. Presumably they were cooking too. He tried to push himself up from the deck but something heavy and shaking was on top of him.

It was leaking blood and shouting, 'My legs. My f…..g legs. Help me. Help me. For God's sake help me.'

Jacot pushed hard and the body rolled off him – shrieking face down on the steel deck. Every instinct, every message from the brain was telling him to get out. Get out. Get out. Get some air. Get off the ship before it blows sky high. But he could not go – not just yet. He turned the body over and reached for a morphine syrette hanging round his neck. If he could get the casualty to be still there would be a chance of carrying him to safety. The body writhed and shuddered. Jacot tried to find a place to inject but as he pulled up the arm of the casualty's combat jacket a mixture of burned material and cooked skin started to come away in his hands. There hardly seemed to be man there at all just a bundle of smoking rags and wildly staring eyes with no lids. The young man was saying the word 'Mam' over and over again. Jacot did not recognise the voice – and there was no face left and no eyelids. Just eyes staring with fear and puzzlement. And blood pumped from the shredded bottoms of combat trousers where the legs had been. Jacot found a patch of unburnt skin just below the neck and injected the morphine. The young guardsman shook and the burned head fell forward. Jacot at the top of his lungs shouted 'Don't worry I'll get you out'. But it was too late. Jacot held the young man's shoulders and began to recite the Lord's Prayer. 'Ein Tad yn y nefoedd, Our Father in Heaven.' A final shudder and the young guardsman was gone. He had taken the full force of the blast. Jacot pulled off the identity discs – chunks of neck-flesh came away too. Mortar ammunition, British ammunition – over a thousand rounds of it stacked at the other end of the tank deck was 'cooking off' – exploding because of the heat. Jacot could hear the angry whizzing and whining of shrapnel doing its deadly work in a confined space – pinging and hissing as it hit the steel superstructure. Time for the rest of the Lord's Prayer later. He had to get out – fast.

His hands smarted. The skin on his hands had begun to peel off. The pain was starting. Not just his hands but his face and chest. His legs damp with blood did not feel so bad.

It all seemed so strange. One minute clear blue South Atlantic sky and the ship at anchor in a calm bay. The only sounds the breeze, the thuds, creaking and sometimes muttered cursing of over-laden soldiers climbing down rope ladders into landing craft. The occasional clang as a rifle hit the side. Invariably followed by the gruff admonishment of a non-commissioned officer. And then Jacot's radio operator had shouted, 'It's Red. It's Red. Air Raid Warning Red, sir.'

It was a bit late. They appeared to have escalated from Air Raid extremely unlikely, or whatever the precise definition was, to Air Raid Warning Red meaning an air raid was imminent or under way, without any of the intermediate levels. Such was life. But there were no planes thank God. Maybe it was just a false alarm.

Still definitely time to get off the *Oliver Cromwell*. Jacot's heartbeat began to return to normal. And then it came. The radio operator screamed 'Handbrake, Handbrake, Handbrake' – the single word most feared by the Task Force.

It was the warning for an Exocet attack. Jesus no, thought Jacot. Then the massive concussion from the blasts threw him off his feet.

Jacot could not concentrate. His mind was wandering and the pain second by second was becoming unbearable. Above all he wanted to get out. Get into the open air. Live. But he could not think. He was tired. Maybe he was dying. Was this what it was like? An arm grabbed him from nowhere and dragged him through a door pushing him upstairs. 'Keep going sir. We're nearly there.' It was his platoon sergeant. Where was the rest of the platoon? One final push and suddenly they were on the deck. Jacot collapsed. He wanted to cry.

'Don't worry I've got you now sir.' Sergeant Jones turned Jacot over and injected morphine into his thigh. And the pain began to go away.

A Chinese crew member walked vacantly by – stunned by what had just happened to his ship.

'*Kung Hee Fat Choi*', Jacot called out. It was the only Cantonese he knew, picked up while living in Hong Kong as a teenager with his parents. Happy New Year. They grinned at each other.

The sounds from the ship began to change. The dying were dead. Their screaming – the sounds of men trapped and burning to death – animal cries of claustrophobic anguish and agony – had stopped. And the wounded were calmer or sedated – many of the burnt faces bearing a single or double M in military crayon on the forehead to show that they had been given morphine. In the background the noisy hum of helicopters as the wounded were evacuated, the rotors biting into the air as the Sea King helicopters hovered over the deck. It was too dangerous to land. At the back of the boat a chopper hovered low over an inflated orange life raft using its powerful downdraft to push the raft and its occupants away from the burning ship. Nearby the shouted instructions of officers and non-commissioned officers and the grunting as men were lifted onto stretchers were oddly re-assuring. The panic and shambles of a few minutes ago was slowly being transformed bit by bit and thanks to deeply ingrained discipline into a military operation. And some protection was at hand. Jacot could hear the thud thud of the British half-inch machine guns in the bay as they put up a curtain of tracer to deter further attacks. They were firing 'four bit' – every fourth round was tracer leaving a burning trail in the sky. It allowed the firer to see his fall of shot and deterred enemy pilots. But the Rapier anti-aircraft missiles which really could make a difference moved crazily around in their stands – pointing first at the sky and then straight at the ground – their radars could sense enemy aircraft but their gyroscopes, still not bedded in properly after a month at sea, were confused as to which direction was up and which down. It was too late anyway. The Mirage Super-Etendard bombers would have launched their missiles from many miles away.

More than the fear and pain Jacot felt humiliated. They had sailed 8,000 miles just to get themselves caught in a stupid military fuck up – without even landing a blow on the Argentines. But worse than the humiliation was the ghastly realisation that flooded Jacot's consciousness and seemed to surge into every part of his body: his platoon, his men would not have been caught in the inferno on the tank deck if he had listened to Jones' advice. God knows how many were dead or dying or burnt beyond suffering.

And then Jacot heard another roar. Faint but growing stronger. Jet aircraft flying low and fast, straining at maximum capacity. He prayed that they were British Harriers…

Jacot got up from his chair. The fire was burning low. Most of the Calvados was gone.

VI

It had been a mainly frustrating day consisting of long talks about police procedure and fairly tedious alibi checking on some peripheral players. The low point had been a difficult telephone conversation with Verney's deputy, a prickly Air Vice Marshal who wanted minute by minute updates on the investigation. When Jacot declined he made it pretty clear that he ate army colonels for breakfast. In the end Jacot had referred him to Lady Nevinson but it had been a humiliating and bad-tempered exchange. The arrival of Charlotte Pirbright in his rooms just a few minutes after the Air Vice Marshal had hung up on him lifted Jacot's spirits – helped also by the arrival of the cocktail hour. Jones was right thought Jacot – she was extraordinarily good looking. Every lovesick poet in the book had tried but no one had ever pinned down in words that kind of beauty. Some had come close. Jacot liked Philip Marlowe's great reaction to being shown a photograph of Mrs. Lewin Lockridge Grayle. "It was a blonde. A blonde to make a bishop kick a hole in a stained glass window." She was blonde but she wasn't that at all. The curves were interesting enough and she was well dressed to make the most of her figure but the allure did not come from an in your face sexuality. It was the face itself. It was perfect. And perfect in what seemed to Jacot a perfectly English way. A high forehead descended into a strong nose – not a Barbie doll nose so popular amongst Hollywood actresses. No one would ask her plastic surgeon to reproduce it. Neither would a Jihadist on the brink of detonating his backpack think to find such features in Paradise. The teeth were white. She was wearing a little make-up but the skin appeared near flawless. And the eyes were an intense but pale blue. But what clinched it was a kind of moral quality. The gaze wasn't innocent but knowing. She seemed happy, content with whatever she was doing. In a slightly crazy world that seemed to prize tension and edginess above all else, this beautiful girl was happy in her own skin

Jacot felt himself about to gawp so smiled and quickly turned to his drinks tray. 'Sherry? I have a Manzanilla.'

'Golly, what's that?'

'It's a very dry sherry, supposedly with a salty tang because the vineyards are almost on the sea. It's have to have stuff, I assure you.'

'Thank you. Sounds great.'

Jacot noticed that she was looking at his hands. Encased tonight in black Thai silk.

'What happened to your hands?' she asked, her eyes moving from the hands and gazing directly at his.

'Oh, I was burned in the Falklands War. An Argentine missile attack.'

'Oh dear. Were you on that ship the Oliver whatshisname?'

'Alas, yes. The silk gloves soothe them a little.'

'It's strange seeing a man indoors wearing black gloves. They're usually for thieves and assassins.'

'Well white would make me look like a waiter or a magician. So I settled on black many years ago. Occasionally, I branch out into more jazzy colours.'

She sipped her ice-cold Manzanilla. 'Sherry still seems to be traditional in Cambridge. And I have to say I rather like it.'

She sat down in an armchair by the fire. Jacot took up position on the red leather club fender that surrounded the fireplace. The rooms had a faint smell of wood-smoke. Jacot noticed that Mr. Jones had laid a single layer of coals beneath the apple wood that was used only in the fellows' rooms – it made the fire roar and crackle.

'You knew General Verney.'

'Yes, very well. I met him in the Antarctic. I was at the American base at McMurdo on Cape Evans for a couple of months gathering data for my PhD. In the summer it gets quite busy with over a thousand living and working there – people not penguins. I became a sort of unofficial guide to Scott's hut, about fifteen miles from the base. The one from his first expedition is within walking distance but you need transport to reach the hut he built for his second and fatal expedition, the one everyone knows from the photographs. I was the person organizing the tours. Most people heading for the Pole pass through. One day this British general turned up and I showed him round. It was fate really. Captain Scott has always been my passion – an unfashionable one of late to be honest. And then suddenly out of nowhere and in the middle of nowhere there was another aficionado. We kept in touch. It turned out that Verney was privately wealthy and he helped fund some of my research, supplementing my meagre fellow's stipend. We were both working on various aspects of Captain Scott's last expedition. Verney provided the inspiration and I provided what you might call the academic muscle. I completed my PhD a few years ago and I know my way round the Scott-Wilson Austral Studies Institute, SWASI we call it, here in Cambridge. You know, the modern world underestimates Scott and his achievements. Curiously, he doesn't play well in the United States whereas Shackleton has been adopted as a magnificent example by various American leadership gurus. But General Verney and I had no doubt whose side we were on.'

Jacot like many men of his generation was awkward asking personal questions. His analytical training had overcome this to some extent but he didn't like it at all. So he forced himself to ask, 'Were you having an affair?'

She laughed. 'Good Lord, no. He wasn't at all attractive and to be honest I didn't really like him that much.'

'Why work with him then?'

'Well. It's funny. I enjoyed working with him to be fair. We were both obsessed with "Captain S" as we called him. We both felt he had had a hard time historically. We both felt that he was a great man. Also, and I shouldn't really say this as an academic, we both despised most of Scott's detractors – as chippy a crew as you could wish to meet. And we both had a sneaking suspicion that despite the lionization of Shackleton in recent years there was something not quite right with him. Scott, of course, felt this too. His diary entry for the day they get further south than Shackleton had done some years before talks about being 'beyond the record of Shackleton's walk'. Funny way to put it and I have always detected a double entendre in his use of the word 'record'. It was as if he didn't believe Shackleton's account.'

'But that's unfair', interjected Jacot. 'Shackleton was a

leader there is no dispute about that. His epic journey from Elephant Island to South Georgia in an open boat puts him up there with the greats, surely. During the Falklands war we trans-shipped from the QE2 to the Canberra off South Georgia in the teeth of the Austral winter and I can tell you it was dodgy enough in a 50,000-ton liner let alone a small lifeboat.'

'Of course, Colonel. Shackleton had and has his admirers and I think Scott's rivalry with him was one of the motors for his own competitive instinct. It may not have been his fault but part of my preference for Scott it is that Shackleton became the kind of leader lionized on Wall Street. Imagine all sorts of extremely dodgy bankers flocking to leadership seminars as their balance sheets went down the tubes. They would not have dreamed of going to a lecture about good old-fashioned Scott. Anyway, the next paragraph in Scott's diary is even more interesting – it was one of the things that got old Verney and me going.'

'Pray, do tell.' Jacot smiled. He was enjoying his talk with this striking and intelligent young girl.

'Well, as you know Scott experienced some strange weather on his way to the pole. Lots of people have put this down to whingeing but we now know that he was unlucky – March 1912 really was the coldest March. It was a big breakthrough when an American scientist called Susan Solomon, whose main interest was the ozone layer or rather the hole in it over the poles, explained all this in her 2001 book of that name. She used the temperatures gathered by both Amundsen and Scott and modern automatically gathered readings to show that Amundsen experienced comparatively warm temperatures. Of course he makes it to the pole six weeks before Scott which helped, but it's clear that the temperatures experienced by Amundsen are at the warm edge of the mean whereas Scott's are closer to the mean itself or slightly below. When you add it all up most of what Amundsen had to put up with was between minus ten and minus twenty degrees Fahrenheit. Scott's party was fending off between minus twenty and minus thirty.'

'But so what? If the two explorers experienced radically different temperatures surely it was just the luck of the draw.'

She smiled and looked up at him under her eyelashes. 'It was warmer for Amundsen. Made it easier for him but also made it different in many other possibly significant ways. We have concentrated very much on what it must have felt like for the men and dogs and in Scott's case the ponies. What effect it had on their discomfort, energy levels and above all with Scott on their intake of food. The colder it gets the more calories you need to walk and haul equipment. In the end Scott and his companions just ran out of calories. Rotten luck really – they were just a few square meals short. A bit more food and a bit more paraffin and they would have been home and dry – even with the ghastly weather they had to put up with. Remember they were only 11 miles from One Ton Depot. Eleven miles. Or in Cambridge terms a walk through Grantchester to Byron's Pool and back twice. It must have been hard.'

In her account the expedition had come to life again. Jacot continued 'To think it's the centenary of Scott's last expedition this year and here we are talking about some of the men involved as if it were current affairs. But back to Verney.'

She tilted her head back and took a long sip of the ice-cold Manzanilla. She uncrossed her legs and leant forward. 'More Manzanilla please colonel.'

He took her glass and turned for the bottle.

'Are you sure Scott was second to the Pole?'

It was an extraordinary thing to say and he nearly spilt the refilled glass of Manzanilla. Jacot laughed. 'I bet you say that to all the boys – it's a good chat-up line. But...'

'All right. All right. Just messing about but I hope you will read our paper on Scott when it's ready. I keep a copy close to hand on a little memory stick tucked away in a private place.' She pointed coquettishly to her bra and laughed. 'Back to Verney. He was an interesting man too.'

'In what way?' Jacot was alert now.

'He was incredibly indiscreet about his intelligence work. I think he sensed I didn't like him that much and certainly wasn't interested in him in any other way. I think he told me stuff to jolly me along. It was a rarified form of flirting.'

'Did you know anything about his family?'

'Yes a bit. He was married and there are some grown up children. I think a boy and two girls. But he was a cold fish. He spoke of them with affection in the usual way but not with any great passion. He appeared neither uxorious nor over-interested in his children. What really fired him up was his career. I always thought making general was pretty good but he seemed determined to become an even bigger sort of general. In a way it was all-consuming for him with a little time off every now and again for some Antarctic studies.'

Her mobile pinged with a text message. She finished her sherry and stood up.

'Listen, Colonel Jacot.'

'Dan is easier.'

'Listen Dan. I have an urgent appointment to go to. Academic stuff. Why don't we reconvene another time? I was horrified by General Verney's death. I hope I haven't been rude about him. We got along OK. It's just that he wasn't very inspiring. Unlike you I don't think there was anything untoward about it but I still want to help you get to the bottom of the whole thing.'

And with that she was gone. Jacot heard her light steps on the staircase and watched through the window as she crossed the court with long-legged strides. A young woman at the peak of her powers and attraction. She was perfect of her type. As ever it was a cause of joy – for a moment or two you felt close to the driving life force of humanity – hope, the future, the fun in the present – all the good things. Some of those who saw Nureyev at his peak told of a weird sense that at the top of some of his famous balletic leaps he seemed to almost hang in mid air defying gravity. Of course it was a trick of the eye or the senses. In the same way the beautiful and clever young seemed just for a moment exempt, free, not subject to mortality. In part it was their own obliviousness. In part an exhilarated wishful thinking by the observer. But as with Nureyev's leaps there was a quick falling away that only multiplied the underlying melancholy.

> 'Golden lads and girls all must,
> As chimney-sweepers, come to dust.'

She was a golden girl for sure. At least she wasn't thinking about coming to dust just now.

Jacot decided on more Manzanilla, lots more and some Mozart. Kiri Te Kanawa's voice came through his iPod speakers. It was as if she was in the room. *'Ruhe sanft, meine holdes Leben'*. Sleep soundly my beloved. Zaida's ravishing lullaby for grown ups lifted his melancholy and soothed the long buried guilt re-awakened by his earlier interview with Jones.

My, young Charlotte Pirbright was a head-turner. It was still not late. Time for a little more sherry. His mobile pinged with a text message. Lady Nevinson's driver would pick him up at King's Cross at 2230 – she was working late.

VII

The car drove at top speed from the station and Jacot arrived in Lady Nevinson's Number 10 office a few minutes before 11 o'clock. He expected her to quiz him urgently about Cambridge. Instead she kicked off with 'Do you remember in the 1970s those vigilante films starring Charles Bronson?' Lady Nevinson seemed to be in a beneficent and chatty mood and the whisky would follow soon thought Jacot.

He replied, 'Yes, of course. They were a huge hit at school. Michael Winner directed. Bronson was also in those other staples of preparatory school life in the 1960s and 1970s *The Great Escape* and *The Dirty Dozen.*'

She picked up the decanter, poured two glasses of whisky and slid one across her desk to Jacot. 'Winner is mainly known as a restaurant critic these days. People forget how powerful his films were in their day. You are younger than me Jacot and so you probably can't remember the sense of breakdown that the adult, or recently become adult, world experienced in the early and mid 1970s. Bit like today really. People had little faith in the system and so vigilante films of all kinds touched a chord. Shame he never got round to directing a Bond film. It might have been fun.'

Jacot had known and worked for Lady Nevinson for nearly two years. They shared many attitudes and got on well. But they were not intimates or even friends. Curiously, since the start of the General Verney affair they had grown closer. They were both in on the same secret. Indeed, if in truth she wasn't sharing Jacot's findings with anyone else or rather she wasn't keeping the prime minister in the loop, they were co-conspirators of a sort. He realised that he didn't know much about her beyond her entry in *Who's Who*.

'I don't know how they went down at your dingy prep school but they went down a storm in diplomatic circles even in far-off lands. I read French at Newnham and spent a year at the Sorbonne as part of my degree and so I spoke and speak it fluently. I passed the Foreign Office exam rather well.' She looked up at him. 'As you would expect.'

Jacot smiled. He wasn't at all sure that she had been making a joke. Getting to know someone was one thing, understanding their sense of humour quite another. Like many senior civil servants he had met she was proud of academic achievements long ago. The first class honours degree and the high place in the civil service exam still mattered to her in her early 60s.

Lady Nevinson continued, 'I spent a few months in London and was looking forward to my first posting which I assumed would be Paris. I had it all worked out. But my first posting was, inevitably looking back, Viet Nam. In the Seventies I spent much of my time in Indo-China. We watched Winner's films at the embassy. Oh those old film nights with a slightly cranky projector and intervals when the reels were changed. The embassy servants would bring drinks and the most wonderful cocktail eats – small chow we called them. Every time I see Michael Winner on TV or advertising something the films and the memories come right back.

'I was posted as a young Third Secretary in Saigon in 1972 just after Cambridge. Had a great time. Most of it in the famous Continental Hotel, where all the journalists and senior American officers congregated. 'Hung out' they called it. Some young officers too. The most glamorous were not the soldiers but the US Marines. They had an impressive swagger and nice manners to boot. They were also fighting a different style of war to the US Army, much more the sort of thing our troops had tried in Malaya some years before. Anyway, they seemed to have thought about war a little whereas many of the army officers seemed obsessed with 'free fire zones' and Agent Orange. It really was like something out of Graham Greene. I was young and clever and not bad looking. Things were great.

'And then the Americans began to withdraw and the whole thing fell apart rather quickly in April 1975. I had been dispatched up country to see what was happening and got back too late to be evacuated. I was lucky to get back to Saigon at all in fact. I had been in Da Nang which fell pretty easily and had then got caught up in the hundreds of thousands of refugees pouring south. There was panic and despair. I got swept along to a small town called Xuan Loc where the South Vietnamese army made an extraordinary last stand. The South Vietnamese infantry division that held the town for eleven days was despised by the Americans for its poor discipline and cowboy attitude. In the end it fought with astonishing energy to the end. Few others did. They were charming too and made sure I got out well before the town fell and was transported safely to Saigon. I shall remember till the day I die saying good-bye to them. They didn't know where their families were. They weren't especially enamoured of the South Vietnamese regime. Many of them were personally disreputable, black marketeers and so forth. But they loathed communism and would rather go down fighting than live under it. Some of them got away in the end but not many.'

She looked wistfully out of the window overlooking Downing Street. 'By the time I tipped back up at the embassy our ambassador had already left for the airport. Famously, he travelled in a silver Jaguar and the pictures were broadcast across the world. The British Ambassador leaving was felt to be a key moment. It was my fault. I wasn't frightened but I felt on my own and wondered what would become of me. A young French diplomat, Gilles Navarre, who was a close friend, came up trumps. To be fair the Americans would have got me out. They are good like that. But I certainly felt safe once I had reached the French Embassy.

'I always felt a little sorry for the Yanks. They had a rough time of it – 58,000 of their young men were killed – they got little thanks for trying. Many were from poor backgrounds. Needless to say urban blacks were 'over-represented' as the modern politically correct jargon would have it. Basically, the poor blacks and poor whites did most of the fighting. Some were volunteers, others conscripted. Most tried to do their duty. Some were extraordinarily brave. There were a few shirkers no doubt but they were rare in the front line. Until the late 1960s the army and the marines were impressive fighting forces – well led, reasonably motivated. I liked the GIs and their young officers up to a certain rank were good and cared about their men. Or at least the ones I met.

'The further away from Saigon you got the better the American soldiers were. It was in Saigon itself that I developed an abiding dislike of the senior American military, their State Department and above all the CIA. Everyone in air-conditioned offices and pressed uniforms or smart Brooks Brothers suits working out how to claim extra allowances and having a good time. All revelling in the fact that they were at war. Except they weren't. They were enjoying the prestige and appurtenances of war without ever risking their own necks. Indeed they were sending young men into harm's way and asking them to do stuff that they had never had to do. Obviously not the senior officers who had fought in the Second World War and Korea, but most of them hadn't.'

'So you don't like staff officers either Lady Nevinson', interjected Jacot with a smile. 'The Blackadder effect you might call it. They are necessary you know. I am one technically. Most of the really big cock-ups in war are as a result of poor staff work. If Captain Nolan or Lord Cardigan had been to a proper staff college we wouldn't have had the Charge of the Light Brigade.'

'Oh I'm sorry. I didn't mean to be rude.' She almost blushed. 'And I loved all things French – including the men although some of them were a pain. Later I spent some time in Bonn and then Berlin. I found I liked and admired the Germans too. Our disagreements with them seem so strange now.' She looked at Jacot 'I had forgotten to English public school boys the Germans remain something out of a pantomime.'

'Actually I am a great admirer and speak a little of the language after three years in the Rhine Army.'

She continued unperturbed. 'All in all it meant I never fell under the American spell. You saw the television pictures.'

'Yes I did as a teenager living in Hong Kong. And we realized all was not going well as our flights out from school took longer the further south the North Vietnamese penetrated. I can remember in the early days the BOAC pilots pointing out the site of Da Nang which is somewhere in the middle. By the end we were taking the long route round the South China Sea.'

She poured more whisky for them both, got up from her desk and walked to her office windows again. 'I've seen what it looks like – leaving in a hurry and beaten or too exhausted to carry on. Saigon was a frightening place in the final days and hours. Weird things happen. The world gets turned upside down. For instance money became absolutely worthless – even dollars, or perhaps especially dollars. The only currency that was any use at buying a passage on a boat or an aircraft was gold. Krugerrands were popular. We Brits have done it ourselves time and time again. We got out of India just in time. Palestine. Too many places, culminating in our scuttle from Aden. As the helicopter carrying the last British governor of Aden out to a waiting warship lifted off from the grounds of government house the rebels burst in and began looting it. And yet we cannot help going back. It's in the military, political and diplomatic DNA.'

She was in full philosophical flow. Jacot sipped his whisky. It had been a long day but he admired her and respected her judgment, mostly.

'How do you extricate a lost army? Nobody really tried to get our people out of Singapore in late 1941. They were left to defeat and their fate. At least after that disaster we didn't have the generals appearing on television every five minutes telling us how the battle for Singapore was a 'journey'. I bet that's the sort of thing the Roman generals, unworthy descendants of Caesar, were saying just before their game was up. "Emperor, the defence of Rome is a journey." Colonel Jacot where do you get these people?'

'To be fair, Lady Nevinson I think the man who talked about "a journey" was an Air Marshal.'

'Well, the Romans were lucky that they didn't have an air force.'

'Lady Nevinson the government which we serve has decided that we are going to stay in Afghanistan until 2015. I understand it's probably now going to be 2014. It's a democratic decision taken by parliament. "Period" as our American allies would say. It's above my pay grade I know but whatever anyone might feel about the way the current government does its business no one can say that it's not keen on getting us out of Afghanistan. It appears to come from the very top.'

She was certainly in a strange mood but he had some sympathy. If you were a cog in the machine as Jacot was you wrote your paper or gave your advice and went home for supper or out to a party. And when it was time to sleep, you slept well enough. But if you were at the top there was never any rest and the implications and ramifications of your advice must haunt your off duty hours. In a way it was not so bad for politicians. Huge egos and extraordinary drive are par for their course. But it was different for Mandarins. It must be particularly hard for the individuals at the pinnacle of the intelligence establishment. Worse for Lady Nevinson.

'Everyone wants the troops out now. My God I am happy not to have sons.'

'But we don't have conscription.'

'No, Colonel Jacot but I have some understanding of the male psyche. The thirst for glory is a powerful motivator. I saw it in Saigon. I know I have just been rude about the whole American military establishment and made fun of the legions of desk warriors in their air-conditioned portakabins. But many of the young officers I met wanted to go to war, fighting in the Mekong Delta was integral to their view of themselves and their masculinity. Every generation is the same and British or rather English youth is especially prone to this. My view is that it is a hangover from Empire lingering in the English public schools. Do you know Jacot I went up to your old school Harrow a few years back to give a talk on diplomacy? Nice dinner, nice boys, nice setting. But the room I spoke in appeared to be a mausoleum to the war dead of both wars but particularly the Great War.'

'Well that's hardly surprising as the whole complex was built as a war memorial. I think many families felt very strongly at the time about their lost sons and brothers – some lost husbands too of course. The great public schools suffered very badly. Disproportionate numbers of young officers were killed. If you want to feel impending tragedy, have a look at photographs of Speech Day at Harrow in 1912 or the Fourth of June at Eton that year. All the boys that you see in those photographs were born between 1894 and 1899. All would reach military age during the war. A fifth would die in action. Many more wounded and many more permanently marked by their experiences. Imagine the heartbreak.'

She turned away and sighed. 'Just as we have finished one bloody war there could be another one on the horizon.'

Jacot slipped away quietly from the room. It had been a strange conversation. She was clearly sounding him out on something. He wondered what exactly.

Lady Nevinson's ex-military driver grinned as he got into the car. 'You'll make the last train and I've arranged a taxi for you at Cambridge. Her ladyship has been working very late. I think there's a flap on about the Falklands.'

VIII

Gibbs' Building, King's College, Cambridge

'I understand that you have no official status here but that you have been sent down from the Cabinet Office to oversee things'. The Cambridge Coroner wasn't at all what Jacot had been expecting. Tall, expensively and well dressed in a Savile Row suit and wearing an Old Wykehamist tie, Professor Michael Livesey looked more like a traditional university don than a pathologist who worked in a basement. But there was an unexplained note of hostility or possibly disdain in his voice.

'Exactly, Professor Livesey. You don't have to see me or answer any of my questions. I am not part of the investigating team but it would be helpful. I should make clear that although I work in the Cabinet Office I am neither a political appointee nor a career civil servant. I am a military man who now works for the National Security Adviser, Lady Nevinson. I am a servant of the Crown, not any political party.'

Livesey smiled. 'Of course, of course, I'm sorry. To most people Cabinet Office means the political side of the government. Bad reputation under the last lot and little better today. Is your office close to the deputy prime minister's?'

They both laughed. 'And I consider it my duty to help you and Lady Nevinson out. It's not often that the Regius Professor of Pathology gets asked to carry out a post mortem, although I do them from time to time to remain current.'

'What can you tell me about the body?'

Livesey frowned. 'Strange, really strange. General Verney appeared to be in pretty good health. Obviously, he was in his late fifties and was a smoker but frankly not in a bad physical state at all. No excess weight. Lungs not too bad for a smoker. Nothing wrong with the heart or the circulation. No bleeding anywhere. No injuries. Nothing. I have checked everything and asked another senior member of the medical faculty to have a look as well. It would appear that a man in late middle age in perfect health just died in his bed one night. It happens.'

'But what was the actual cause of death?'

'I think he just stopped breathing – passed away in the night. There are no bruises to suggest that someone suffocated him. He didn't choke on anything. The only thing I would say is that he appeared to have had quite a lot to drink – a bottle and a half of wine and something a little stronger to finish off.'

'In St James' it's always Calvados.'

'Yes quite, Colonel. Even against a background of embalming fluid and disinfectant I could detect an appley smell. I have drunk the stuff myself. It's rather good.'

'Since the Litvinenko murder is not so long ago I suppose I should ask – any traces of radioactivity?'

Livesey looked hard at Jacot. The penny had just dropped that this was an intelligence matter. 'No. The police asked me to check for that. Not surprising given what the Russians have been up to. But no radioactive substances at all present. It's one of the easiest things to check for.'

'Poisons?'

'The toxicology report is clear. We have tested for all the

usual stuff and most exotics. There was no curare if that is what you are wondering about or any of the modern derivatives. Although a drug like that would suffocate in the way poor old Verney seems to have died. It's a very unpleasant way to go. You suffocate but are still conscious until the end. Horrible I should think. But there is no sign of it.'

Jacot flexed his hands. 'What's your view?'

'Obviously, I don't know the background. Don't worry I won't ask you. To a pathologist it looks like a natural death. But then if he was killed by opponents from the sort of world that you represent I suppose it would look like a natural death. There are a couple of more tests we need to run to exclude a couple of the more exotic, very exotic poisons. I can't do them here but the Home Office are coming for a sample tomorrow and I understand the FBI have offered to help. I have prepared samples for them.'

'What sort of exotics, Professor?'

'The kinds of things used by those who might wish this country harm. Stuff that is used by other countries' intelligence people and, of course, these days terrorists. I am not naïve Colonel. And it is not the first time I have received a visit from the intelligence services.'

'They sent someone up about Verney already?'

Livesey laughed. 'No not at all. Cambridge has in the past been full of spies. It still is. One head of house is a former "C" and they have people at all levels of the university in various guises nervous about our laboratories and some of our international students. And shall we say there is lots of sponsorship.'

Jacot looked out of the window over the Backs. The bulk

of King's College Chapel loomed to the right with the south front of Clare just behind running down to the river. It was an odd feeling. He was inside one of the most famous views in the world, inside the postcard.

Livesey understood what Jacot was thinking. 'For some reason the Regius Professor of Pathology is a fellow of King's. Funny gang. Lots of women parsons and the ugliest undergraduettes in the university. But the view is glorious.'

This was going well thought Jacot. There is no more powerful bond between modern men of a slightly old-fashioned disposition than a secretly shared political incorrectness. 'Professor, forgive me, but I have a question.'

'Do go on?'

'If you wanted to kill someone quickly without making it look like a murder, how would you do it?'

'How do you mean?'

'No funny stuff. No 1930s thriller stuff. But a simple effective poison that would not be detected by the authorities.'

Livesey went to his bookshelf, crammed with medical books but also with shelves of amusement and civilisation. Jacot noticed row after row of PG Wodehouse, beautifully bound in dark blue Morocco.

'I see you have spotted my secret vice – Wodehouse first editions rebound. He keeps you going if you are a pathologist. Let me make it absolutely clear Colonel Jacot that I would never discuss poisons with anyone outside the medical profession. I probably would not discuss them with anyone who wasn't a qualified and practising pathologist. Poisons are funny things, tempting things to some people. Some perfectly innocent chemicals can quite simply be mixed into powerful poisons. Some quite powerful poisons can be administered in such a way that it would be easy to allay the suspicions of observers or even the police. All of us live in terror of a rogue doctor like Shipman. That's why medical schools are so strict on personal discipline and character. Becoming a doctor is a bit like being ordained. It's not just a matter of the medical or theological knowledge. Suitability is all. Worse much worse than a Shipman who was a General Practitioner would be a pathologist who turned rogue murderer. If the back office can't be trusted we have all had it.'

'Professor, I understand. Believe me.'

'Well, Colonel I will make an exception for you.' He took a paperback from one of the shelves, one of those French paperbacks where you have to slit the pages yourself with a knife and gave it to Jacot. 'Marine toxins are what I would use. It's all in this book. It's in French because the French keep an eye on these things because of their possessions in the Caribbean and the Pacific. These are basically toxins, naturally occurring poisons, produced by various types of algae in small quantities usually in tropical waters. The algae are ingested by creatures like oysters which are then eaten by small fish which are then eaten by large fish. Usually ones that live on reefs like barracuda. The toxins are not poisonous to the fish themselves but they build up in the food chain. By the time you get to a barracuda that's been feeding on this stuff it can be very dangerous. They are all different and produce different symptoms but basically they interfere with the chemical messaging system in the body causing respiratory failure – sometimes quite quickly. The toxins are heat resistant so cooking does not help. But there is one upside from the safety point of view –

eat some of this stuff and you are normally sick as a dog. Vomiting and all the rest of it, so very often the body is purged quite quickly.'

'I suppose faking a virulent stomach bug would be a good way to murder but wouldn't it be a bit obvious? In our scenario we are trying to kill without being found out,' said Jacot.

'Quite, Colonel. And some of the toxins have strange effects to say the least – there is one found in the Pacific and Caribbean which affects the nervous system in such a way that it changes the heat sensors in the mouth – hot will feel cold and vice versa. Bit obvious that one too. Poisoning of this sort can happen in northern climes as well, rarely though, and only with imported fish – most doctors learn something about it at medical school and then forget all about it.'

Livesey handed over the book. He seemed hesitant. 'There is one toxin that stands apart from any of the others. But please don't discuss it with anyone other than your professional colleagues. Other than Lady Nevinson in fact. I don't want to put ideas into people's heads. I would use something called Saxitoxin. It is a toxin, therefore naturally occurring, derived from certain types of shellfish. In the way I have described oysters, say, ingest a type of rare algae that produces the toxin in minute, really minute quantities and even then only in certain unusual climatic, tidal and other marine conditions. Most of the time in quantities that do not affect humans – even after two dozen oysters at Wilton's. Through the way molluscs feed – they filter stuff out of vast quantities of water and vegetable matter – occasionally, if the water they are in has a glut of the unusual algae responsible, a harmful algal bloom, these potent toxins build up in their flesh. If a whale or an otter or human eats the oyster or whatever it is – bingo. Something called Paralytic Shellfish Poisoning occurs – PSP. The toxin, through a chemical process which I will not bore you with, shuts down the signals to and from the respiratory system. Paralysis can be very quick, usually within a few minutes of ingestion – maybe up to an hour. The unfortunate individual is usually dead within a couple of hours. It's a kind of dry drowning. Nasty form of death I should think because you know what is happening but can't do anything about it. And here's the killer fact if you like – it only takes about .2 of a milligramme of this stuff to kill a normal man or woman. Bit more if you are very heavily built. And afterwards it's very difficult to find. The tests for it are unreliable in some ways but between them the FBI and our Forensic Science Service should be able to detect it, although not necessarily.'

'Very interesting, Professor. But there are no signs of a stomach upset with Verney. So we are back to square one.'

'Not quite. And again you must not pass this on to anyone. We checked everywhere. But some poisons, like Saxitoxin, if injected or even inhaled, can work very quickly, at extremely low doses. The digestive system is bypassed so no vomiting or diarrhoea. Paralysis would be almost instantaneous although unconsciousness would not follow for some time, as I have said. I hasten to add there were no signs of any injections on Verney's body. I checked thoroughly, very thoroughly.'

'And who is likely to have this sort of stuff?'

'The Americans used to make it. But President Nixon ordered the supplies destroyed. There is still some around in research institutes and hospitals for nervous diseases – it works by obstructing sodium channels in the nervous system.

But nothing else – all the other channels remain open. So incredibly useful in research into various unpleasant diseases of the nervous system.'

'But difficult.'

'Difficult. Very difficult. Although if you had an oyster farm and a chemistry degree you could probably have a go. From time to time there is a worry that somehow Jihadists have synthesised a small quantity. Interestingly, it's what the US used to give to their spies – just in case. Gary Powers the U2 pilot shot down over Russia in 1956 was rumoured to be carrying a suicide pill made of the stuff. I very much doubt that there is any of it left and it would have lost its power by now, chemically degraded. There was an antidote as well, if I remember rightly, with even more complex chemistry. I have little doubt that both the FBI and our people will draw a blank. But for what it's worth that's what I would do. One final thing. Despite my oyster farm image, if it were a poison of this type I would expect it to have been synthesised by a state, an advanced state.'

'So not terrorists?' Jacot spoke slowly emphasising every word.

'No', Livesey clearly understood what Jacot was asking and the implications. 'No. It would have to be a state.'

'And the FBI and our spooks are coming tomorrow for their samples?'

'Yes. Someone from the embassy in London and an official from the Home Office.'

Professor Livesey was used to dealing with the authorities and clearly enjoyed dealing with people "from the other side of the green baize door". Somehow Jacot needed him to believe that he Jacot represented a more senior authority. It was time for a little bluff.

'Well I think we should have some more tests done. I would be grateful if you would prepare a sample for the National Security Adviser. You know Lady Nevinson of course.'

'Well yes, a little. I mean I met her once at something in Cambridge.'

'She wants me to arrange some more tests.'

Livesey looked nervous and undecided. It was time for Jacot to go in for the kill. 'You understand, of course, the constitutional position – not only is she the Prime Minister's personal adviser on intelligence matters, but also she has operational control on his behalf of the entire intelligence set up – a different creature altogether. In effect she controls promotion within the services and budgets and curiously the allocation of honours. You know MBEs, knighthoods and peerages.'

He was bluffing like mad. But it was enough. It was a tiny flash – almost unnoticeable – there just for a moment in Livesey's body language. He had stiffened like a shooting dog waiting to retrieve a pheasant. Livesey did care. He obviously liked good suits. Who did not except for wealthy politicians trying to look poorer than they really were? His rooms were beautifully decorated and filled with lovely things, watercolours on the wall and porcelain figures on the bookshelves, which were a conscious effort to display good taste. It was expensive stuff and somehow Jacot doubted that it had been inherited. Being a senior Cambridge don was certainly comfortable and could make you money, particularly in the scientific or computer spheres. Soon Livesey would almost certainly be knighted. It came with the job. But the momentary stiffening of the body had come a split second after the word "peerage". Lady Nevinson had certainly arranged for a couple of deserving spooks to be elevated to the House of Lords. Livesey probably knew this.

Napoleon was right enough. Men were interested in baubles – but for soldiers they were there for a reason – they encouraged bravery. For civilians it was different – some of the more humble medals meant a lot and were awarded for years of hard work or dedication. But at the more senior levels it was Buggins turn. And the awarding of peerages was little more than a form of spiritual corruption. Otherwise perfectly normal and honourable people seemed to lose the plot at the thought of ermine and gilt and calling themselves Lord something or other. Anyway, he had Livesey hooked.

'I am operating under her orders. Do you want to speak to her? I can get her on a secure phone now.' Jacot took his red iPhone from his pocket and made to look as though he was about to get through to her.

'No, no. Not necessary. Give her my compliments when you return to London. Of course I will prepare another sample. You can have it tomorrow. Have a glass of sherry.'

'Yes, Professor. Thank you.'

Jacot took a long sip. Trekking around Cambridge trying to solve a murder was proving tough on the liver. They both moved to the window to admire the view. It was like peering out of the Doge's Palace or the Taj Mahal. There was a slight companionable feeling in the air, as if a deal had been done. Jacot had no idea what kind of a sample was required for exotic toxicology tests but he decided not to ask lest the spell of a possible peerage was broken.

'I'll have the sample sent over to St James' tomorrow.'

'No, thanks. I will pick it up from here.'

'But that would be most irregular and the refrigerated box will be bar coded.'

Jacot was relieved – at least the sample, whatever it was, would be in a refrigerated box. He would go back to London immediately after picking it up and seek instructions from her ladyship. He hoped she would approve. But for now he must continue in costume and character as it were.

'No bar code, please professor. It will be a matter entirely between you and Lady Nevinson – and just between the two of you. Not the Home Office or the American Embassy. Please do not discuss the matter outside this room or with anyone other than Lady Nevinson herself.'

'Of course, of course.' Livesey quivered with secret satisfaction. 'I'll let you know when it is ready and will probably have the final results of the tests we can do here.'

IX

Jacot was getting used to the Cambridge train. This time he had not been summoned but had returned to London at his own volition to update Lady Nevinson. He had never liked the term National Security Adviser – the Cabinet Office was not the White House after all. But it looked good on the brass plaque on Lady Nevinson's door inside the Number 10 complex. He knocked and went in. She smiled and motioned for him to sit on the leather sofa and pour himself a cup of coffee. She was talking on the telephone, apparently to the prime minister.

'He's young enough to be my son,' she commented, putting the phone down and joining him on the sofa.

'Surely not', volunteered Jacot.

'There is no need for your bogus guardee gallantry.' She laughed though and her eyes shone.

Nevinson was unusual in that she was not exalted by her closeness to the centre of power. Jacot had never seen this before. Even civil servants privately deeply opposed political-ly to a particular government or policy usually enjoyed working in or close to Downing Street and found it difficult to disagree in person with the prime minister of the day. Nevinson's attitude wasn't just unusual it was invaluable. But he wondered how long the prime minister would tolerate her concealed disdain. Like all politicians he was acutely conscious of the attitude of those he felt were not fully onside. The charismatic always agonized about those impervious to their charisma.

She didn't actually think very much of the current incumbent, if her asides and small talk were anything to judge her opinions by. From time to time though he did appear to win her stern approval. The usual chippy reasons for not liking him were entirely absent from her horizon. Private wealth and a good education were in her view good things in a professional politician. But she worried about his judgment – not political judgment – but what she called "wisdom". She just could not see or accept that a man in his early forties, with little experience outside politics, could make good decisions. The consequences were that she often acted on her own initiative – using her work title which everyone knew from watching the American television series about the White House, *West Wing*, was an important and powerful one – to look into areas which really were not her responsibility and to bypass established systems.

To be fair to her, she was scrupulous in maintaining a good relationship with the prime minister, as was her duty. She even learned a little about modern music and football, which the prime minister was keen on in order not to appear stuffy and old-fashioned. What irked her was having to send all intelligence papers to the deputy prime minister as well. She had started with good intentions but Jacot wondered how much actually got through. There were a thousand 'Yes, Minister' type reasons why the distribution of such documents should be restricted. Her views on him were unprintable but colour-

ful. One of the many good things about working for an educated and civilised woman was that she never swore. Jacot
didn't mind swearing and had enjoyed the vivid and fruity language used in the army, particularly when things went wrong.
But in the end it was over-reliant for effect on the all-purpose
epithet that sometimes smothered the joke. Lady Nevinson's
language was cleaner but the humour darker and more savage.
Her descriptions of the deputy prime minister's incompetence
and vanity were elegant mini-*Haikus* of disdain and abuse.
Jacot had secretly started noting the best ones down on the
pads of pale cream Joint Intelligence Committee writing paper
on which he wrote his notes. The "Haiku" file was kept in his
safe under a suitably extreme "Top Secret" classification.
Perhaps one day, thirty or forty years hence, he might be able
to publish a selection.

The deputy prime minister's staff seemed always to be in
pursuit of various documents which they felt their boss
should have seen. They became very worked up one day when
they somehow discovered that the Palace had received the
Queen's copy a day before their man got his. Lady Nevinson
was at her most gracious when she explained that intelligence
documents of this type had always been sent to the Queen
first. She pointed out that if the unfortunate staffer were to
cast his eye over the distribution list at the back of every Joint
Intelligence Committee paper published since the Queen's
Accession in February 1952 he would see the same formula –
"Copy Number One – HM The Queen."

The Queen had been reading Joint Intelligence Committee
papers for sixty years, possibly longer. One rather hoped that
she might make up for the callowness and inexperience of her

current and recent ministers. Although a monarchist at heart and by principle, part of the current allure of the monarchy for Jacot and many others was that it answered that age-old question – "Who guards the guardians?" Or as Lady Nevinson sometimes liked to put it "Where the hell are the grown ups?"

In a way not perhaps obvious to the elected and professional politicians the monarch, or certainly this Queen, really did command the loyalty of the armed forces – every last man. Formal real power lay of course in Downing Street with the prime minister who, like the centurion in Chapter Eight of St Matthew's Gospel, actually decided who went where and did what. But God forbid, if push ever came to shove in some political nightmare scenario, the army and the other armed services would act or refrain to act on the Queen's orders and no one else's.

It was an odd situation. Jacot was slightly wary of Lady Nevinson but it was part of his military training to obey orders. He wondered if increasingly she was out to do her own thing. He briefly took her through further developments in Cambridge. She listened intently. 'Lady Nevinson, the problem is essentially a locked room mystery.' Jacot looked eager and rather pleased.

She sighed. 'Jacot, now is not the time for one of your know-all performances. Intelligence work is not like appearing on University Challenge. I like to think I am a reasonably educated Englishwoman. On a damp holiday last year in the Lake District I watched just about every episode of Agatha Christie's Poirot and Miss Marple. I therefore regard myself as an expert in detective fiction. And, if it helps, partying wasn't the only thing Gilles Navarre and I got up to in Saigon and afterwards. He was and is a fan of the Maigret books. Can't say they especially enthused me but I was young and I faked it. Gilles was obsessed with "the psychological angle" of these books. He would expound on them for hours. Still, better than an existentialist or a man obsessed with football. So in a way I am an expert in French detective novels too. I have spent many hours inside that little flat in the Rue Richard Lenoire.'

'You are interested after all', enthused Jacot. 'Not sure Maigret ever solved locked room stuff. In the meantime just one recommendation for you. My personal favourite is an American called Jacques Futrelle. He wrote perhaps the greatest locked room mystery of all time, *The Problem of Cell 13*, in which his detective manages to escape from a hermetically sealed cell.'

'Well, OK can you get me a copy – might be fun to read on the beach.'

'You are most gracious. But in a way I was being deadly serious. In detective fiction there are about twenty or so ways in which a locked room or something similar can apparently be breached. For instance, take a yacht found at sea with no one on board. The Marie Celeste problem, if you like. How do we explain it?'

Jacot beamed like a schoolboy. Nevinson looked bored but she was prepared to indulge her sidekick. Very often he was on to something.

'Do tell, Colonel.'

'The yacht's cook had poisoned everybody on board and then thrown their bodies into the sea', he continued. 'Unfortunately, he was seen doing so by the yacht owner's ever-faithful baboon who consequently strangled him in revenge and tipped the body into the sea. It then hid in a secret place above a wardrobe.'

Lady Nevinson tried to look interested.

'The least interesting stuff is about secret passages and revolving drinks cabinets allowing the murderer access. Useful if you live in a medieval castle or one of those manor houses with priest holes. Even here in Downing Street we have underground passages. The prime minister can access COBRA without having to come to the surface. I think he can even make his way to the command centre in the MOD without having to emerge in the street. Annoyingly, he cannot walk to the House of Commons underground. Something of an oversight. The Old War Office also has them. Profumo as Secretary of State for War is said to have smuggled his mistresses in by one for secret assignations in his office. There are some quite good stories in which fiendish devices are activated once the victim is safely behind his locked doors and windows. What about this: the bed on which the victim slept was hooked from outside with a strong fishing line and moved so that it faced a different direction? The victim was then woken by a very strong light being shone directly into his eyes, and, thinking that he was moving towards the bathroom to switch off the light, stepped through an open balcony window to his death. But if you read enough of this stuff gradually you begin to understand the best techniques. Bereaved baboons are amusing but hardly serious. We are not looking for a bereaved baboon. The best stories, the ones which seem most real are those where the victim is actually killed before entering the hermetically sealed room.'

Nevinson was suddenly alert. 'Go on.'

'Well, we know Verney was alive after the feast and we know he was alive when he went to bed and sufficiently *compos mentis* to bolt his inner door and slide a small chock under it. The rooms in the older parts of some Cambridge colleges have an outer door with a key to lock it and an inner door with a bolt. It's just like that unfortunate Russian Litvinenko. He was alive when he left the *Yo Sushi* restaurant on Piccadilly. But he had been done for. The polonium had been administered in his food and he died in agony two weeks later. The murder to all intents and purposes had been carried out. There is no antidote to radiation poisoning. The body can handle a little but not very much.'

'But there was no radioactivity in Verney's room,' said Nevinson. 'The police are on to Russian dirty trick techniques. And it doesn't look as though Litvinenko's murderers cared about covering their tracks, unlike whoever did this. The West End was lit up like a Christmas tree with radiation. And Jacot, the authorities are confident that there are no poisons either.'

Jacot went on, 'But the real interest from our point of view lies in the basic truth behind all the plots and stories. They are always disappointing. Once we see how the murder has been carried out we always feel slightly disappointed. It never turns out to be as clever as we thought. Like a magician's trick, once we know the technique we can see how simple it was to pull off.'

'What do you mean?'

'It's something simple. Very simple. Staring us in the face stuff but we can't see it.'

'So, in summary, Colonel, you have come up with very little. But just to make sure you have acquired a part of the late

General Verney which is in that ludicrous little box; what an Australian would call an "Esky". And you have acquired the specimen illegally and off the record by suggesting to a Cambridge professor that I might at some point be in a position to get him a knighthood.'

'Possibly even a peerage. But yes, that's about it Lady Nevinson.'

'Who would want a peerage these days Jacot? I received mine a couple of years before the hereditaries were ejected in 1998. I was proud of it: a reward for my distinguished service and an opportunity to serve my country in the future at the highest level. But once most of the hereditaries went the heart seemed to go out of it. The House used to have the civilized custom that when you were breakfasting or lunching on your own you sat at a general table. Some London clubs do this I understand. And you take the next available seat. A kind of pot luck with a bit of speed dating thrown in...'

Jacot giggled. 'You would not have been at home in a Foot Guards' Mess Lady Nevinson. At breakfast the places are laid with an extra space in between and if you don't want to speak to anyone you wear your hat.'

'A bearskin, surely not!' exclaimed Nevinson in mock horror and continued 'I was able to sit next to all kinds of people. There was a hereditary who was a dentist. Another I remember who was a bookie. And many who had had distinguished careers in the military – not as generals but as fighting soldiers in the last war and the various campaigns since. Plenty of spooks too. But now they are all political apparatchiks of one sort or another. An awful crew. Simply awful.' For a moment she looked deeply depressed. But then she rallied.

'Well done anyway Jacot. It is for these difficult events that I keep you on my establishment. Let's hope this professor Livesey keeps his mouth shut. I am sure I can wangle him a knighthood if necessary so don't worry.' She smiled.

'Take me through why exactly you did it though?' She leaned back into her leather chair and waited for Jacot's explanation.

'Most of the people I talked to, including both a hard-headed provincial policeman who has seen it all, and the military police's brightest detective, think Verney died of natural causes. Even the Regius Professor of Pathology, er, our new best friend, has his money was on it being a natural death. Apparently, it does happen even though Verney appeared to be in good health for a man of his age. The routine toxicology tests have proved negative. No radioactivity or anything like that present, as you said. Just a couple more very exotic poison tests to go and then that's it. Both the Home Office, and very kindly, the FBI will take care of those but everyone expects them to prove negative.

'But I am just not convinced. Although I am not a police detective my instincts and capacity for legitimate suspicion have been finely honed working for you these past few years. There is something not quite right. Something we are not seeing. Curiously, Livesey seemed a little uneasy as well when I spoke to him. He was very reluctant to discuss with a non-medical professional the details of exotic, untraceable poisons. There are apparently ways of killing people with poisons that would make our eyes water.'

Lady Nevinson smiled. She was definitely onside and Jacot was relieved. 'So why the body parts?'

'They're not body parts. Or at least I hope not. Inside the "Esky" as you call it are just a couple of small test tubes with swabs in them. That's what Livesey said anyway. I certainly haven't had a look.'

'Charming. It would appear that you trust neither the Forensic Science Service nor the FBI with its extraordinary laboratories to get it right. Perhaps you were going to send them off by post to an address you found on the Internet.' Lady Nevinson enjoyed her own joke.

'Well, actually I was going to dispatch them to Vienna. There's a clinic there, the Rudolferinhaus, which dealt with the poisoning of the president of Ukraine.'

'Yes. I remember. And I take the point. That whole business about the poisoning of President Yuschenko is still reverberating. One of the counter-allegations is that the Americans doctored the blood samples to make it appear that their man had been poisoned by the Russians to clinch the election for him. It's nonsense I know, but at least this way we will get an independent second opinion. And no doubt you have friends there. Do you know I can't remember the name of the Austrian spook organisation? That lovely Count Von something with the beard is their head of station in London. Wonderful party he gives at Christmas in their embassy.'

'My contacts are with the *Heeresnachrichtenamt*, the HNA, which is part of their military intelligence.'

Her frown softened. 'I had forgotten you speak German. Vienna is all very well but what about your contacts in Berlin?'

'Berlin and Munich. I don't think the move from Munich will be complete for another couple of years. Pretty good too.'

'I am sorry to hassle you. Of course they are. Don't worry

Jacot. You have done exactly the right thing. Keep them in your fridge and you can bring them with us to Paris tomorrow.'

'Paris, Lady Nevinson?'

'Yes. Paris, Colonel Jacot. You make it sound like a dirty weekend. Yes, Paris. Official visit to French intelligence. And you are coming with me. We are off on a jaunt Jacot – you and me and General Verney in his "Esky". The French are another group independent of the Americans and I am sure their toxicology laboratories will be on the ball. The car leaves for King's Cross at nine o'clock tomorrow. What was the name of that detective story writer you mentioned? I think I'll send the car to Hatchards right now. Be fun to read on the train.'

'Jacques Futrelle.'

'Funny, I had never heard of him until you mentioned his name a few minutes ago. I hope he is as good as you say.'

'Well he was a one story wonder in many ways and his career was cruelly cut short.'

'Oh dear, how?'

'He went down on The Titanic.' Thinking this a suitably dramatic punch line Jacot shimmered out.

X

Direction Centrale du Renseignement Intérieur, Paris
7 Rue Nélaton (near the Eiffel Tower)

Jacot always enjoyed the Eurostar. It was an aspect of modernity he never really got used to. As a child a trip to Paris meant a long bumpy car ride through Kent and then sailing on a rather grimy ferry to Calais and then onwards slowly on often cobbled roads to Paris. He had been in Paris with his parents in 1968 and he always remembered a smelly and rather inconvenient city. On his first tour of Northern Ireland nearly twenty years later he realized what the smell had been – stale tear gas. But the Eurostar was a marvel. He settled back with a book and took a sip of his champagne. Very senior civil servants like Celia Nevinson travelled in style and their sidekicks went along with them.

Jacot had been surprised to be asked to accompany her on a visit to the DCRI, the French domestic intelligence service. After his dressing down in St James' Park over his tensions with the CIA's London Station he assumed he was not in her good books, least of all for a visit to the French, the trickiest of the intelligence allies. On their visits to London they tended to complain about the food, make disparaging remarks about the Americans and flirt inappropriately with the waitresses. All very tiring. But Jacot like many Englishmen of his type was securely Francophile and looking forward to the visit. On a professional level he also heartily approved of the way French Intelligence was set up. The inevitable and recurrent insecurities of French history ensured that France's post-Napoleonic rulers had always kept a close eye on the popular mood, particularly in Paris. The organisation put in place by Napoleon's minister of police, the utterly repellent but completely brilliant Fouché, had metamorphosed into a low level intelligence gathering outfit – the *Renseignements Génereaux* (General Intelligence) with offices across the country. The government in Paris had a good handle on what was happening in the suburbs and provinces. As a result the French had been less surprised by the emergence of Al Qaida and its various franchisees. The French also had a version of MI5 responsible for protecting the French State from external and internal threats – the *Direction du Surveillance Territoire* (DST). Although like all the other French intelligence agencies it emerged somewhat murkily from the Second World War – it had had an enviable record since. The DST claimed with some justification never to have been penetrated by the Russians. They had one clear advantage over their colleagues at MI5 – they were essentially part of the police force and regarded themselves primarily as policemen. Thus they were happy doing bread and butter work like surveillance, hanging around in dingy bars and mosques. They never hankered after the James Bond life or the lifestyle of their intelligence counterparts who worked abroad. Protecting France and its way of life in France was a high enough calling. They had an additional advantage in that most Frenchmen had a certain idea of France.

President Sarkozy had re-organised the French intelligence establishment a couple of years before combining RG and DST into a new organisation. It made sense and worked well: combining a great tradition of collecting and considering valuable

low-lever intelligence with the more traditional skills of a security police set up. But the new headquarters in an upmarket
suburb did not appeal to some of the old hands who preferred
their traditional stomping ground close to the Eiffel Tower at 7
Rue Nélaton, where today's meeting with Celia Nevinson and
Daniel Jacot was to take place.

As Jacot looked out at the French countryside speeding past
his window he was struck by one difference between the two
countries. The French had no intelligence heroes. Police heroes
yes, but the spy had a different status in France. He or she
remained not quite respectable in the popular mind. To work
for the state was good – too good perhaps in these austere
times. But the intelligence agent had been forever compromised
by the war. It was unfair of course. Not every spook went to
work for Vichy but the damage was done. But the Brits had
James Bond. Jacot enjoyed both the books and the films but
could not help wondering if the whole thing wasn't an exercise
in nostalgic fantasy. One of those scraps you clung onto when
everything else familiar and re-assuring that propped up your
status and national self esteem was gone. Like a pensioner of
the Habsburgs we clung on to our trinkets and our past. All else
had gone but at least we had a good analytical handle on our
decline.

Like the remote wolf ancestors of today's pet dogs who
abandoned their independence in exchange for being looked
after by men, we made a deliberate decision. Anything would be
better than facing the full implications of our lost status. We
preferred domestication by the United States to international
insignificance.

The French had had much the same experience of decline

but had internalised it through seeking to influence the EU.
Jacot wondered if the French national mood would darken if
the various crises afflicting that organisation got out of hand.
But for now the French seemed very onside, especially since
Libya. The newspapers suggested that there had been some
kind of rupture between the French President and the British
prime minister, but the word inside the cabinet office was that
relations were as warm as before. It certainly made sense.
French calculations had changed. The one clear effect of the
current instability was to increase the power of Germany.
Anathema to most Frenchmen. A renewed *Entente Cordiale*
with their old adversaries the British to offset German hege-
mony would be preferable for many.

A Jaguar from the embassy met them at the Gare Du Nord
and whisked them to the Rue Nélaton. They walked up to the
security desk.

'Madame la Baronesse Nevinson', a voice boomed from
behind them. They both turned. A large man with an olive
complexion moved forward nimbly to kiss Nevinson on the
cheeks – many times.

'Madame Le National Security Adviser' he chuckled.
'*Enchanté.*' He bowed low.

'How nice to see you Monsieur Directeur. Monsieur le
Directeur Gilles Navarre – this is my assistant Colonel Daniel
Jacot.'

'Mon Colonel'. And with that he swept them both into a
lift which, in the way of French lifts, creaked slowly up to the
fourth floor.

It was one of the most beautiful offices Jacot had ever
seen. Decorated in the Empire style – all mirrors and striped

material – you half expected the Empress Josephine to waft in. A portrait of Napoleon hung on one of the walls. Behind the director's desk three large French windows overlooked the street with a good view of the Eiffel Tower beyond. In a corner a table was set for lunch – for four. They sat down around the gilded First Empire desk.

'Monsieur Directeur, it was good of you to find the time to see us', Lady Nevinson began.

'Madame la Baronesse, I am as ever at your service. We have much to discuss.'

'Colonel Jacot is a distinguished colleague of mine who shares many of my views. One view in particular.'

'Of course.'

'But I have not yet explained to him how it works.'

'I think explaining over lunch would be in order.'

They moved to the small table in the corner. Jacot as well as being hungry was interested to see what they would get to eat. The catering in the Cabinet Office was like a works canteen in the 1950s. Jacot kept a small fridge in his office out of desperation and filled it with a few good things. Lady Nevinson occasionally asked to borrow some of his white burgundy or a salad. She had viewed him as something of a gourmet until she had discovered him eating corned beef sandwiches one day at his desk – an old army habit that was impossible to discard. MI5 and MI6 had better food. "C" was rumoured to keep a fine cellar – particularly strong in claret.

Navarre pressed a buzzer on his desk before sitting down. 'Let me introduce you to a colleague.' A few seconds later a young woman entered the room. She had obviously been waiting to be summoned. She nodded at the director and at

Celia Nevinson whom she must have met before.

'Monica Zaden – Daniel Jacot.' The introductions were made.

She was in her mid thirties probably. Dark shining hair and olive skin. She was one of the most striking women Jacot had ever seen. And tall. Nearly six foot he reckoned. She sat down next to him.

'Mme Zaden is one of our most experienced operatives. She has been undercover for some time in various grisly suburbs of Paris keeping an eye on some of our "bearded chums", if I can put it like that. But it is time for a change of scene and I am pleased to say that she has been posted to our London Embassy. Part of her duties will be to liaise with your intelligence people.'

'You say "part of her duties"', Jacot intervened.

'Yes, yes. Part', replied Navarre.

Zaden herself continued, 'Don't worry. I won't be under-cover, I won't have to live in Londonistan, and I won't be on the front line but I will have overall responsibility for our agents in London who are concerned with Islamist extremism.'

Navarre had the decency to look embarrassed. 'I am afraid that we prefer to keep our own eyes on some of the hotheads you appear to be willing to put up with in London.' He shrugged.

Lady Nevinson did not seem put out, so Jacot did not pursue the line any further. Despite the presence of this beau-tiful girl and the congenial Navarre, Jacot was feeling increas-ingly uncomfortable. But Nevinson was all smiles. The waiters started to serve lunch.

Navarre dispatched his plain green salad with walnut dressing at speed and took large sips of ice-cold Chablis. He laughed, flashing his teeth at Nevinson. His mood continued to improve over a thick slice of cold beef fillet served with green beans, accompanied by two glasses of an unidentified but silky and strong red burgundy.

As Jacot tasted it Nevinson laughed, 'I can see you are trying to work out where it's from. It is extraordinarily good but you won't get the answer. French intelligence have their methods. They also have their own vineyards.'

Navarre grinned. 'What is the point of being the director of French Domestic Intelligence if you cannot have decent wine? Austerity yes. But not for Monsieur le Directeur of counter-terror. Anyway in France we organize these things better. In your country it is not the done thing to earn more than your prime minister if you are in public service. Here no one cares – as long as your cellar is not better than the Elysée.'

Everyone laughed. Jacot relaxed and got stuck in too. There may be no such thing as a free lunch in the intelligence world, and he certainly got that feeling, but he was going to enjoy it anyway.

Admiring a thick slice of Roquefort, Navarre finally came to the point. Looking at Lady Nevinson he said just one word, 'Magenta?'

'Magenta', replied Nevinson.

All three smiled conspiratorially at Jacot.

Jacot was puzzled. Extremely puzzled. Actually he was alarmed. He thought Magenta was an entirely British affair. Here he was in the grand office of the head of the French equivalent of MI5 along with the British National Security

Adviser no less. With possibly the most dazzlingly pretty French lady spook imaginable in attendance. And it seemed as if there was a private secret between them. He felt he was playing intelligence gooseberry.

The waitress left closing the doors behind her.

'Madame La Baronesse?'

'Yes I suppose I should. Jacot, I have come here for a meeting with my old friend Gilles – routine business really. We go back a long way – Saigon in the early 70s. We were both there when Saigon fell. I told you if you remember.'

Jacot now understood the strange nostalgic 1970s inter-lude in Nevinson's office a few days previously. He was being pre-introduced to Gilles Navarre – not just the part he had played in the private life of her youth but the part he played in the intelligence life of her maturity.

Navarre chuckled. He looked like a Frenchman who had led a full life so far and though now in his early sixties fully intended to keep going to the end. 'Madame Nevinson helped us at a critical time and ever since I personally – and France too I suppose – have been in her debt. We are part of a group – a kind of Franco-British liaison team and we think you should belong as well Mon Colonel.'

She nodded at Navarre.

Jacot said still slightly bewildered, 'I had assumed, Lady Nevinson, that it was an all-British affair.'

'Well, it's not. It has a branch office in France. Indeed the Magenta codes and ciphers and various bits of kit are a joint Franco-British venture.'

'You're joking, of course.'

'No. And as I said in London I want you to be part of the

group. It's small for now anyway but all of us are absolutely on side.'

'Who else? I mean who else apart from these good people?'

Navarre said, 'Never mind. It's too dangerous. Not for our lives I hope but for our careers and our nerves. Madame La Baronnesse and I still have some secrets from each other.'

Jacot was stunned.

Navarre continued, 'Your GCHQ works very closely with its American counterpart NSA – no doubt it gives you many advantages of which frankly our people are jealous. But it gives you two great disadvantages. One is that your system is completely intertwined with the Americans. The second is that you think like them technically. I can't pretend that the French do not have their own methods, Mon Colonel. Unlike Captain Reynaud in *Casablanca* I am not shocked. It is true that we used to bug the seats in First Class on Air France. Nor should I explain that we are doing this just because of my friendship with Madame La Baronesse Nevinson. We are doing it in the interests of France as you would expect. But our interests coincide.'

He took a sip of his Burgundy and went on. 'We had been worried for some time about our own communications. In particular the communication network surrounding our nuclear deterrent, which seems to have been subject to a sophisticated technical attack. We assumed initially that it was the usual suspects, but we do not think so now. It was almost certainly a technical attack by the United States. We are not sure whether the Americans wanted to find out how our command and control worked or whether they were actually trying to take control of it. Unlike yours our nuclear deterrent is not just called independent, in fact it really is. It can actually be launched by the President of the Republic in concert with a few others – all of them French. The codes and technical and engineering procedures required to get the missiles in the air are all under exclusive French control. As are the communications and the targeting. None of those apply to the English system I understand. But I digress.

'To cut a long story short, last summer various ministers from your Coalition government spent their holidays in southern France, some quite close to where some of our nuclear facilities are. Two of the ministers, as far as we could tell, were required to be in touch with London and were receiving highly encrypted information for I think what you call their electronic red boxes. After some embarrassments a few years ago we do not as a rule try to intercept English communications.' His eyes twinkled. 'But we had hardened our nuclear communications to confuse the Americans. How shall I say – one of our command and control installations is in a part of France well known for its English tourists? We began to pick up indications of what might be a technical attack. But on investigation our system was not the target – one of your minister's encrypted communications were. And yes it was the Americans. And we believe that they were able to read what your minister was sending and receiving. We have a more modest signals capability than you but because we don't trust the Americans we are more sophisticated at keeping them out.'

'I am afraid it get's worse Daniel.' Celia Nevinson looked appalled.

'Yes, Mon Colonel. Indeed it does. As a result of our findings last summer we sent a small detachment out to

Afghanistan – to make sure that our communications there are secure. They are but… and I think you know what I am going to say – yours are not. Some of the messages between your generals in the field and London are being read in real time in Washington. The scale of it surprised even us wearily cynical French.'

'But Lady Nevinson – if this is the case we should take our information to GCHQ. The third party rule would apply – we can't tell our people that the French told us, but at least we could improve our own security. A country has to have some secrets after all. Surely, Monsieur le Directeur, that is what a patriotic Englishman should do.'

Navarre stared down at the table avoiding Jacot's gaze. There was silence. Nevinson looked out of the window. Only Zaden looked at him.

After several seconds Nevinson turned her head back from the window and looked him straight in the eye. 'Daniel, we have thought of that. And you are right that would be the correct thing to do. But there is one rather crucial detail you still do not know about. We are not sure, the French are not sure, but there are some additional oddnesses about the comms attacks picked up by the French last summer and a few weeks later in Afghanistan. French technicians believe that on both occasions our systems alarmed, warned our people that some kind of attack was underway. There's a protocol for that; what an outside observer like the French should have been able to see was some kind of adjustment of the system – a change in the transmitting frequency or the levels of encryption – a defensive manoeuvre, for instance. It should be like Chess. But nothing. It's possible that we were trying to be clever – a kind of Donald Rumsfeld action – we know that you know, but you don't know that we know. But it's strange nevertheless. When our strongly encrypted stuff is attacked by the Chinese or the Russians our system behaves differently. In the case of these attacks it's as if we don't care.'

'Or maybe you do but the people who saw the alarm don't, or maybe someone did raise the alarm', said Monica 'and didn't live to tell the tale.'

'That's absurd.' Jacot looked weary. 'So in summary French spooks are telling us that the Americans are reading chunks of our strongly encrypted data and we don't seem to care.'

'I am afraid, Daniel, there you have it. And times are changing which means we now will have to act more vigorously. Both the French and ourselves have been picking up signs in both intelligence and diplomatic reporting of increased paranoia in the Americans. Not so much the elected politicians but the officials, what some call the permanent government. We know – the world knows – that parts of the American set up got out of control post 911. Even the most sceptical minds underestimated the sheer vengeance of what they were up to all over the globe. They got mad and then tried to get even. It doesn't work. If you really want to screw your enemies you need to keep a cool head.'

'But we know all this Lady Nevinson. What's different now?' asked Jacot.

'I am trying to explain that. It was possible just for us to rub along, the French included. Keep a gentle eye on what the Yanks were up to and make sure they didn't get out of control. Always much easier in France even under Sarkozy.

More difficult in the UK but until recently doable. But the whole Arab Spring has almost unhinged them. Black ops plans, for instance, to keep the Bahraini king in power. And of course plans for a strike on Iran – the timing to be decided by the American presidential electoral cycle. How crazy is that? Another driver for the tougher attitude was the whole Wikileaks affair. Why seek extradition when we could kidnap or kill seemed to be a strong view both at Langley and the State Department. These guys are on edge and it worries both the French and us. So now we need more people on side. In France as well as the UK. Who guards the guardians Jacot? Well, it's us.' She turned to Navarre, 'Oh and Gilles, as I mentioned the good colonel has something for you.'

'Yes, yes.' Jacot got up opened his briefcase and took out the container of forensic samples from General Verney.

Navarre nodded, took it, and pressed the buzzer. One of his staff came in opened the container peered at the test tubes and swabs inside. '*C'est suffit*', he said and then left.

Navarre turned to Jacot and Nevinson. 'It's enough for two tests. We will split the samples and re-ice them. One will leave with a courier from the *Gare de L'Est* in forty-five minutes. It will be at the *Centre Antipoison* in Strasbourg in a few hours. We have trusted people there who will let us know the results as soon as possible. It may take a little time though. I understand that we are checking for exotics, in particular marine toxins. These can be difficult and the expertise in Europe is good in theory but few scientists will have experience of these things. The other sample will leave tonight on the weekly military flight to Papeete. Our people in the *Polynesie Francaise* understand these poisons. But again it will take time as you might expect.

'I understand you are not expecting anything to be found but that you are using our scientists as a kind of independent control. I commend you for your caution, Mon Colonel.'

They drank a little more. Jacot and Monica flirted. The UK's National Security Adviser flirted outrageously with France's top spy. Some young romances ended in marriage. Some brought heartache. Jacot had not seen it much but sometimes old flames remained the best of friends. Their time in Saigon had obviously been intense and dangerous.

It all seemed so natural. The surroundings and the food and wine softened if not smothered the implications. It was a shaming experience to be told by foreigners, however civilized and helpful, that you could no longer trust your own country-men.

The Wikileaks affair and the US diplomatic cables that were made public as a result should have made it obvious to even those, in Lady Nevinson's favourite phrase, with "a room temperature IQ" that the UK's central government machinery was heavily penetrated by American intelligence. The leaks also showed the treachery of the United States in revealing to the Russians the details of the UK's independent deterrent – an act worthy of Judas himself.

But if what Navarre had told them was true then the Americans had British allies on the inside. People whose patri-otism and moral sense had been so dulled by years of sub-servience that they could no longer tell the difference between our own interests and those of the United States. Or worse, people who saw an advantage in allowing the US access to everything. In exchange for what – a place at the top table?

That was it thought Jacot. That was the ultimate source of the difficulty – why some Englishmen were so prone to corruption by the Americans. It was all about status. Like the poor old Duke of Windsor endlessly fretting whether his friends and countrymen were going to curtsey to his duchess, a certain kind of politician and Mandarin endlessly fretted about our lost national status. The Americans could sense this, at all levels, and used it to their advantage. Whether it was a British prime minister happily carrying out chores for an American president or an ambitious army officer planning his next promotion, ultimately they were all piggy-backing on American power.

Most galling of all the only way to fight back was through a different betrayal. Nevinson and he were no longer colleagues but conspirators. He felt sad and ashamed. Had it come to this? The only way to be a loyal Englishman was to conspire with the French. Navarre and Zaden were all very well – the very picture of modern Frenchmen. But what of the other side of France – the ugly side that you saw during Vichy. The vainglorious side that you saw during the French Indo-China war that persisted with the absurd cult of Napoleon, in many ways the author of their misfortunes. The brutal side of the Algerian war. He didn't trust the French either. It was in Jacot's view a proper country with a strong identity far removed from the drivel of political correctness. But that strong identity involved something elemental, true only unto itself. And much of that had evolved in opposition to the English. The *entente cordiale* had been such a big deal because it was so new. It was a turning against the past and an always incomplete one at that. There was another catch, another alarm going off in his mind – was the process he was going through mentally what happened to a previous generation as they were preparing to betray their country? Is this how Philby, and Burgess and Maclean justified it to themselves? Yes I may be doing a rubbish on my country but it's all in a higher cause. And the Islamists?

Pretentious humbug thought Jacot – nearly a bottle of Chablis at lunch meant not befuddlement but clarity – four letter thinking. It was time for a choice. How had that overestimated and pretentious American poet put it – it's a turn in the road. But for now the French would make better friends than anyone else Jacot could think of. And they were the only people available. Nelson and Wellington would be turning in their graves. But then again a previous generation of English generals and admirals had fought the Americans – Cornwallis who had found George Washington so boorish and provincial at Yorktown might smile indulgently. Perhaps we were about to return to an older world, a different order. Jacot wondered when the switch had come. Queen Victoria for instance had been very reluctant for the Prince of Wales to visit the young United States in 1860. He crossed the border from Canada having begun his visit with a re-union of Canadian veterans of the war of 1812. For the first time since 1776 prayers were said for the Royal Family in churches across the Union.

At the end of the day from Winston Churchill onwards the deal had always been that to be a loyal Englishman you had to be pro-American. Not any more. He looked at Lady Nevinson sitting opposite. She must have been very good looking in her day and energetic in a way that women coming into professional life in the 1970s and 80s had to be to get ahead. Anyway he trusted her and her judgment. They sat opposite each other in the Eurostar on the way back, drinking more wine. She made no reference to the events of the day but instead asked him about the events of thirty years before. Despite working for her for over two years she had never asked him about his experiences in the Falklands. She kept the conversation in the past, mostly, but it was clear on occasion that she was desperately worried about the security of the islands in the present day. Just before they got to London she came to the point: she wanted him to visit the islands on her behalf, just to re-assure her that everything that needed to be done was being done.

XI

Jacot stepped forward to be searched by a US Marine. The American Embassy was getting more and more difficult to get into. After 911 and a series of attacks on American embassies across the world, it was hardly surprising. Security everywhere. Barriers everywhere. No wonder the local residents were up in arms. But it had certainly outgrown the Grosvenor Square site.

Apparently there was a plan to move the whole operation south of the River Thames to Nine Elms. He wondered whether the codename for the CIA station in London, "Grosvenor", would change as well. The head of the station sat ex-officio on the British Joint Intelligence Committee behind a neatly typed place card which said "Grosvenor". "Nine Elms" did not have the same ring to it.

The Embassy itself was hideous and made no concessions to the surrounding area and architecture. Grosvenor Square had always struck Jacot as an odd place. It was essentially a piece of the United States of America in the middle of London. During the war General Eisenhower had established his headquarters in the square, promptly nicknamed "EisenhowerPlatz" by irreverent Londoners. The square was filled with reminders of American power and how it rose at our expense. The statue of General Eisenhower in the north-east corner certainly looked like the "Ike" of the newsreels, but which "Ike"? The one who led the allied forces at Normandy, or the "Ike" who became president and then pulled the rug from beneath us at Suez?

Jacot was escorted to the grand staircase through the grand entrance hallway. The walls were filled with paintings and various items of Americana. It was a curious experience walking through the hall – half reading a comic book and half walking down the nave and aisles of a medieval cathedral. There were simple messages embedded in the décor, statues and decoration. Like every other US Embassy in the world the room was dominated by a copy of the famous Lansdowne Portrait of Washington. It showed the first president renouncing the possibility of a third term in office. It was huge, eight feet by five feet and filled with symbolism. As with so many things American it was seventy percent magnificent, twenty per cent ridiculous and ten per cent total absolute lie. Washington was a great man no doubt about it. And like Cromwell before him in England he could have been a King if he had wanted. But just before the portrait was painted Washington had received a new set of false teeth. It made him look faintly ridiculous, like a child trying to pretend that it's mouth isn't full of sweets.

Jacot admired George Washington hugely. Unlike, say, Napoleon or even Wellington, the more anyone read about Washington the more impressive he became. This came across in most of the official representations of his image which did homage to his strength of will and essential nobility. The face, whether in portraits or statues, radiated his patriotism. This seemed to Jacot his most powerful legacy to the American people and spirit. They, like their first president, were never afraid to display their patriotism. It sometimes took some distasteful forms but love of country was never sneered at on the other side of the Atlantic.

The Lansdowne Portrait still loomed large as Jacot climbed the stairs. It was this portrait that was supposed to have been rescued by the fourth First Lady, Dolley Madison, as the British closed in on the White House just before the end of the War of 1812. And that was where the lie came in, a characteristic lie for the Americans. The portrait had indeed been rescued from the advancing British who attempted to burn the White House down. But it wasn't the First Lady who did the deed. The rescue was in reality organized a by one of the Madison's slaves, a certain Paul Jennings, who was lucky enough many years later to be able to buy his freedom for the then colossal sum of $120. Presumably he made a lot from tips mused Jacot, as he was ushered into the office of the head of the CIA Station on the second floor.

Jacot shook hands with John Dixwell, the third or perhaps it was the fourth – Jacot could never remember. Dixwell was tall and rangey. Dressed in a dark grey Brooks Brothers suit with a button down shirt and horizontal striped tie, he was the epitome of the successful preppy American. Anglophile, fond of opera and with an encyclopedic knowledge of the James Bond books and films, he was precisely the sort of man to be in charge of the CIA's large and formidable London Station. The UK intelligence establishment loved him. He had a pretty wife and twin, very handsome, teenage sons who spent their vacations from Duke in London charming all the English girls. He and Jacot got on well enough but Jacot never forgot for a moment that Dixwell was an accomplished intelligence operative for a foreign power. And for all the charm, genuine charm in a way, there was something about the man's eyes that made Jacot uneasy. Dixwell knew that Jacot was a man on whom his blandishments and old-fashioned Southern manners cut little ice, but he kept trying anyway.

He asked Jacot to sit, filled two shot glasses, embossed with the CIA's ubiquitous logo of an eagle atop a compass rose, with a fiery bourbon and pushed one over. They downed them in a single gulp and Jacot pushed his glass for a refill. The etiquette of bourbon drinking was as subtle as the Japanese tea ceremony. Jacot enjoyed it. For all the hatchet faced women in the boardroom and in senior positions in the government, under the surface American society retained a kind of frontier masculinity. Jacot even enjoyed watching American Football occasionally. Dixwell's team loyalty was on display in his office – the light blue colours of the North Carolina Tar Heels were omnipresent.

Dixwell cottoned on. He grinned. 'Yep, I played college football. I was a quarterback. Actually it was my footballing prowess that got me a college education in the first place. But I wasn't good enough to turn professional. I was disappointed at the time but there you go. Nevertheless, I follow The Tar Heels still. One of the great, perhaps the great effect of the internet revolution for me is that I can watch them live every week in season – wherever I am.'

'Why Tar Heels?' asked Jacot. He could turn on the charm as well, when it suited him.

Dixwell warmed to the theme. He wasn't a fan of Jacot's but the question had carried with it a genuine inquisitiveness. 'Something to do with tar from the pine forests of North

Carolina which was the state's main export for many years. It's a nickname for all North Carolinans. To begin with it may have been semi-insulting but it was adopted enthusiastically after Robert E Lee put a glorious gloss on it. Dixwell pulled a small card from somewhere on his desk and read aloud:

"'During the late unhappy war between the States it was sometimes called the "Tar-heel State", because tar was made in the State, and because in battle the soldiers of North Carolina stuck to their bloody work as if they had tar on their heels, and when General Lee said, "God bless the Tar-heel boys", they took the name.'"

Oddly, all senior Americans, whether in government service or the private sector tried to reproduce elements of the presidential Oval Office in their own offices. The shape was difficult to replicate but the fittings could be imitated easily enough by all budgets. Dixwell's office was no different. The reproduction Federal furniture with its striped upholstery was straight out of an episode of *West Wing*, another cultural reference point that seemed universal in American government circles. And like the characters in that series many US officials seemed to hold most of their conversations while on the move. They didn't walk down corridors, they strode. Always in a hurry. Always making decisions. Jacot usually found it a little exhausting. He wondered how anyone could watch *West Wing*. Even the poor old president of the United States seemed always to be on the move. Dixwell had the habit when he visited the Cabinet Office but Jacot was relieved that this meeting at least would be held sitting down and in an office.

'Hell, I am sorry to hear about General Verney. It's a bad

business and anything we can do to help of course we will. I gather the Feds are having a look at some stuff. Since the Russians started killing people we have had to be extra careful. I understand the British police have run a Geiger counter over the room and so nothing radioactive is suspected. But there are other things the Russians may have been up to we need to check out. And of course there are the Islamists. Any senior British official is at risk from some of those guys. I don't want to be unkind to you Brits but your borders are a joke. You just don't know who you have got here.'

Jacot agreed wholeheartedly with this sentiment but it was not why he was there. 'There are always the Islamists. But to be frank I can't see someone going for Verney at Cambridge. He's been a much easier target on his travels around the world and numerous visits to Afghanistan.'

'Maybe you are right', said Dixwell. 'The bad guys on the ground in Helmand soon got wind of the new prime minister's first visit didn't they? Jeez, I know the Secret Service are constantly having kittens anytime POTUS visits the troops. Another thing, I know your universities appear to be hotbeds of Islamist radicalism but mainly the third grade ones, not Cambridge, surely. Those colleges are closed societies. It would be difficult to get someone on the inside. Anyway I hear it's natural causes. Sad, but it does happen to men in their late fifties, particularly on the squash court.'

Jacot took all this in and knocked his Bourbon back. Was Dixwell saying a little too much? 'You could be right', said Jacot. 'Verney died in bed though, not the squash court. The police and military police are covering most of the angles and as you say the money's on natural causes. Nevertheless, I am the guy who has to look at the areas that are too sensitive for the police. One of those areas is you and your colleagues. I am interested in who exactly was there that night from Langley?'

Dixwell looked out of the window. 'Me, obviously, and Johnny Downes, the Deputy Director of the Agency. He was going to be in town. Comes from a dirt poor mid-western background and I thought he might like to taste the glories of Cambridge.' He added, conspiratorially, 'To be honest Jacot we are from different backgrounds entirely but we have always got on. America is more class-ridden than you think or we like to pretend. There is a place for everybody. Ivy League is Ivy League. The Midwesterners tend to stick together. We Southern gentlemen get on well as long as we don't fly the Confederate Flag at home or whistle Dixie too much or too loud at the office. The cowboys do their own thing. But it's still difficult if you're from a really poor background. And when they do make it they tend to have a kind of difficult brashness. Even if their success means that they can handle the Yalies their wives can be tricky – first wives that is.' Dixwell grinned. 'But Downes and his good lady fit the scene like a glove. He has done me a lot of favours. We get on. Hey, he loved Cambridge. And you know what Jacot, Downes is very welcome at the White House. The CIA gets to see a lot of the president but there aren't many of us who get invited to the presidential weekly cocktail parties in the family quarters. Downes and his wife do. Yeah, the Martinis are fabulous and the finger food out of this world. Sometimes there's a little US Marine string quartet.' Dixwell looked wistful. 'Johnny could easily be the next director. And if that happens I am going up with him.'

This seemed to Jacot an awful lot of personal information from an intelligence professional. Sure, Dixwell's apple pie family was helpful in creating the right impression in London but this was a layer of detail too much. The art of human intelligence is to get others to give information away. Sometimes it's the intelligence information an agent has been specifically tasked to collect – where the chemical weapons are hidden for instance – or if there are any chemical weapons at all. Sometimes, an agent is on a general trawl for personal information that can then be exploited to turn the target into a source. Very often the opening into exploiting a target can be very simple – some aspiration that can be fulfilled – a child that could do with some help to get into a good American university and a visa. Or a career disappointment that can be put right by a strong American endorsement in the right ears. Or a personal vulnerability like debt, or gambling or girls or boys. Very often it was just plain vanity that gave the intelligence people the opening. As always when dealing with professional spies, even our own professional spies, Jacot felt he was being manipulated in some subtle way. If the manipulation involved so much personal information about Dixwell himself was he trying to hide something behind that? If he was prepared to admit to a foreigner the importance, personal importance, of his relationship with such a senior CIA figure there must be a reason.

'And Mr. Downes came straight back to London that night by car?'

'Yes. It's an easy ride late at night. Johnny would have been back in the Connaught by one thirty or two.'

'The Connaught Hotel?'

'Yes. That's where our really senior guys like to hang out. Good bar too. It was Nixon's favourite hotel if I remember accurately. Incidentally Jacot, never spill the beans in the bar of the Connaught Hotel, the CIA could just be listening.'

Jacot was finding Dixwell less convincing by the minute. 'And you went with him?'

'Yes, absolutely. We went straight from the Fellows' Combination Room, wow what a name, to the Great Gate where our limo awaited. We were let out by the head porter. We did have a couple of night caps on the way down the motorway.' Dixwell smiled again.

'Did you say good night to Verney?'

'Yes, in the Combination Room in the usual way. I know him reasonably well. Johnny Downes went big on the Combination Room. For him candlelight meant a power cut when dad couldn't pay the utility bill. That someone would still want to light an entire room that way wowed him out.'

'I am sure it will be good for your career. But back to Verney. Was he friendly?'

'Yes.' All of a sudden Dixwell's long answers were mono-syllabic.

'If I wanted to ask Mr. Downes to confirm this story – he would?'

'Or you could ask the embassy chauffeur who drove us back.'

'Did you notice anything else about the dinner that was odd?'

Dixwell paused. 'There was a bit of what you Brits call an "atmosphere". Most of your top people were there and I know there have been tensions.'

'What sort of tensions?'

'Well, over Afghanistan and other stuff. You know the score Daniel. We don't actually need you militarily as the good Donald Rumsfeld once put it. We can go it alone. But you give very good cover. If the Brits pulled out early then it would make it even more difficult for us.'

Jacot said, 'Hang on. Our top general, who's in and out of Downing Street every day, has a map of Afghanistan above his desk in the ministry. And I understand his apartment in Kensington Palace is a kind of shrine to the country. He's a what we used to call in the days of Empire a Sepoy general through and through. We are unlikely to leave before the agreed time. And Verney, for all his faults, has always been a strong supporter of our intervention in Afghanistan. Maybe he had been getting cold feet recently but he's not in a position to call the whole thing off.'

Dixwell looked out of the window again. 'Yeah, you are probably right. But our people in Washington worry. And guess what Daniel? I believe in a higher power that controls our lives. It's not called God but Washington. Anyway, who is going to step into Verney's shoes?'

Jacot knew perfectly well but wasn't going to say. 'I am sure it will be announced in due course and that it will be someone sympathetic, as ever, to American concerns. Listen, it has been very good of you to see me. Don't worry, I will find my way to the lobby.'

'No way, Daniel. A Marine has to take you down. This may be London but this is the US Embassy.'

Jacot nodded and within seconds a smart young US Marine corporal entered the room and saluted. They strode down the corridor together like extras in *West Wing*.

As he walked down the steps at the front of the embassy and past the statue of Eisenhower he looked back at the great gold American eagle that hovered over the embassy façade. It looked magnificent in the soft evening sunshine. Jacot walked to the other side of the square to the memorial to the victims of the terrorist atrocities of 911 to pay his quiet respects. The entire Western World still lived in the baleful shadow of that day. He remembered his small part in it. The Cabinet Office had been due to have a tele-conference with colleagues at Langley. He couldn't even remember what it had meant to be about. They had settled into their seats in COBRA and waited for the satellite connection. But no one from Langley had appeared on the screens – just buzzing and a blank green screen. And then Jacot remembered the sound of running. Something he had never heard before in Downing Street. "Never run it panics the men", he had been told on joining his regiment. He knew immediately that there must be something terribly wrong. As the tragic drama of the day unfolded he worried about American colleagues in Washington and New York who may or may not have survived the day. The public only discovered later but the intelligence world knew all along that the CIA's huge New York office was in the World Trade Centre.

In the days that followed, Jacot and his British colleagues did what they could to show solidarity with the members of Grosvenor. Jacot took his opposite number to watch the Changing of the Guard the next day when the bands, on the direct orders of the Queen, had played the American national anthem. It was a moving moment for both of them. They had stood side by side and worked hard in what had seemed the common cause of humanity and freedom. They had drunk a lot together in various spots around London.

When the Americans had a crackdown on expenses the Brits picked up the bill. And when the Cabinet Office was having one of its periodic fits of austerity there was always the prospect of the CIA's monthly lunches at Rules in Maiden Lane off Covent Garden to sustain morale. The CIA were a broad minded bunch with huge experience but most of them could never quite get over the idea of silver tankards filled with Black Velvet. Mixing golden bubbly champagne with black stout to the American mind seemed outrageous. But they drank it well and good times were had. There seemed to be a trust between the two countries. The Brits went the extra mile to help the Americans. The CIA reciprocated, releasing information and judgments to their allies that would get them into trouble with Washington. And yet. And yet. As Jacot stood in front of the memorial deep in meditation he knew that in the matter of the death of general Sir Christopher Verney, Chief of the UK's Defence Intelligence, the head of Grosvenor, the CIA's London Station, was not giving him the whole picture. What was it he was concealing behind those intimate details of the White House, lovingly retold, but designed to dazzle and distract?

XII

Headquarters of the Secret Intelligence Service,
85 Vauxhall Cross, London SE1

Jacot walked from the Cabinet office to the headquarters of the Secret Intelligence Service at Vauxhall Cross on the south bank of the Thames. It was an unattractive building originally built to house commercial offices but bought by the government to house its foreign secret intelligence service. It was a funny decision – better to have left them in anonymous offices dotted over London than house them all in one very obvious building. But maybe that was Jacot's military sensibility intervening – soldiers liked to keep things split up and hidden until the critical moment. It was really none of his business but none of his colleagues who worked there thought the building suitable. They had a variety of uncomplimentary nicknames for the place. Legoland was the most used, but Babylon-on-Thames was the most accurate in Jacot's view. With its ziggurat like shape and weird architectural detailing it could easily have been designed by one of Saddam Hussein's kitschier in-house architects.

Jacot had been invited a few years previously to a preview of the latest James Bond film held for the staff of SIS at an anonymous cinema in north London. It was a formal and elegant occasion with drinks and small eats available. Just before the lights went down "C", the Chief of the Secret Intelligence Service, and the six directors of the principal departments took their seats in the front row, accompanied by some senior movie executives and actors from the film. Everyone craned their necks to see if Dame Judy Dench, "M" in the latest films, was going to be sitting next to her real life counterpart "C". SIS were very proud of their good taste and good manners. It was a gala occasion. Jacot had been hugely flattered to be invited. One of the pleasures of working in the intelligence world was that you were in-the-know even if you could not tell anyone. It was a huge treat to see the latest Bond film weeks before anyone else and in the company of Bond's present-day successors. The atmosphere had been slightly spoiled at the start of the film when as the SIS building was blown sky high on screen a huge cheer went up from the cheap seats. "C" himself failed to see the joke and left at the end with a face like thunder, his aides trailing nervously behind.

It was "C", Sir Valentine Walton, Jacot had come to speak to. As it was a formal visit Jacot was in uniform. Khaki service dress, highly polished Sam Browne belt and the dark blue 'forage cap' of his regiment, the Celtic Guards, with its cap badge of a gold embroidered Celtic cross. In his gloved hands Jacot also carried a thin highly-polished leather cane.

He passed swiftly through security and was ushered into "C's" private lift which ascended with slightly uncomfortable speed to the fifth floor. He expected to wait a few minutes in the small anteroom dominated by a good copy of Annigoni's portrait of the Queen and a rather obsequious and over-tailored male private secretary. But the door opened within seconds and the impressive figure of Sir Valentine Walton KCMG, OBE, Chief of the Secret Intelligence Service, came out of it. Jacot only got halfway through a smart and guards-man-like salute before being grabbed by the arm and guided towards a chair by the side of a large and highly polished partner's desk on which there appeared to be a large decanter of sherry.

'Well, Colonel let's get down to business', said Valentine taking a large glug of sherry. 'General Verney. Can't say he was quite my cup of tea. Very sorry he has come to a sudden end and all that.'

The *mis en scene* was impressive. It was a glorious office with a great view of the Thames. The glass in the windows allowed you to appreciate the view, but as a result of the compounds in it that deflected both light and radio waves it had a metallic hue that reinforced the aura of secrecy and security. It was as if the whole building was wearing rather cheap dark glasses. Walton was at the same time paying coded homage to his boss Lady Nevinson – you are her emissary and I will treat you well – and trying subtly to overawe Jacot with his own status as head of SIS. Fair enough, thought Jacot. Whatever the realities of the UK's faded position in the world SIS, as a result of the connection with Bond, remained one of the world's premier and most powerful brands.

'Are you aware of any reason why Verney may have been disposed of – if I can put it like that?' asked Jacot, taking a large sip of sherry – an impressively dry Fino.

'That, I think, is one for the police. As you know we had a problem ourselves a couple of years back with an unexplained sudden death just across the river from here. Very Agatha Christie. The jury is still out on that one. The poor man was discovered zipped up in a hold-all if you remember. He had been working in an area of interest to the Russian Mafia. So there was reason to be in a frightful flap. Verney's I understand was a sudden death behind a locked door but not otherwise suspicious in any way. The toxicology tests show nothing and his rooms were checked thoroughly for radiation.'

The interview lasted half an hour. Walton went into some detail about the projects Verney had been involved with that might have put him at more risk than usual. Jacot questioned him in some detail about Verney's involvement in planning for any pre-emptive action in Iran should the country get even closer to manufacturing a nuclear weapon. Walton was most forthcoming. Verney had recently travelled to Cyprus to inspect the intelligence facilities on the island. The listening stations on the island would play a crucial part in building an intelligence picture of what the Iranians were up to. Jacot pressed the issue – no it didn't seem that Verney had much confidence in a pre-emptive strike against Tehran. And yes relations with some of the allies had become a little strained. While Verney had been in Washington a few weeks before a senior US official had insisted on referring to The Falkland Islands as the Malvinas – repeatedly throughout the meeting. Verney, unusually for such a thick-skinned man with a great admiration for the US system, had taken grave offence.

There were a number of the details about allied plans for Iran that Jacot found astonishing. In the press and on television the Western allies were often portrayed as relying on the brute force of air power. In reality they were capable of great subtlety and guile. A number of famous spies had become novelists, but none as far as Jacot could remember had been members of the Magic Circle. Shame. Their tricks were impressive. Valentine was less forthcoming about Verney's tensions with the Americans.

Jacot thanked Walton and left the office. Thankfully the lift descended at a more leisurely speed. As he walked along Albert Embankment he ran the conversation back through his mind. It was always difficult dealing with SIS personnel. Their principal training was not, as the James Bond films would have us believe, in pistol shooting, scuba diving or flying Q's latest pocket-sized helicopters, but in psychological manipulation and concealment. They wanted information from other people and to protect what they gleaned from prying eyes. They were good at it too. The training started from day one with young recruits sent out into town centres across the country to collect personal details on casual acquaintances and passers by. Jacot was used to it and military intelligence also had the habit of extreme discretion. In areas Walton did not want Jacot or Lady Nevinson peering into had he had parried, evaded and avoided like the master he was. In other areas he had perhaps been too free with the information. He had no choice but to speak to Jacot – Lady Nevinson controlled his service's budget.

Ultimately, Jacot had not been re-assured by his meeting with "C". Walton had been most forthcoming about plans for Iran. In fact he had told Jacot too much. Perhaps he was meant to be impressed. But other than a throwaway remark about Verney's annoyance at American rudeness while in Washington, Walton had given little else away.

XIII

Jacot's Flat, Montagu Square,
Marylebone, London W1

Jacot stood by the tall windows of his first floor flat in Marylebone, looking out at the square in the twilight. The square gardens were ordered and attractive. The residents' association who owned the square had insisted that it should look like what it was – an English Georgian square; one of those unspoilt and glorious remnants that lined the West End just north of Oxford Street. The English inhabitants were actually in a minority. There were American and European bankers, diplomats of various types and a number of young families from various parts of the Middle East – Jews, Muslims and Christians. The residents' meetings could be disputatious and difficult but only in a gentle way. All were agreed on one thing: the square was a beautiful and private amenity and that it should remain true to its roots. Jacot still smiled at the thought of the very senior Australian television presenter who suggested at a meeting that a dying oak tree should be replaced by a eucalyptus. The wife of an Arab ambassador went pink with horror under her headscarf.

'In Sydney, yes. But not in London.'

The gardens looked more pleasing than ever. After six weeks of digging and construction the garden was enclosed for the first time since 1940 with a black painted wrought iron fence. It looked magnificent and well worth every penny the inhabitants had contributed or raised. Every resident of the square had done something and the nearby embassies had been generous, but nearly half the necessary money came as a personal contribution from a foreign banker who lived in one of the few remaining undivided houses. The original fence and gates had been removed just before the Battle of Britain as part of a national campaign to gather scrap metal for the war effort. "Weapons from scrap metal – all boys can help" ran a poster put up in schools. Aluminium pots and pans could be melted down to make urgently needed aircraft parts. But wrought iron had no modern military uses. Ironically it wasn't just the Luftwaffe who wanted to destroy and despoil. The great national, even global, emergency of 1940 needed nerves and sacrifice by many people but somewhere in the government machinery there were officials who wanted to disfigure London's beautiful squares, at a time when preservation should have been a priority. Who knows what the motivation was – probably the usual British vice, chippiness, but on this occasion dressed up in the more respectable clothes of patriotism.

Jacot was jolted from his resentful melancholy by the appearance of Monica at the front door below. He pressed the buzzer to let her in. She walked into the large mirrored hall and then up the stairs. Jacot was at his own door to let her in. They shook hands and he ushered her into his sitting room and presented her with a glass of ice cold Manzanilla which she took gratefully.

He looked pleased to see her.

'I thought we should go to my favourite Italian. Just round the corner. This part of London has really come up in the world since I first came to live here in the mid-eighties.'

'Italian sounds great.' She sipped her sherry. She was pleased to see him as well. The flat was impressive with high ceilings and full-length windows looking over the square. It was plainly decorated in white with beige carpets – the English fashion as she was quickly learning. A large mirror over the fireplace dominated the room. On either side were two oil paintings with picture lights above. On the left was a portrait of Jacot in his ceremonial uniform. The scarlet of the tunic and the gold and silver of the medals, buttons and accoutrements glittered in the light of a small chandelier. The detail in the portrait was extraordinarily lifelike. The fur of the bearskin so truthfully rendered that she was tempted to stroke it.

Jacot saw her looking at the portrait. 'It's for my mother really.'

Monica laughed. 'I don't believe you. Anyway it's lovely and lifelike. It makes the room.' She looked around. On the right hand side of the fireplace was another portrait. No scarlet in this one, instead the khaki service dress of a British Great War officer sitting at a desk in a dugout – lit by candles stuck in empty wine bottles. The expression on the face of the moustachioed officer was wistful, as if his mind was far away from the horrors of war. On the back wall of the dugout appeared to be pictures of Can Can girls torn from magazines – a splash of colour in a drab setting. The way the artist had painted the various candles round the dugout suggested the lighting in an orchestra pit. Perhaps the officer was looking forward to his next leave – the pleasures of a show in London and a good dinner or just being above ground for a few days and away from the mud and the danger. It was a powerful painting and Monica moved towards it for a closer look. She saw the signature and turned to Jacot.

'It is a beautiful painting. It's not Lady Nevinson I assume.'

Jacot smiled. 'It's not by her but a man called CRW Nevinson who was an official artist in the First World War. He painted French soldiers as well.' The telephone rang in the next room. 'Hang on, I'll be back in a moment.'

Monica sipped her sherry and looked at the bookshelves on the back wall of the room. You could tell a lot about a man from his bookshelves and she was under instructions to get to know Jacot well. Row after row of beautifully bound books in green leather with gold lettering. She had been briefed in Paris on the likely tastes of this type of Englishman. Lots of Second World War military history and books about Rugby Football and Winston Churchill was what the briefers had said. She looked at the titles and was puzzled. Most of the military history appeared to be about the First rather than the Second World War. And much of it seemed to be about the French, German and Austro-Hungarian armies, most of it in the original French and German editions. It was unusual to see in an English house the sixteen volumes of the *Histoire Illustree de la Guerre de 1914* and she was pleasantly astonished to see Marshal Petain's *Verdun* – the definitive account whatever the world thought about his later activities. At the end of the shelves on the Great War were editions of the English poets who found their voice and their muse at the front but also a collected edition of Anton Schnak – the German Army's Wilfred Owen.

There seemed to be nothing at all about the Second World

War except Von Manstein's selectively amnesiac memoirs and a superbly bound over-sized edition of *Catch 22*. France featured again with a number of volumes about Dien Ben Phu and Algeria. She smiled. No Rugby Football at all. It was not what she was expecting. But she did notice a shelf of books by and about Churchill. The briefers had said that Jacot had been to the same school. He was not an intelligence target as such but she had been briefed in some detail about his background and experiences in life. It was clear that Navarre and other senior officials in the French Intelligence Services were determined to have the closest possible relationship with the British. No ifs, no buts and certainly no "Anglophobie", was how Navarre had put it.

He came back into the room. 'Sorry about that. Let's go.'

They finished their sherry and left for the restaurant in a small street tucked away behind the huge Roman Catholic church of St James', Spanish Place. She pleaded ignorance and let him choose from the menu. Jacot seemed well known there. The food was superb. Mozzarella, tomato and avocado salad was followed by penne with a Puttanesca sauce. The strong black olives and anchovies appealed very much to her southern Mediterranean taste. They shared a bottle of an ice cold, light but alcoholic white wine from Sicily, according to Jacot, and finished with fresh figs and coffee. They were meant to be talking business. Instead they just got to know each other. They made a handsome couple in the restaurant. She, in particular, drew admiring glances from both the waiters and most of the other male diners and as she noticed from Jacot himself. Like all intelligence agents she had been trained in understanding body language, particularly in men.

Englishmen were more difficult to read perhaps but the signs were there. Initially, Jacot sat upright. He was polite and attentive but in a way you would expect at a professional meeting. As the wine and intimate atmosphere took effect she sensed Jacot leaning a fraction closer across the table. Instead of looking down or away after making a remark he held her gaze. His gloved hands, hidden under the table unless in the process of eating or pouring wine, relaxed and rested on the crisp white table cloth. They discussed her recent experiences as an undercover agent in one of Paris' most dingy and most hostile suburbs.

Playing the part of a widowed Algerian cleaning woman had been demanding – the work had been hard. She washed not very frequently and wore dirty and baggy clothes. As a widow she had little status and was generally ignored by both men and women. But cleaning ladies have access. Many of the people she worked for were Islamist militants of one sort or another, always looking over their shoulders in case the authorities were onto them. Hyper-aware in many ways. They did not notice women except as items of property or objects of their own or other people's lust. There had been a lionization of some Islamist terrorists in the media over the years. They had the capacity to cause chaos in a modern democracy for sure. But warriors they were not. Not in their private lives at least, and she had seen them close up. Bullies most of them, and what passed for their passionately held beliefs were usually a set of brutal and self-satisfied prejudices. It had been a difficult and frightening time for her and it was good to go through it with someone who would understand, to have a kind of elegant decompression, with an Englishman of all people. Towards the end of her account she noticed Jacot started to make quips and comments in an effort to lighten the conversation. Her grim story had been told and it was time to laugh at the ridiculousness of it all, exactly the right tone to adopt in the circumstances. She felt that he understood.

'You know Daniel, I was taught at spy school that the British routinely talked up the capabilities of the IRA so that they could look like a worthy enemy rather than the gang of dysfunctional thugs they really were. And to disguise your own unwillingness to take them on con brio.'

'You are probably right. They weren't that good. The average IQ was low and their personal habits let the side down a bit. I always thought of them as similar to murderous football supporters. But they could be effective. You saw the steel door to my flat. And my bathroom functions as a safe room. I can lock myself in there and probably survive a direct hit. All thanks to a run in I had with the IRA as a soldier in Northern Ireland. There are a few of them still around.'

'I wasn't just having a go at the British.' She laughed. 'I think we do the same with Islamists. Most of the ones I saw in Paris were stupid and brutal.'

'Well I think you have a point, Monica. The threat is there but it is difficult for us to gauge it properly because of what happened on 911. We all assumed it was the opening overture and by the time they got to Act Five the world would be left a smoking, toxic, radioactive wreck. But the more I look at what happened that day it looks as though our enemies were at the limits of what they could pull off. Everything pretty much went their way on the day. And just about everything that could go wrong for Uncle Sam did go wrong. The US Air

Force was unlucky not to shoot down the second plane into the twin towers to be frank. And the whole thing wasn't helped by the shoddy construction of the towers that allowed such a quick collapse. I doubt if the Empire State Building would have fallen apart quite like that. Chunks of it would have been missing and hundreds would have died in the fires but the butcher's bill would have been lower.'

'Where were you on the day?'

'In COBRA – the UK's crisis management organisation. I ran back from lunch when I heard and did not emerge like everyone else for several days. Like Asterix and Obelix, we thought the sky was going to fall on our heads. But it didn't and despite 7-7 it hasn't since. The more I look at that day the more it reminds me of that long jumper, Bob Beamon I think he was called, who made that freak long jump at the Mexico Olympics in 1968. He jumped so far that the officials' tape measure wouldn't reach to measure it.'

'I see what you mean', said Monica. 'I have an early start in the morning but am dying for a glass of brandy. You have mentioned Mozart a number of times tonight. Play me some.'

'Shall we go back for a nightcap?'

They walked slowly back towards Jacot's flat, not arm in arm but very close to each other. At the corner of George Street and Montagu Square they stopped to cross the road. They were the only people waiting to cross. It was busy at this time of night with many fast-moving cars zipping by. Jacot pressed the button on the pelican crossing. The little green man came on and the bleeping began. Jacot looked both ways – noticed a black Mercedes twenty feet to his right which had plenty of time to slow down – and stepped into the road with

Monica at his side.

The horn and screeching of brakes made him realise that all was not as it should be. Time went into its slow motion mode. It always does if you are about to be shot, bombed or run over. Slow motion is not a gimmick invented by film directors. That's how it happens for real. Pulling Monica with him he jumped for the pavement. They both ended up in a winded heap. He could feel the hot air from the brakes of the Mercedes as it slithered by stopping in the centre of the crossing. As he twisted round he could see that the traffic light and the pedestrian light were both green – just for a split second. And then they went back to normal.

The driver got out and ran over cursing. 'For God's sake look out I could have killed you. F.....g idiot. Couldn't you see the light was green?'

Monica was crouched just by the railings with her right hand in her handbag looking up and down the street. There was no movement.

'I am sorry', said Jacot. 'I hope you are all right. Sorry. I hope your car is OK.'

'Yeah. Yeah', said the well-dressed man. 'Are you guys OK?'

'Yes, thanks', they both replied.

'Listen sweetheart', he addressed Monica, 'your boyfriend is going to get you killed if he doesn't wake up'. With that he got back into the car and drove off.

They both leaned against the railings.

'I saw the lights', said Monica. 'Both green.'

'We should ring the police and tell them', said Jacot.

'Come off it. These things never go wrong. Let's just get

into your flat. I'm not sure what's going on out here.'

They just about fell into the safety of Jacot's flat. The brandies were larger than they might have been but the Mozart was on a lower volume thanks to their jangled nerves. Monica warmed her brandy by holding the glass in both hands and looked out of the window. The square was quiet. Jacot was listening intently to the *Marriage of Figaro* – a good anti-dote to the tension.

'Daniel, it was a hit or at very least a warning. Clever technique. They must have a way of messing up the lights. Police cars can change them can't they?'

'Yes, I believe so. There is a gadget. They, whoever they are, have probably modified it so both signals show green. It's rather clever.' He laughed. 'But they missed'.

'I looked up and down the street. I couldn't see anyone. The driver would not have been in on it. I will let Paris know. I have to go now.'

'Yes I will have a word with Lady Nevinson in the morning. Take care on your way home. I will walk behind you until you are the other side of Oxford Street. You could go through the park if you want. All sorts of weirdos in there at night but difficult for you to be followed.'

'Don't worry about me', she smiled pointing at the MAB PA-15 standard military issue pistol in her hand-bag.

'Nice weapon. I didn't know they still made them. Eight rounds in the magazine rather than the usual six.'

Jacot hadn't turned the music off as they put on their coats. Just as they were leaving the glorious sound of Susanna and the Contessa singing their duet Sull'aria from the third act of Marriage of Figaro filled the flat. Monica stood at the door listening intently.

'It's beautiful. I have heard it somewhere I think, not at the opera though.'

'They used it in an American film a few years ago – that one about a prison, *The Shawshank Redemption*.'

'I haven't watched many American films. It's a love song, yes?'

'Yes, in a way. One of the greatest but at the same time it's a plot or, in our jargon, an operational plan to expose a husband's infidelity. All is never quite what it seems in Mozart's operas.'

'Tell me about it', Monica laughed.

They walked towards Hyde Park. He scanned both sides of the road. It was late. There were a few people coming out of the tube station. Either no one was following them or they were very good at hiding themselves.

They reached the high railings around the park. Jacot kissed her on the lips in a rather non-committal English way. She drew her head back and smilingly kissed him on both cheeks in the French manner and then once more enthusiastically on the lips. Jacot turned her round with both his hands around her slim waist to check that his silk gloves would not slip on her coat and then lifted her onto the railings. She jumped down into the park and disappeared into the night.

Jacot felt curiously responsible and protective of Monica. She had been through a lot in a short time. But she could look after herself. Indeed, with her background, she could look after Jacot as well. He felt reassured by her presence. She was after all a clandestine agent of French intelligence who had spent many years in deep cover. There was no gallantry in espionage and no sexism either. Men and women competed and co-operated on a level playing field. Come what may she would be safe in the darkness as she crossed Hyde Park. He hoped no one tried to mug her – for the mugger's sake.

XIV

Falkland Islands
– self-governing British Overseas Territory, South Atlantic

The ancient RAF airbus shuddered on the descent into Mount Pleasant airport, buffeted by the strong winds regular in these latitudes. It wasn't so much due to the fact that the Antarctic Continent lay not far away to the south, more that the next landfall to the east, other than a few frozen French Islands, the Kerguelens, was Australia.

'I think Daniel we should bring your visit to the Falklands forward by a week,' was Lady Nevinson's only comment on hearing of Jacot's adventures on the George Street pelican crossing. 'I am increasingly nervous about the place. You say there's the off chance that this Verney business may have a Falklands connection so you can kill two birds with one stone. And it may be a good idea if you were out of town for a while. I'll have MI5 keep an eye on your flat. Oh, one more thing – I have written letters to the Governor and the Commander British Forces South Atlantic. Just putting the final touches to them now. The copies for despatch will be handed to you at Brize Norton. I think you know what's in them. They must be destroyed once read. Have a good trip.' As he turned for the door she added, 'I hope you enjoyed dinner with your glamorous French colleague.'

Jacot half turned back towards her. She should have smiled at this point but she didn't and he was dismissed.

Jacot looked out of the window as Port Stanley passed below the aircraft. It had been nearly thirty years. As is usual in a military transport the passengers sat with their backs to the cockpit. It always seemed strange but was in fact logical – if the plane crashed for any reason more of them would survive. As they flew into Falklands airspace a pair of RAF Typhoon fighter-bombers had appeared alongside each wing tip. It was both a routine precaution and an impressive show of force. The aircraft touched down at RAF Mount Pleasant, the huge military base constructed to defend the islands opened by Prince Andrew three years after the end of the war. As the airbus slowed to a halt the escorting Typhoons roared deafeningly past, afterburners aglow and climbed almost vertically into the far sky. They were certainly impressive bits of kit, thought Jacot, literally able to massacre any assault on the islands by the Argentine Air Force. If just one had been available in 1982 the butcher's bill would have been halved. And they were marvellous to watch.

He would not be on military premises for long. Lady Nevinson appeared to be a friend of everyone's and that seemed to include the current Governor of the Falkland Islands. Too young surely to be an ex-admirer, but somewhere along the way no doubt he had fallen under her spell or had become in some way indebted to her. Jacot was grateful. It meant avoiding a stay in a small barrack room, sparsely furnished by an over-stretched budget. He had always found military bases depressing.

The governor's signature black taxi was waiting. The chauffeur grabbed his bags and they set off cheerily for Port Stanley thirty miles away by a slow cinder road. Sitting in the back,

Jacot marvelled at the scenery. The rolling and sometimes jagged hills set against the stormy blue-black South Atlantic reminded him of the Western Isles but on a grander scale as if built by a Hollywood studio. He got out at Government House where he was to stay. It was an odd looking building, similar to a rather grand boarding house in a windy part of Devon. The lawn was well tended and the glass panels in its large conservatory highly polished. Jacot was ushered to a small ante-room outside the Governor's office and a matronly and most welcoming housekeeper spirited his suitcases away upstairs. It might be a small colony and the governor to most was more like a headmaster than an imperial representative, but the proper ceremonies were still observed, just as they had been all over the grander parts of the British Empire years before. The door opened and Jacot went in standing stiffly to attention in front of the governor's desk and calling him 'sir'. He handed over a sealed envelope.

'Ah, yes Colonel. I understood you had something for me.' The governor slit open the envelope and extracted a single sheet of paper which he read.

'Good God.' He looked at Jacot. 'Is this true?'

'Yes, as far as we can tell, sir. We should remember that the Argentine army and navy may not have been up to much but their intelligence people put up a good show.'

'And their air force come to that', said the governor looking at Jacot's black silk gloves.

'Quite so. I have only two copies, one for you and one for the Commander British Forces who I am seeing shortly. Lady Nevinson would like both copies destroyed. I think the intelligence is from a particularly exposed source.'

'And does this refer to something about to happen or what?'

'Not today or tomorrow but sometime during the 30th anniversary year. All the necessary action has been taken upstream. What you and your military commander have to do is make sure that nothing can happen once the stuff is on or near the islands.'

'I assume you will be discussing it in detail with the military. Let me know the outcome.'

Charming and understated in the way of foreign office officials, his Excellency the Governor gave Jacot coffee and pointed out some of the historic features of his office. Behind the desk was the large three part bookcase, famous to admiring Argentine schoolchildren as the backdrop in numerous photographs to "Mario B Menendez, General de Brigada and Gobernador Militar" of the Islas Malvinas. It's always there in the frame whatever the caption and activity of the photograph – Menendez working, Menendez planning, Menendez in conference with General Galtieri, Menendez talking to the grateful people of the liberated Malvinas. To its left in the photographs was invariably a chalk drawing of Ernest Shackleton which Menendez curiously kept on the wall. It was still there. Restored to its rightful place in the room was a print of Annigoni's portrait of the Queen which the Argentines had taken down after the British surrender and left in the corridor. Perhaps they always suspected theirs would be a temporary occupation. The governor wished Jacot luck on his tour of inspection and looked forward to seeing a little of him over the next couple of days. And then Jacot departed, once again in the taxi, for his first appointment at the headquarters of British Forces South Atlantic Islands.

In view of the tensions over the Falklands, stoked by the re-elected president Christina Kirchner in late 2011 and early 2012, Lady Nevinson had had a mini episode of the vapours. These were thankfully rare but usually reflected a genuine inner worry bordering on panic. The usual signs were there – irritability with underlings, including Jacot. Drinking too many cups of coffee through the day and early evening appearances in Jacot's office where she knew his tiny fridge was stocked with salads and reasonable white Burgundy. Her deep worries about the islands had surfaced in the train on their way back from Paris and from then on the clock had been ticking on Jacot's mission. He had rather been looking forward to a trip to see the Defence Attaché and the SIS Station in Buenos Aires and had dropped a number of hints to Lady Nevinson about the importance of "getting on the ground" in Argentina, as well as the islands themselves. But, to his abiding disappointment, it would appear he could chat to them when they were in London.

Ultimately, the safety of the islands was her call and she had only been partly re-assured by the chiefs of staff that the islands were indeed secure, for the moment at least. She seemed to agonise more over the Falklands than the other military and intelligence problems she faced every day. 'It's British territory lived in by British people loyal to Queen and country', was her refrain. She wasn't particularly interested whether the islands could be retaken after being lost, again. Her view was that if we were negligent enough to lose them again then they might as well become Argentine. But she was very committed to making sure that everything was in place to give Her

Majesty's Government the best possible warning of any hostile intent in the South Atlantic and she wanted Jacot to check up on and audit the intelligence assets involved. That an emissary of the National security Adviser should travel South to poke his nose into intelligence matters was one thing. She also wanted Jacot to have a good look at the military arrangements for defending the island.

The Governor's taxi arrived at the headquarters of British Forces South Atlantic Islands where he was met by the commander, a naval commodore of the old school, who had been a junior officer on the nuclear powered hunter-killer submarine, HMS Conqueror, that had sunk the Belgrano.

'Good morning Colonel.' Jacot saluted and then shook his hand. 'Commodore Simon Mayne, Royal Navy. At her ladyship's service I suppose.' Mayne had a cheery grin coupled with a distinctly Nelsonian air. Like many submariners he appeared to have no interest at all in the regulations governing naval uniforms. He looked like a character from a Pinewood Studios film about Second World War submarines – big leather jacket and big leather boots with his naval forage cap set at a jaunty angle. But he clearly knew what he was doing and Jacot noticed immediately and approvingly, that his subordinates seemed slightly nervous in his presence – definitely a good sign. In small faraway garrisons it was too easy for the military formalities to be dispensed with and a familiar and ultimately inefficient atmosphere to take hold.

Jacot handed over the envelope to him.

After reading it he seemed unperturbed. 'Sneaky bunch, the Argies. Have to hand it to them, it's a clever wheeze. I will give the necessary instructions and thank the good Lady

Nevinson for her concern. I will modify the exercise we are due to show you the day after tomorrow to take into account this intelligence. We had intended to practise what we would do if the Argentine Special Forces, the *Buzo Tactico*, managed in some way to blow up our four Typhoons; instead we will assume that they have pulled off the little scheme your signals intercept suggests and that our aircraft are immobilised through deliberately contaminated aviation fuel. In the meantime I will summon the head RAF ground wallah and tell him to tighten the checks on fuel purity. I am pretty sure they do quite a lot of checks anyway. These Typhoon fighters are amazing and the RAF certainly know how to fly them, but the maintenance is a bit of a nightmare I gather. I think we will also tighten physical security on our fuel supplies. I am going to enjoy bullying the RAF.'

'I am sure that will be a good idea Commodore.'

'Oh and Jacot I'm under no illusions who you work for and I know she is worried. I will put down the new measures on paper so you can show her.'

He had an enjoyable, if tiring, couple of days in discussions with the military and was taken through various "event scenarios" and the plans to meet them. It was clear that the J2, Joint Intelligence, staff were seriously on the ball in this part of the world. Jacot was mentally drafting his report for Lady Nevinson throughout the process and those he met clearly understood this. He hoped they didn't find him awkward, but he knew the kind of awkward and difficult questions Lady Nevinson would ask him and the kind of awkward and difficult questions the prime minister would ask her. It would be political, reputational and historical suicide for any British

Prime Minister to lose the Falklands – again.

It had been a number of years since Jacot had carried a rifle and he was struck by just how much more potent certain weapons systems had become in recent years. The huge interactive radar map in the underground operations room at Mount Pleasant showed precisely the locations of our submarines in the South Atlantic. Most people thought of submarines as platforms on which to carry mechanical torpedoes, but they were much more than that these days. Their electronic intelligence gathering capabilities were state of the art. Their improved torpedoes couldn't miss and would send Argentine ships to the bottom of the sea without warning, just as the *Belgrano* was tragically and reluctantly despatched all those years ago. And if push really came to shove they could launch cruise missiles at bases on the Argentine mainland – even the defence ministry or the *Casa Rosada* itself, the pink and very kitsch presidential palace in the heart of Buenos Aires, would not be safe.

He was impressed too by the young soldiers from a traditional English county regiment who formed the garrison. Most had served in Afghanistan, some more than once, and had the easy grace and calm unhurried efficiency of men who knew what they were doing.

But still Jacot was uneasy, as Lady Nevinson was in London. Our defence and early warning arrangements were well planned and well run but they were still designed to meet the kind of threat we expected the Argentines to pose. A seaborne attack would be suicidal, like jumping into a pond at the bottom of which lurked a Great White Shark in the shape of our latest submarine. Jacot noticed from the ops room that the submarine on station was the appropriately named *HMS Ambush*. An airborne attack likewise. A commando raid to disable the four RAF Typhoon fighters permanently based on the islands might have a chance but Mount Pleasant was ten miles from the coast – it seemed unlikely that commandos could land undetected. They might try a landing on remote West Falkland but with no air or sea superiority any Argentine troops who got ashore could be easily rounded up at leisure.

All this was obvious enough and within the capabilities of the British to handle. But what if the Argentines tried something different – carried out a raid that they knew would fail or started a war that they knew they would lose? It was the intelligence analyst's ultimate nightmare. It was exactly what the Egyptians had done in the Yom Kippur War of 1973 – as a result they came within a few hours of pulling it off. Even a lost war forced the Israelis to the negotiating table.

As part of the training programme and as a courtesy to Lady Nevinson, during Jacot's visit the garrison would practise one of its defence plans for the RAF base at Mount Pleasant to counter a particular Argentine attack scenario. It was one that Lady Nevinson had expressed an interest in personally – in other words it was keeping both her and the prime minister awake at night.

On the third day of his visit very early in the morning Commodore Mayne arrived to pick Jacot up in a white Land Rover Discovery. He was clearly in a good mood and keen to show Jacot what the garrison could do in a crisis. He smiled a lot and gave the odd chuckle as he outlined the exercise scenario.

'Basically the whole thing has been going on for some

hours. We've seen the *Buzo Tactico* off. I really wanted you to see the climax. Our aircraft are out of action but we have established that even if the Argies manage to get a few special forces types onto the airfield, they can't do it in strength. And we doubt they would be able to bring with them the stores required to deny the runway to British reinforcements. They would have to bring in additional aircraft. HMS *Dauntless* the new destroyer which is steaming to our east just within territorial waters can track and destroy forty-eight air or surface targets at any one time. Its Sea Viper missile travels at Mach Four. One enemy aircraft might get through but not much more and the airfield has its own protection with the latest Rapier Missiles and anti-aircraft guns.' Jacot was impressed. Mayne chuckled 'Haven't had so much fun since I was down here for real. But just to set Lady Nevinson's mind at rest we have for the purposes of the exercise cut the length of the runway by two thirds.'

They were waved through the front gate by a heavily armed detachment of RAF Police. Commodore Mayne, driving at breakneck speed, drew up to one of the fortified hangars where the RAF Typhoons were stored supposedly out of harm's way. A number of disgruntled looking fast jet pilots were in attendance. Scrambled in the early hours of the morning they had rushed to their aircraft only to be told that all four Typhoons were out of action because of contaminated fuel. It was a fighter pilot's deep instinct to take to the air and they were unimpressed to be left out of the exercise. After all, the entire defence of the islands was supposed to revolve around them and their extraordinarily capable machines.

A military Land Rover pulled up. A tall, tough looking man

leapt from the driver's seat. Jacot could see from his badges of rank that he was the Sergeant Major of the infantry detachment. He couldn't have been anything else. He saluted, smiled conspiratorially at the Commodore and started unloading SA 80 rifles, GPMG machine guns and boxes of blank ammunition from the back of the vehicle.

'Don't just stand around', the Commodore bawled at the group of RAF personnel, 'go and help the infantry.'

Once the pilots and their ground crews had been deployed at the double into what passed for a defensive position around the hangars, the still grinning Sergeant-Major disappeared off at high speed to rejoin his men on the other side of the airfield.

'Let's get back in my vehicle Colonel. I need to listen to the radio.' The Commodore drove rapidly to the side of the runway, lit a cigarette and listened intently to the air-traffic control net. There was only static. 'We might have a couple of minutes to wait. Let me explain one thing quickly. I said we had shortened the runway by two thirds as if the Argies had managed to block it off in some way. See that red and white marker post – that marks the end of the usable runway – for the exercise anyway. We haven't put any barriers up – too dangerous.'

The radio burst into life. 'Mount Pleasant Control this is Blackbuck leader, over.'

'Mount Pleasant, send over', the control tower replied.

'Blackbuck leader, entering Falkland Islands airspace in figures five. Are we clear for low-level pass, over?'

'Mount Pleasant, yes, over.'

'Blackbuck leader, roger. Blackbuck Three is a few

minutes behind us and looking good. Out.'

The Commodore smiled. 'Here we go'.

They waited for a few minutes. The Commodore's binoculars were fixed on the Eastern approach to the airfield.

Jacot caught a glimpse of sun glancing off something metallic in the distance and then heard that strange tearing noise made by fighter jets just before you can hear the roar of their engines. A pair of RAF Typhoons, perfectly aligned, screamed in from the East and flew the length of the airfield. They banked and disappeared over Wickham Heights, the hills to the north of the air base and into the distance. It was suddenly quiet again and along with the moaning of the wind Jacot could hear cheering from the troops taking part in the exercise.

'I didn't tell them what was going to happen', said the delighted Commodore before chattering into the radio for a few minutes.

Again Jacot heard that slight tearing noise. This time the Typhoons came in from the West, even lower. As they came into view plumes of red, white and blue smoke billowed from their exhausts. They flew the length of the runway and then soared almost vertically into the sky.

'Marvellous, bloody marvellous', said Jacot. The cheering continued in the background.

'Mount Pleasant, this is Blackbuck leader. We'd love to do it again but we don't want to run out of fuel. Heading for our first tanker rendezvous. Should be back at Ascension in time for tea.'

'Blackbuck leader, thank you and good luck. The weather looks good at Ascension.'

Jacot turned to the Commodore, 'Great stuff. Lady Nevinson will be most re-assured.'

The Commodore replied, 'Those aircraft were not armed. Obviously, if they were bombed up it would take more re-fuelling tankers to get them down here from Ascension Island but it should be no problem for the RAF. They got very good at it once again last year flying direct from their bases in East Anglia to Tripoli, and we did it in '82.'

'Mount Pleasant, this is Blackbuck Three.'

'Hang on, this is the climax', said the Commodore fixing his eyes to his binoculars once more.

A single C130 Hercules transport aircraft hove into view on the horizon, the pilot adjusting his approach with the aid of air traffic control. He was coming into land.

'It will be tight for a Herc on the shortened runway', said Jacot.

'Don't worry these guys have had years of practice in Helmand. If the pilot knows what he is doing he'll be fine. The Yanks once landed an early variant on one of their carriers, without arrestor gear.' Just as the plane reached the start of the runway it was hit by a fierce side wind. The pilot corrected … 'Jeez, he's too high to make it.' The Commodore looked a little concerned.

All they could hear on the radio was the stressed heavy breathing of the pilot. At the last minute he applied full power and with a roar of engines overshot the runway. As the plane climbed slowly they could hear the co-pilot anxiously calling out the airspeed. For just a couple of seconds the high-pitched stall alarm kicked in shrieking its warning. The Commodore went pale. Once he had enough speed the pilot banked, went around, and started his approach again.

A worried looking Commodore grabbed the radio 'Hallo Blackbuck Three this is Commodore Mayne, Commander British Forces South Atlantic Islands. Look, just land normally. Maybe the wind is too strong.'

'Blackbuck Three, sorry about that sir. We got distracted by the in-flight movie. Don't worry we'll make it this time. Out.'

It was a text-book short landing. The pilot dropped the aircraft hard on the runway right at the edge of the tarmac, slammed the engines into reverse, deployed a parachute to increase the drag and crunched to a metallic and smoky halt with fifty metres to spare before the red marker post. The rear ramp came down and a platoon of soldiers from the same regiment as the garrison took up fire positions around the plane. Jacot noticed one of them throwing up. A bumpy flight and a spectacular landing were hardly the best way of keeping breakfast down.

'There we are. I think we have proved the point. Provided we can fly aircraft from Ascension then these islands are safe. We need a drink Colonel Jacot. Do you army types drink pink gin?'

XV

Falkland Islands
– self-governing British Overseas Territory, South Atlantic

The fourth day of his visit Jacot had arranged for personal matters and the military had kindly laid on a helicopter. As he ran towards it at the helipad just outside Government House it was so windy Jacot hardly noticed the downdraft. Tucked away inside his combat jacket were two beautifully wrapped bunches of flowers. The last time he had been in a helicopter in the Falklands he was being evacuated to the field hospital at Port San Carlos – "The Blue and Green Life Machine" – called after the completely marvellous Royal Navy and Royal Marine medics who staffed it. Put together partly in an old sheep shed it was a far cry from the sophisticated medical facilities available to the contemporary British Army and it took many hours for a casualty to get there.

Jacot's painful journey as a casualty had been interrupted by another Argentine air raid coming in. The immediate action was to land the helicopter as quickly as possible to avoid becoming a target for the air-to-air missiles carried by the Argentine Skyhawks and Mirages. Jacot thought they were going to crash and had nursed a dislike of helicopters ever since. As the helicopter took off from Government House it was buffeted by the strong prevailing Westerly winds. It would be a bumpy, lumpy journey to his three destinations. At each of the first two the helicopter deposited Jacot and returned after half an hour spent on navigational exercises.

The first stop was the Celtic Guards Memorial at Port Louis. Twenty or so miles to the north-west of Port Stanley and with a fine natural harbour the small settlement had been the first established on the islands, by French sailors from St Malo, in Brittany – hence Isles Malouines in French and Islas Malvinas in Spanish and, more recently, American usage. Charles Darwin visited, twice, but the capital moved to Stanley in 1845. It was a pretty little place lucky enough to be completely bypassed by the Falklands War until a few days before it was over. A stark granite Celtic Cross in the shape of the regimental cap-badge overlooked the bay where the *Oliver Cromwell* had been attacked all those years ago. Jacot came smartly to attention in front of it. His burned hands snapped in salute to his fallen comrades. Although alone, he said the Lord's Prayer aloud in both English and Welsh according to regimental custom and laid a small posy of daffodils at the foot of the cross. There was no card – he didn't have to identify himself to these men. He stood absolutely still at attention for nearly half an hour until he heard the sound of the returning helicopter, saluted again and got back on board.

The same process was repeated at the next destination the main Argentine military cemetery at Darwin. Jacot had wanted to lay flowers in the beautiful Argentine national colours of pale blue and white but anything suitable was difficult to come by this far south and daffodils would have to suffice. Once again he saluted, and then stood absolutely still for nearly half an hour. The wind buffeted his body and the short slightly greying hair underneath the army beret ruffled in the wind. As the hum of the rotors came to his ears once again his arm snapped upwards to the salute and was then brought down to his side once again. Longest way up, shortest way down as the instructors at Sandhurst had shouted during drill periods.

And then he climbed back on board the helicopter for a third time en route to the southernmost tip of East Falkland, Porpoise Point, dramatically overlooking Drake Passage: the stretch of water that separated the islands from the Antarctic Continent.

There it was, a solitary cottage with a corrugated iron roof held down by turf slabs. There was smoke coming out of the chimney. A huge bear of a man came out of the front door and made for Jacot roaring a happy hallo. But he didn't stick his hand out in the usual way but just stood close and looked Jacot directly in the eye.

'It's good to see you young man after all these years. I hope your hands are more comfortable than when we first met. Come on in.'

Jacot had not seen William Say for nearly ten years. They had first met thirty years before when Will had been helping at the field hospital near Blue Beach at San Carlos. Nearly overwhelmed by the burns casualties on *Oliver Cromwell,* some of the local inhabitants had volunteered to change dressings, reducing the burden on the military nursing staff. In agony and waiting to be evacuated to the hospital ship *SS Uganda* Jacot had been helped and comforted by this no nonsense Falklander. Like many big men Will was both light on his feet and nimble with his hands. His sense of humour and light touch meant that Jacot and others had found the ordeal of changing dressings and reapplying the glutinous Flammazine paste just about bearable.

From the moment they were put on board the helicopters at Port Louis the casualties had been doped with morphine. But you can only rely on morphine for a short space of time. Within a day or two all but the most severe casualties were weaned off it – except at night. Jacot had fainted the first time his dressings were changed without morphine. He was still slightly ashamed of it. But once Will became the main dresser for his little group things really did seem to improve. Will had also written a short note on a "Bluey", the nickname for the official military air letter forms, to Jacot's widowed mother who had assumed that her only son had been killed. The butcher's bill on *Cromwell* had been high particularly among Jacot's regiment but not as high as some of the initial reports suggested.

They had kept in touch and on the twentieth anniversary of the war Will had visited London. It was the first time he had ever left the Falklands. Jacot and various other casualties Will had looked after enjoyed showing him round London. His wide-eyed and innocent admiration had been a joy to behold. It had all been, on the surface at least, a little like that great Aussie film of the 1980s, *Crocodile Dundee*. Jacot's liver had barely survived and Will and he had rekindled their relationship of years before over numerous visits to the opera. Will had insisted on seeing live performances of every one of Mozart's great operas and Jacot had been happy to organise it all. He had been a great hit with Jacot's friends who both liked him and were grateful for his spontaneous kindness to Jacot and his wounded guardsmen during the Falklands War. Will had stayed at Jacot's flat in Marylebone. They had had a ball. Of course it turned out that Will was no ingénue from a remote half-forgotten colony at all but a highly educated and highly sophisticated individual. In his remote settlement on East Falkland he had made a serious study of Mozart's operas that put Jacot's dilettante interest in the shade. Also, he knew his history of England – king by king, queen by queen, battle by battle. He was, like Jacot, both devout and an ardent patriot. But unlike many of those in the modern world who clung to their faith and their monarchy inwardly but didn't make too much of it in public – for a quiet life – Will had no embarrassment at all about these pillars of his personal and professional life.

They had kept in touch by Christmas card and then email. There were few weeks when Jacot's inbox did not have some outrageous message from Williamsay@falklandislands.com in it. Unlike Jacot he had married and had a family who were his pride and joy. Jacot was envious. The children were away at school and his wife was in Stanley. They got inside the house.

'It's good to see you but we could have met up for a few beers in the Upland Goose. Tell me what have you come for?'

'Well it seemed a shame to waste the helicopter. The governor here is clearly either keen on or frightened of my boss. Actually, I need your help Will. I have got a kind of hunch about something. It's a delicate matter. National security and all that stuff.'

Will smiled.

'You were busy during the war weren't you?' said Jacot, deadpan.

'Well amongst other things I helped out at the hospital if you remember.'

'No. I don't mean that I meant your then hobby – the radio.'

'I am still very much an amateur radio man to this day and even in this crazy technological age they still call us "Hams". But yes you were right those were the glory days. In a way I was On Her Majesty's Secret Service listening in to the Argentine radio transmissions and passing on what I could to the Task Force. If they had found out I think I would have been shot. It was like being in the French Resistance. The Argentine military government had banned the use of amateur radios and confiscated a lot of the equipment but they didn't get my stuff, though they had a jolly good look.'

Jacot giggled like a schoolboy at the memory. 'It was hidden under a sheep pen. Very clever for a Falklander.'

'Yes. And the Argies were too dim to find it. They were a grotty lot, most of them. Especially the conscripts from the wrong side of the tracks in Buenos Aires. Felt a bit sorry for them. But they did not like going anywhere near piles of damp and gooey sheep shit. It was still risky setting it up as they did have a direction finding capability. But I was mainly listening and went to the other end of the point to transmit. They were never quick enough off the mark and in the end I hid the whole apparatus up on the rocky outcrop you can just see from this window. Job done. I think I made a proper patriotic contribution to the war effort.

'Actually, I was a bit disappointed when the Task Force landed as there was no further requirement for me to listen in. So as you know I switched to monitoring our own military transmissions – just for fun mind. It was amusing to spot the difference between the official transmissions and what the soldiers and young officers were actually saying on their own nets. You explained it all to me I remember. One tone for the battalion radio net. All "Yes sir, no sir, very good sir. Things are going well sir." And another for what you young officers called "chat nets" on obscure frequencies where you could communicate without the knowledge of your rather heavy handed superiors.

'I can remember hearing your voice somewhere before you ended up in the hospital', said Will. 'And I have got recordings of some of you guys. Didn't give them to the inquiry into the *Cromwell* disaster – you would have all been court martialled for cheek and dissent. The language was rather shocking too I remember. What did they teach you all at your fancy schools? I made some recordings on my old tape recorders. More than two hundred hours in all. Thought it might be in the historical interest.'

'Where are they now?'

'Oh I got rid of them long ago. The tape recorders I mean. But the recordings themselves are still around, digitised, as you would expect for a techie like me.'

'It's those chat nets that I am interested in Will. I don't know if you have heard about the death of General Verney in rather Agatha Christie-like circumstances a couple of weeks ago in Cambridge. Not the ones with me and my mates mouthing off about life. But others, with perhaps more senior officers talking amongst themselves. 21st Infantry Brigade transmissions and Celtic Guards transmissions for the night 8/9 June 1982. And I am looking for a particular voice, a Captain Verney. Now General Verney.'

'I'll help you but you have to tell me why.' His face held no expression but the eyes were serious. He knew enough about what Jacot did for a living to understand the implications.

'OK Will, I'll let you in on the secret but please don't go blabbing about it in the Upland Goose after a few too many beers. And if you defect to the Russian Embassy in Stanley, my career is finished.'

Will got up, went into the small kitchen and re-appeared with a bottle of whisky. 'Famous Grouse is what you young officers used to drink. It's going to be a long afternoon looking for your dead general's voice. We might need a little help.'

The wind buffeted the small house, little more than a shack.

'William, consider yourself back on Her Majesty's Secret Service and here's why. I have been tasked by my boss, the formidable Lady Nevinson, to check up on the circumstances of Verney's death just to make sure that everything is shall we say "kosher". She was not originally a spook herself and basically views most members of the intelligence establishment as lying, devious, double-crossing scheisters.' He knocked back a large whisky and laughed. 'I'm exaggerating of course but you get my drift. Anyway, Verney's death looks innocent enough. Just one of those things for a man in late middle age. He smoked a lot too. The tests and all that suggest that he died of a heart attack or some kind of seizure on his own inside a locked room in a Cambridge College. End of chat as they say. I have been able to find nothing suspicious… except a connection to the Falklands War. The head butler in this college was in my regiment and lost a brother on the *Cromwell* which he himself was lucky to survive. It's a sad story which I will spare you. The details will have us crying into our whisky. Verney was a staff officer of some sort I think, and I just wondered if there was any connection between him and the ghastly affair of the *Oliver Cromwell*? I certainly remember his name at the time. It's a long shot and it's not really why I am here but let's give it a go.'

They drank whisky through the afternoon. Laughing as they heard Jacot's young voice chatting in colourful terms to another young officer. They didn't just talk about the war. They discussed the present. Say seemed unconcerned by the posturing of President Kirchner. 'The Malvinas are a kind of crazy national G Spot. Every shady Argentine politician eventually can't resist pressing the button and President Kirchner is no different. Good-looking lady mind.' Say laughed and drank more whisky. 'Hell's teeth, if I said that in the Upland Goose the lads would throw me into Stanley Harbour.' But the humour was gone as he expressed forcefully what he and some others believed – that the Americans were backing Argentina in the dispute because of the massive oil reserves being discovered in the islands' territorial waters. 'It's oil. It's always oil with the Americans. They can't help it. We are going to have between 8 billion and 60 billion barrels of the stuff. If the islands belonged to the Argies how convenient would that be for the big American oil companies. A guaranteed supply on their own continent.' He returned to the war. 'You didn't like the people in charge of you did you?'

'No we didn't. And that was even before things turned rough'.

It was a peculiar experience for Jacot to hear his voice from thirty years before. The conversations he was having with his brother officers provided a ribald and disaffected commentary on the events unfolding around them. You could hear though the sheer excitement of a young soldier going to war for the first time. Jacot felt nostalgic.

And then a couple of hours into their search, many whiskies and many belly-laughs later... suddenly there was Verney's voice. The other voices were not clear but Jacot suspected who they might have been. The group were apparently organising the transport of some mortar tubes and ammunition on some kind of ramshackle tractor and trailer over a steep hill. It was a task that Verney clearly found absurd, saying over and over again 'This is ridiculous. Why don't we just wait and do this in a properly organised way?' His indistinct interlocutors agreed. It was hardly of great interest, merely the tedium, tension and strain of war. Not everything goes wrong but just about everything becomes more difficult than expected and that's without the enemy even being involved. The recording became more and more difficult to decipher. They could hear the fierce wind in the background and the occasional offstage voice and squelch as groups of guardsmen came struggling past on their way up the hill.

The recording was briefly more audible. It sounded as if another officer on the net had asked a question. There was a pause. The wind abated. You could hear a number of guardsmen walk past. Then another pause and the rasp of what sounded like a petrol cigarette lighter repeatedly struck. Then Verney taking a deep drag on his cigarette. His tone was infinitely weary and sarcastic:

'Why don't we just make it look as if the thing has broken down?'

The hairs on the back of Jacot's neck stood up.

'Play it again.'

Will looked startled.

'OK. OK. Calm yourself.' Will fiddled with the machine.

He listened a second time. 'Why don't we just make it look as if the thing has broken down?' It was definitely Verney.

Jacot stood up and walked to the window. He stood still looking out and flexing his burnt hands.

'Anything wrong Dan?' asked Will.

'Yes, there is something very, very wrong. Dreadfully wrong. But I'm not sure how or why.'

'So what if Verney called off some half-hearted, half-baked attempt to drag ammunition over a hill close to the landing beaches. It's thirty years ago now. Imagine someone in 1975 agonising over some mini-incident in the Second World War in a not very active theatre. Who gives a tinker's fart? You can't define your life by it.'

'Quite. Most of us moved on long ago. But just because a single incident in a small war long ago does not define me does not mean it is the same for everybody. Far from it, single events do categorise some people – being a murder victim for instance. Things that happen in the past pursue people far into the future. It wasn't the marching that stopped us getting over that mountain. We were ordered to turn back because we could not take our mortar tubes and ammunition with us. Each man was carrying two mortar bombs in his pack but that was not enough. If we ran into trouble we needed more. If Verney stopped that tractor from getting its load across the mountain that's the event that kicked off the chain of events that sees us all blown to kingdom come. It's like the ignored ice warnings on the Titanic. But this is more. It wasn't sloppiness or fatigue – forgiveable perhaps. This was disobeying a direct order not because of new circumstances or using his initiative but because he and others thought they had a better idea. If anyone had found out it would have been fatal to his career.'

'But who else could have known? A few squaddies passing by would hardly put two and two together. Sorry, I know you hate the term "squaddies". And as I said who cares now?'

Jacot turned and faced Will. 'It could be a motive for murder.'

'Really. Do you think that? OK. OK. Calm yourself.'

Jacot's hands flexed more powerfully. 'I need to get a message to London quickly. What's the best way –I can't hassle the governor? Poor man has been putting me up for three days. The military at Mount Pleasant?'

'Dan, please. You are talking to a skilled radio ham. Admittedly we are in the middle of nowhere. My satellite phone might take a few minutes to get going but it will easily get through to a landline in London.'

'What's the time in London?'

'We are three hours behind GMT and so four behind the UK at the moment.'

Jacot laughed. 'Easily confused. I remember during the war we all had to operate on London time otherwise everything got muddled up. Will, give me a couple of minutes while I ring my boss in London and pretend to be sober.'

Say nodded, grinned and went into the kitchen.

'Lady Nevinson, Jacot here.' It wasn't exactly a squeal of delight but she was certainly pleased to hear from him. He took her through what he had discovered and finished with, 'Well, it amounts to a motive for murder. Could explain a lot and if it's the case we are all off the hook as it's not a national security matter. It's not a very good line. Would you get someone to contact the Cambridge Police. They had better re-interview Mr Jones, the Fellows' Butler at St James'. Yes, Lady Nevinson. No, Lady Nevinson. I fly out via Chile tomorrow.'

The Austral winter wind shook the house. Jacot was no longer drafting in his mind his report to Lady Nevinson. His mind wasn't focussing on intelligence. It was mulling over murder. Maybe Jones had killed Verney as payback for his young brother's hellish, burning death on the *Oliver Cromwell*. If others were involved in Verney's little scheme to frustrate the Celtic Guards' efforts to leave the landing beaches that fateful night they presumably had kept silent too. Those connexions hardly mattered now, certainly not to the murder investigation. With any luck it would emerge that Verney had died of natural causes before Jones had got around to doing anything in revenge for his brother. He felt sorry for Jones. All those years of grief for a lost brother and their poor, proud mother who had never got over it.

Jacot was going to miss playing the amateur sleuth on a secret mission from the Cabinet Office. He had rather enjoyed himself and it was more amusing than watching yet another unfolding British military disaster in Afghanistan or manically flattering the Americans, which seemed these days to be the bread and butter of intelligence work.

Jacot took another gulp of his Famous Grouse. A malicious mistake nearly thirty years before had set off a chain of events that resulted in the ghastly, claustrophobic deaths of over fifty young men. Jacot did not believe that comforting myth about being burned alive, that the smoke and gases overwhelm you before you actually start to burn seriously. He had been told it at school about Joan of Arc and he had always been relieved that the Oxford Martyrs – Latimer, Ridley and a few months later Cranmer – would have had a mercifully quick, if frightening, death. It wasn't true. He had heard those men dying on the *Cromwell*. They did not suffocate, they burned all the way.

'Come on Dan, let's finish the whisky. The RAF will be here in a couple of hours to pick you up. Who knows, the pilot might even be Prince William.'

XVI

LAN Flight 0045
– Santiago de Chile to London

The flight back from Santiago was long and tedious. Santiago was to all intents and purposes a European city, making it easy to forget just how far away South America was from home. It was a curious custom in the Cabinet Office that certain officials took the status of their bosses even when not accompanying them. The taxpayer had therefore been kind enough to pay for a premium economy seat for Jacot, rightly an increasingly rare occurrence in these straitened times. As ever Lady Nevinson's elegant claws seemed to extend most places and a very attentive British ambassador to Chile ensured that Jacot eventually travelled in what the Chilean airline called "Premium Business" – a rare treat indeed for anyone except bankers in their heyday. The food on the Chilean Airlines flight had been excellent and, sexist though it was even to think it, the air hostesses were gorgeous. Jacot slept much of the way.

His mind slowly purged itself of the emotions aroused by his first return visit to the Falkland Islands since 1982. So far it had been different from what he expected. To his great relief the dead men he had known who had appeared many times in his dreams over the years did not return to him. Nor was he plagued again by the sound of screaming. It used to come in the night and had pursued him for a long time afterwards, well into his early 40s. Even the guilt he felt seemed benign. He had been struck by the kindness of the Falkland Islanders, still grateful after all these years for their deliverance from a brutal invasion. The recapture of the Falkland Islands had led to the fall of General Galtieri's Junta. If those awful men in their comic opera uniforms had not so comprehensively bungled what should have been a reasonably easy military task – holding onto the Falklands – they would still be in power today. Jacot shuddered. They had treated their own people with a cruelty and disdain worthy of the Gestapo, throwing some of them alive from aircraft flying far out into the South Atlantic because they might have been socialists or were students who disliked a police state. Jacot looked out of the aircraft window at the vast expanse of cold grey sea thousands of feet below and shuddered again. God knows how they would have treated the Falkland Islanders if the occupation had been allowed to continue. Every sadist in the secret police would have descended on the islands to ensure its loyalty to the "mother country". As was the habit of the Argentine Junta, no doubt they would have kidnapped babies and children and had them adopted by loyal military families.

He had also been struck, again, by the sheer, wild beauty of the Falklands. The light and the constant wind were refreshing, cleansing, even for a visitor; although some more permanent inhabitants might find the wind particularly trying in the months of the Austral winter. We should make more, he thought, of the environmental cost of the invasion in particular the disgraceful laying of unrecorded minefields – in direct contravention of the Geneva conventions and normal human decency. He hadn't read any of the histories of the campaign but a few years before his mother had given him a book of photographs and reminiscences. His favourite account was by a Royal Marine colonel having a cup of tea with his sergeant-major on a hill high above Stanley which they had captured the previous day. Through their binoculars they can see an Argentine working party laying a minefield willy-nilly on the approaches to Port Stanley – without even consulting a map. A few well-placed mortar rounds soon saw them off.

But most of all and most disturbingly Jacot had been struck by the selfishness of his own reaction. He didn't mind his burned hands. Although they hurt like hell sometimes they had become a kind of signature accessory and part of his appearance and personality. He didn't mind the claustrophobia that seemed to have returned with a vengeance as he grew older. Even the deep guilt he felt about his spur of the moment decision to keep his men below for a few more minutes on that fateful day seemed to have lost its gnawing power. But he did mind his lost youth. Aged twenty everything had seemed so simple. It was his lost youth he missed most.

His mind turned to the task ahead: interviewing Jones 74. He took what was nearly a gulp of Chilean red wine. It would be awkward. He had once known Jones extremely well. There was still a strong bond between them. They were both sur-vivors of the *Oliver Cromwell*, wounded survivors. Their burns had taken a long time to heal. Severe burns to the hands are particularly difficult for doctors to deal with and painful for the victim as well as causing all kinds of little indignities during the weeks of recovery, offset by plenty of laughter and black humour on the wards of their hospital. The Celtic Guards casualties showed exemplary invention and imagination in dreaming up almost endless variations of going to the lavatory with no hands jokes. Even on the bleakest days when many of them were slowly being weaned off painkillers it was possible to be rendered speechless, sometimes helpless, with laughter at the latest variation on the well worn theme delivered more often than not in a strong Welsh baritone. The only officer in the ward, Jacot had been astonished at the richness and ribaldry of their imagination. Although generally outclassed, he had occasionally come up with some good lines and was still rather proud of his efforts. John Jones had shared all these things. And yet Jones had lied to him. Worse, it seemed likely that Jones may have murdered General Verney in a delayed revenge for his brother. It was beyond Jacot's imagination that someone like Jones could murder. He must have seen over the years the hollowing effects of grief on his mother, and the anguish the whole Jones family of Llanbedr had felt over the loss of a much loved younger son. Verney had a family for God's sake. It was a reversion to savagery akin to the deeply cruel and uncivilised so called "honour" killings of young men and women of immigrant descent that so often these days disfigured the Sunday newspapers.

Jacot wondered how he had done it. If it hadn't been for something Jones said in his rooms over champagne he would never have suspected. Jacot was ushered off the plane first, without any need for any landing formalities, to a waiting government car and driver which set off at high speed for Cambridge. The driver assured him that his luggage would follow later.

XVII

Jones was sitting in an interview room in Cambridge Police station on St Andrew's Street where he had been held since Jacot's urgent telephone call from the South Atlantic. He stood up as Jacot came in. He wasn't dishevelled or chain-smoking or distressed, but immaculately turned out as always and completely calm. Jacot was relieved that, with luck, there would not be need for a scene. They sat down opposite each other at the interview table.

Jones looked Jacot straight in the eye. 'I didn't kill him Colonel.'

'But you certainly blamed him for Bryn's death, didn't you?'

'Yes. If they hadn't turned that tractor back, or rather made it look as if it had broken down, Bryn would have travelled on it all the way to wherever and he would not have been on that f…..g ship. Stupid f…..g name for a ship anyway the *Oliver Cromwell*. Maybe none of us would have got on that ship. Who knows? But certainly not our Bryn.'

Jacot decided to let him go on. Maybe the whole story would come out naturally. If he questioned him now Jones might become wary. As a former special forces soldier Jones would have had some counter-interrogation training.

'Useless, clever-clever officers poking their noses where they weren't wanted. Why would you want to make it look as if something had broken down? Why not just let the tractor do its work? I don't suppose you've got any answers have you Colonel? Not that he was the only officer involved was he... sir? And I don't mean those f.....g muppets who were in charge of us. I wanted to get the men up on the deck, but oh no, you knew better. Five of our platoon dead and I forget how many injured. You know what really gets to me – maybe if I hadn't been so busy I could have done more for Bryn.' He held his head in his hands and rocked to and fro on the chair.

Jacot said nothing.

'All right, all right. I'm sorry. I'm sorry. Fortunes of f.....g war.' He looked up at Jacot. 'Colonel, I didn't kill him. On Bryn's soul I swear it.' Jones visibly pulled himself together, the years of military discipline kicking in. He smiled. 'How did you work out I had met him before?'

'Something you said while we were having our little drink. I asked you if you had met Verney before. Do you remember?'

Jones looked nonplussed, 'I didn't think I had'.

'But you weren't quite sure, were you? You had been on that rain-soaked hillside that night too. You had chatted to Bryn as he passed by. You were probably standing quite close to Verney. You knew that. It was in your mind when we were talking. That's why you answered my question with "It was dark" and then you quickly moved onto talking about how good the Bridge of Sorrows looked as it was getting dark.'

'My special duties instructors would not be pleased. Silly detail to slip up on.'

'It wasn't a slip up 74. It was stupid. You should have told me. For God's sake man we spent nearly two months in that hospital together.'

'I am profoundly sorry Colonel. I've made you look stupid I know. I didn't want to say anything that might get me into trouble. I'm not just a Fellows' Butler you know. I read a little. Detective novels and, like many others, I am glued to those easy-to-watch, the murder never takes place on a council estate, things on television. I had motive, means and opportunity for sure – those are the three key things a detective looks for aren't they? I had a motive big time. Verney turns out to be an actor in the *Oliver Cromwell* tragedy which nearly did for us all but certainly did for young Bryn.' He paused and looked away. 'And Mam. Plenty of means from my special duties background. Lucky the IRA never "sported their oaks" or it would have been difficult to break in to their homes and offices. I didn't mind the offices so much but their homes – nasty, grotty unhygienic crew for the most part. Opportunity as well. Fellows' Butlers can go anywhere at any time without anyone getting suspicious. Plenty of time to tidy up afterwards as well.'

It was becoming rapidly clear to Jacot that he had made a ghastly mistake. In a way he was relieved. On the way back from Chile he had been genuinely upset and unhappy at the prospect of Jones going to prison. A judge and jury would take a very dim view of this kind of killing and Jones would probably have had to do a minimum of twenty years. If he was being honest with himself, he also felt betrayed. How could this man with whom he had gone through so much lie to him? Jacot's deep sense of loyalty had been deeply offended. Most of all though, Jacot's moral world had been profoundly disorientated and unsettled. Jones had throughout his career been a model soldier. He had fought the IRA with distinction. More than that, in the hellish inferno of the *Oliver Cromwell* he had conducted himself with great bravery. Unable in the end to rescue his own brother, he had devoted his considerable leadership abilities and physical strength to rescuing a group of three young guardsmen who attached themselves to him by chance in the thick smoke of the tank deck. Jacot, like many Englishmen of his type, believed physical courage in the face of extreme danger to be the ultimate virtue and that if a man possessed or showed the kind of courage Jones had displayed then he must be virtuous in other important areas of life.

Jones continued, 'I did go up to General Verney's rooms after the feast was over. I don't know what exactly was in my mind. I certainly did not intend to harm him, maybe confront him. Maybe, I don't know, make him apologise. Possibly, I wanted to clear my own mind. Listen, Colonel ultimately like you I think I'm a grown-up. Blaming Verney for killing Bryn as a result of his little scam would have been crazy. It was a stupid f.....g way to move the mortars anyway.'

'I am going to get you out of here. No questions asked. And there won't be a problem with you going back to your old job. Lady Nevinson will square it with the Master. Better say there was some problem that had to be dealt with dating back to "The Troubles" in Ireland. But on one condition – that you give me a detailed account of everything that happened in college during General Verney's fatal stay. I mean everything that might be of interest to me, even if it casts you in a less than flattering light. You promised to help me last time but when push came to shove you took the easy way out. Most unguardsmanlike in my view.'

Jones looked upset. It was, in its way, quite an insult – a Guards version of "conduct unbecoming" or "lack of moral fibre" and with the same bite. 'Of course, Colonel.'

'One final point. You were trained at vast expense to the British taxpayer in the various esoteric skills and drills required to make an effective special duties soldier, these included extensive training in observation and memory skills. Use them. Let's use them to find the bastard or bastards who killed General Verney. I'll take notes and we may need some alcohol along the way.'

It was a long afternoon in Jacot's rooms helped along by a bottle of Veuve Clicquot. Champagne, in small quantities, of all the ways of drinking alcohol did most to shake up the memory and sharpen the wits. Jones had indeed seen and heard a great deal. Close questioning by Jacot, guilt on the part of Jones and the Veuve Clicquot combined together to build a detailed picture of events on the night of Verney's death. Jacot took copious notes on his scarlet Cabinet Office iPad. Jones' account was very much as he had expected. On his way up perhaps to confront Verney he had overheard a heated argument coming from Verney's room so he stopped in the corridor to listen. The words were there again, 'Make it look as if the thing has broken down', repeated several times by both Verney and the man he was arguing with. That the man had an American accent was hardly surprising to Jacot given the direction his investigation was now taking. But he was puzzled by something Jones said. According to his account the American who had been at the dinner became so incensed during the argument that he had an attack of asthma.

They parted friends and comrades once more, each apologising profusely to the other.

That night the dreams came back, or one of the dreams at least. It was a pay parade at their barracks in London thirty years before. Jacot sat at a wooden table with a ledger and piles of crisp bank notes. Sergeant Jones stood behind him. The queue was short, only five guardsmen, the five from his platoon missing presumed dead on the *Oliver Cromwell* – their bodies had never been recovered. As each one stepped smartly forward and stated his name Sergeant Jones said the same thing "Shall I bring the men up on deck now?" After each man had been paid he would salute, turn to the right and march to the back of the queue...

XVIII

The Scott-Wilson Austral Studies Institute, Cambridge
– basement laboratory

Charlotte Pirbright thought life was good. She hadn't liked Verney that much and she was saddened and a little frightened by his death. But the impact on her was very slight. There was so much else going on. Anyway, it meant that she could take forward their research on "Captain S". Yes, she could dedicate her thesis and her book to his memory, but the glory would be all hers. She felt a bit guilty but what could she do? At last she would be able to realize her ambition of becoming a proper Cambridge don. Currently she held a very junior, very temporary, research fellowship at St James' but it finished at the end of the academic year.

Verney had wangled the fellowship for her but to have any chance of a permanent post she would have to write a well-received book or publish a piece of original and startling research pretty soon. People just did not understand how difficult it was to get "tenure" as they called it on American campuses. There was great demand for research students to assist with teaching undergraduates and to undertake a range of academically menial tasks around the university, but the goal of a permanent fellowship in a decent college remained elusive for most. But their, her, research on Scott would change everything. A grateful country would ensure that the grind and petty jealousies of academic life would be overcome. Golly, if the world only knew where the research had been taking them – was taking them still. It was going to be one of the biggest stories in Antarctic studies ever. Maybe even a film – with Angelina Jolie or perhaps someone a little younger playing her part and a big star as General Verney – Jeremy Irons or Kenneth Branagh. She was sure of it. Now was the time. She was about to get her big break.

She didn't like older men much but that Jacot fellow seemed sweet. He looked very cool and mysterious in his black silk gloves. She had become used to seeing him around the college in the past few weeks. He dined in hall most nights. But then he had disappeared off to the Falklands on some mission or other. Apparently he was now back, according to the head porter. He had that neatness and smartness of turn-out that you often saw in military men. It was his gloves that attracted her attention though. She knew why he wore them but they had a strange effect, making him seem old fashioned and out of place. They also distracted from his eyes. Despite years of training in a girls' boarding school and a strong natural sense of consideration for others, she had looked long and hard at his hands when they had first met a few weeks before. Strong hands, not slim but not stubby and with long fingers. On the left hand she remembered just above the cuff of the glove a burn scar, still red after all these years, where the metal of his red-hot watch had seared into the skin.

She was going to miss Verney's intelligence stories. It gave her an insider's frisson of pleasure whenever she read something in the papers that Verney had given her background on. He had been very indiscreet. Jacot would be surprised at what he had told her. Come to think of it maybe she should ring him now, but no, all in good time.

She walked through the cold Cambridge evening. The cold wind straight from the Urals whipping in her face. It was dark, damp and foggy. The street lights had that Jack the Ripper feel. She turned into the Scott-Wilson Institute. Her tiny office as ever was a mess. She shared it with two other graduate students. No one appeared to be around. But then it was a Friday night. They had probably all gone to the pub. She might go along later but first of all she had to check something for an experiment the following week.

She went down to the basement into a large storeroom. Fitted out when the building was put up in the 1920s, it was full of solid mahogany drawers with stout brass handles, filled with dried animal and plant specimens and other Antarcticana. She was always surprised by how oddly reassuring the hardware of the past could be. Everything seemed organized and built to last – perhaps it was in the craftsmanship. And yet the world had been hurtling through space just as it always had, and being human on it was the same chancy business it had always been, chancier even. There were no antibiotics and at the time the institute was built the world had just gone through a ghastly war, itself only a pale imitation of an even ghastlier war to follow. And yet Scott's world was the more reassuring. He did not have the comforts of religion although his boon companion Dr Wilson certainly did – a deeply devout man who saw all the glories of nature as expressions of God's beneficence and glory. You could see it in his beautiful and haunting watercolours. They died with courage – almost indifference according to Scott's own account at any rate. At least they missed the Great War – others on the expedition were not so fortunate. Perhaps that was the fascination with Captain Scott and all his works. No happy ending for sure, but Edwardian and dependable all the way. Somehow for all the harshness of the Antarctic Scott's world was an ordered place – we can see it still in Herbert Ponting's great photographs. A well built, sturdy, warm and tidy hut. There is plenty of food and lots of laughs. Parties even. The officers and men sleep in different parts of the hut – it's a bungalow but an invisible line separates the upper and lower decks. During the long Antarctic winter few venture outside into the raging blizzards. But within there is honey still for tea.

Charlotte had been allocated a drawer by the director, Professor Stapley. It was lined in dark blue baize. Inside were three instruments – the keys to her and Verney's research. One was a theodolite – the surveying instrument used to navigate and fix positions accurately while travelling to the pole. There was also a sextant. The third instrument was a watch, or rather a chronometer, a variant of a ship's clock of a type similar to those used by both Scott and Amundsen. Curiously, for a set of navigational instruments there was no compass. But then compasses don't work well at the poles – for obvious reasons the needles are attracted to the magnetic poles which are neither in the direction of true south or true north. This caused both expeditions considerable problems. Indeed until the advent of the Global Positioning System it was always quite difficult to work out exactly where you were in the polar regions.

There were two key issues she had been working on with Verney. In order to work out latitude – for Scott and

Amundsen working out how far south they were – a precise measurement with a theodolite was necessary which involved a measurement of solar, stellar or lunar position above the horizon. It works everywhere on earth but you need both a horizon and something in space to measure from. You need to be able to see clearly. And your instruments need to be unaffected by the extreme temperature, hardened against the cold.

There was a further complication. In order to measure longitude – how far east or west you are – you need to be able to measure the solar position at noon and at a second known time. So you not only need to be able to see, but also to tell the time accurately. If the conditions are not right and your clock isn't working you cannot be sure exactly where you are – no ifs, no buts the wrong conditions would have turned the early 20th-century version of Satnav off. No amount of post-expedition checking could make up for this fact. And this is what fascinated her. No one had ever checked how theodolites or Edwardian watches worked in extremely low temperatures. Indeed, Amundsen did not have a theodolite with him when he reached the pole.

Charlotte cleaned and oiled the outsides of the instruments. Scott was always worried about time-keeping. Like all sailors before satellites their lives depended on accurate arithmetic and accurate navigation. That life could be split in half: one part depended on accurate time keeping, the other half depended on the sun. To back it up they used dead reckoning – plotting as accurately as they could their course and speed taking into account tides and currents. Generally the Royal Navy did this well. Scott had his own watch as the primary time-keeper, like a ship's clock. The back up was carried by

Birdie Bowers, the stocky and imperturbable officer from the Indian Navy, and we know from Scott's diaries that it went wrong on at least one occasion.

She was hugely excited. She and Verney had nearly achieved their goal – checking and auditing the navigational instruments on both Amundsen and Scott's expeditions. They were not quite there yet and it was possible that their hunch was wrong. These things were difficult to prove either way a hundred years later. But Verney had certainly intended to give his audience at the Charles II Lecture a taster of what was to come. It would have electrified the room, with journalists dashing out to make contact with their editors. Both she and Verney would have been instantly famous.

A couple of days before he had died Verney had asked her round for a drink in his rooms. He seemed anxious, distracted and angry. He gave her a file with the learned paper they had nearly finished together, plus all the background data and bits and pieces about their collaborative research. He told her to keep it under lock and key in her own room. He had then downloaded the same data onto a tiny memory stick. Smiling, he had handed it to her 'Just to be safe.' It was now slung low on a tiny gold chain around her neck that was tucked into her bra for extra security. Just as well. The police or the military police or the various other people who seemed to be more than ordinarily interested in Verney's death, like Jacot, would no doubt have confiscated them "as evidence".

The director had agreed that she could conduct a controlled experiment the following week in the cold chamber. The institute maintained a sealed room in which it was possible to conduct experiments at very low temperatures – exactly replicating the conditions at the South Pole. What Charlotte really wanted to do was to exactly replicate the journey to the Pole of both expeditions, but it would take too long. Instead she was going to cool the instruments down to a low temperature, similar to the levels they would have experienced in the long trek to the Pole, and then replicate a single day at the Pole itself for each expedition. It had been much colder for Scott than for Amundsen. Her colleagues thought it hare-brained but science was science and it would give her verifiable data on how instruments of this type would actually have behaved on the day. She could, from the comfort of 21st-century Cambridge, reproduce the conditions exactly as experienced by Amundsen and Scott a hundred years before.

She had been allocated two whole days to herself. Other members of the institute were most put out. They needed the chamber for what they called "more relevant" experiments on materials and structures that might be useful at the Pole today and for experiments on global warming, the dullest in Charlotte's view of all the aspects of polar research. What was it about global warming that seemed to attract the most fanatical and unkempt of her colleagues? Most of modern man's great ideas had originated in Cambridge, originally an obscure market town deep in the fens. But one idea that was unlikely ever to bear fruit in this freezing, college-studded fen was that the world was getting warmer. Perhaps it was, but Cambridge was certainly getting colder.

The theodolite, sextant and chronometer were not only impressive aids to navigation. They had been beautifully made. No plastic bits or computer displays, just solid mainly brass instruments – a joy to hold and operate and always, apparently, accurate.

Her mood changed. Suddenly the room lost its re-assuring character. The rows of trays and drawers going up to the ceiling turned darker, bringing to mind the poverty and diffi-culties of life a hundred years before and the turmoil in the Edwardian mind. The solid craftsmanship no longer repre-sented the solidity the Edwardians had enjoyed, but under-lined what they were about to lose in the carnage of the Great War. Suddenly the polished brass and mahogany seemed threatening – the rows of drawers like the slide-out cabinets in a mortuary. The hum of the cold room and the clinical stark-ness of its huge white door at the end of the corridor brought to mind both death and the vast pitiless coldness of the Antarctic. She was afraid. But the feeling would pass and the breath of the night-wind would soften. What she needed was warmth, company and a drink. All available at The Eagle, her favourite Cambridge pub and long time haunt of the younger element at SWASI. She would go and join them. She placed her notebook in her handbag and got up. Who knows, The Eagle was already famous as the place Watson and Crick unlocked the secret of DNA, maybe it would become famous in the Antarctic Studies world as well. It was funny how quickly the prospect of a Friday evening get-together cheered her up. Charlotte was calm and optimistic again when she heard light footsteps in the corridor.

'Hallo. Who's there?' she called out. 'I am just off to the Eagle. If you are doing some work then lock up and put the alarm on.' She applied some lipstick. There was no reply. 'Hallo?'

'Hallo. It's me', replied out a muffled and indistinct voice from the dark corridor outside. She couldn't quite place the voice – probably muffled by a scarf on a night like this, or laid low with a sore throat. She continued looking into the mirror of a small powder compact as she applied the finishing touches to her make-up.

'Hallo,' from the muffled voice again. The door into the store-room opened. She still couldn't see who it was. The face was in shadow. But the trademark black silk gloves were obvious enough.

'Ah the good Colonel Jacot. No doubt on some sleuthing task. I am off to The Eagle. Would you like to come along for a drink? Normally a big turnout by us SWASI types on Friday night.'

In the split second of consciousness left to her before the end of her young life a kind of alarm went off. The hands in their gloves looked like Jacot's but there was no burn scar above the left cuff.

He thrust the sharpened tip of the eight inch hollow ice pick into the back of her head, passing within inches of the cells where that memory had been stored. The pick penetrated into the cerebellum and then into the brain stem: the part of the brain that connects it to the spinal cord. At the same time he pressed a small button at the bottom of the handle activating a charge of compressed air right up the hollow body of the ice pick and shooting six thick steel needles in an umbrella shape deep into the recesses of Charlotte's dying brain. In effect her body's control centre was destroyed in an instant. There was no gentle falling away or dimming of the lights. The hollow ice pick caused massive destruction inside her brain and instant death. Other than strapping an explosive charge to her head it was the quickest way. The movies always underestimated how long it took for someone to die. A cyanide death was not an easy one. Even for a hard man like himself they were distressing – too much thrashing around. This was better.

He remembered a lecture about killing quickly. Dr Beaurieux a 19th-century French doctor had conducted an experiment at an execution by guillotine. After the head had been severed Breaurieux called out to the victim. Apparently the eyes remained clear and blinked in reply. Maybe. But this way really was quick and death was instantaneous. How could she complain?

He let the body fall gently to the ground. She was pretty. He shut her glassy eyes. The ice pick would remain inside her skull. Too messy to take out. Its steel and plastic construction would give nothing away. Why not leave the gloves too? The Cambridge police were unlikely to be that stupid, but it would amuse him if the ludicrous Colonel Jacot got a run for his money. He dropped both gloves to the floor but kept the surgical gloves beneath firmly in place, walked slowly up the stairs and into the dark and foggy street. He was sure no one had seen him – not that he cared.

XIX

The Scott-Wilson Austral Studies Institute, Cambridge
— basement laboratory

Jacot entered the room to find Chief Inspector Bradshaw of the Cambridge Police. A plump man with a shaved head, he looked very unhappy indeed and barely glanced at Jacot.

'The Chief Constable got a call from London earlier to say that you were to be informed immediately and shown the crime scene if you wanted Colonel. And that we are to co-operate with you in every way. Straight from Number 10, I understand'. His disgust with this arrangement was apparent.

Charlotte's body was lying parallel to the banks of mahogany draws, neatly laid out face up. Her arms had been folded across her body and her eyes closed, almost as in a ritual killing. There was no outward sign of violence, the only clue to foul play was a small patch of clear liquid lying beneath her head. If Jacot hadn't known that she was dead she could have been a young woman taking a quick lie down just after washing her hair. She was a beautiful girl, almost more so in death and repose than in life. The features were perfect. She could have been a marvellously carved funerary statue set above her own tomb. But the animation, the soul as Jacot certainly believed, was gone.

Once his initial, disorientating aesthetic response to the death scene had waned what Jacot really wanted to do next was to sit down in a corner and cry, and then afterwards rage at the stupidity and waste that had caused this beautiful young English girl to be murdered. Time for that later, if ever. Jacot took himself in hand. He had seen death before, close up. He must master both his sadness and his anger and channel them into a controlled intellectual and emotional aggression – a drive that would produce results, unravel what the hell was going on.

'Chief Inspector, I would be grateful if one of your team would check the body for a small gold chain and a memory stick that I think she was normally wearing. It should be tucked away somewhere in her bra.'

Bradshaw gave him a distinctly odd look but quickly summoned one of the women on the forensic team. Sure enough the tiny memory stick was still on her body – hung on a small gold chain, tucked sideways for extra security into her bra. It was a small thing, but in it had been wrapped up all the hopes of this young Cambridge don. Hopes for professional advancement and glamour and fame. All come to nothing now.

There was some argument with poor Chief Inspector Bradshaw over Jacot taking possession of the memory stick, only resolved after another telephone call to the Chief Constable. Some might have got a kick out of invoking the Official Secrets Act or aggressively dropping Lady Nevinson's name. Jacot just found it depressing. Ultimately, he didn't approve of a secret official world and he hated the arrogance of the modern state – at its most arrogant in matters of state security. And he felt sorry for Bradshaw. After a little gentle toing and froing the deal Bradshaw laid down, quite rightly, was that Jacot could take immediate possession of a copy of the data made by the Cambridge Police's computer laboratory but that the original belonged to the police investigation. Jacot readily agreed, adding that under no circumstances should the original be surrendered to anyone else – not even GCHQ. Of course Jacot meant "especially" not GCHQ. This triggered something in Bradshaw who appeared to realise that Jacot and the National Security Adviser had no intention of concealing anything or trying to change the course of the investigation. The memory stick was sent away to be copied at the police station a few hundred yards away and Bradshaw handed Jacot a copy before he left the crime scene.

Jacot walked back to St James'. A police forensic team was already in attendance; no doubt forewarned by the newly co-operative Bradshaw, Jacot was waved through the cordon and allowed into Charlotte's rooms accompanied by a police-woman. The rooms were not as grand as the sets allocated to Verney or even Jacot. There was no river view and no gilding. They were pleasant nevertheless and immaculately clean and tidy. Charlotte had decorated the room with six 18th-century prints of her college at Oxford. Her bed was covered in a dark blue duvet. As fellow of a Cambridge college she found it amusing to underline her Oxonian antecedents. The room was exactly as Jacot had expected it – a fairly ordinary junior fellow's set with the personality and habits of its occupant imprinted on a neutral background.

The police forensic team were clearly going through the motions. The rooms were neat and tidy and bore no traces of having been forcibly entered or thoroughly searched. They were much as Charlotte had left them before embarking on her last journey to the Scott-Wilson Institute. He spoke briefly to the policewoman in charge who confessed that, as the rooms were not technically a crime scene, they would seal them off for a few days until Detective Chief Inspector Bradshaw had had a good snoop around and then release them back to the college.

Jacot was suspicious. It takes one to know one – the rooms had been searched meticulously and methodically by a team of professionals. He had carried out the same procedure himself in Northern Ireland years ago, against the clock. One man would remain on look-out outside. Two men would break into the house or office usually belonging to a senior IRA figure who would have been detained by the police for a few hours on some trumped up offence or other. The RUC's favourite was usually "Thought to be in possession of illegally distilled alcohol"; ironic given that the police themselves distilled the best moonshine or poteen north of the border. The version made with pear drops was particularly prized by the British Army.

The first action would be to take Polaroid photographs of the lay out of the room as an aide memoire. It was easy to forget small details when in a hurry – exactly how were the copies of *An Phoblacht* (The Republic) the IRA's over-the-top but sometimes well written propaganda journal stacked by the filing cabinet, or the precise lay out of a tray of pipes, tobacco and pipe cleaners. They would also check for basic security measures – was there a hair or a small piece of paper laid in a certain way on the handle of a briefcase, say? The most popular defensive trick was to insert a small piece of paper inside a book on a certain page. Searchers in a hurry had a tendency to flip through books and it was easy enough for the piece of paper to slip out and be replaced between the wrong pages. Luckily, the British intelligence teams had been well-trained and were able to spot the techniques. They were useful even, as they contributed to a sense of false security among the IRA capos. But the biggest danger for even a highly trained, highly experienced team was the temptation to over-tidy once the search was complete. When restoring a room, supposedly to the status quo ante the spooks breaking in, it was almost impossible to resist the temptation to impose order – squaring off magazines and books on tables for instance or straightening books on a shelf – like an obsessive housewife.

Even the best-trained search teams made mistakes. The team that went through Charlotte's room must have been under immense time pressure. Charlotte's sitting room certainly had that overtidied look.

But to confirm Jacot would look in the bathroom. It was small and the shelves were crammed with an immense array of scents, creams and potions. These were difficult to search properly without leaving a trace. The usual procedure would be to open each pot and insert a knitting needle, or something similar, to probe for anything concealed below. But the knitting needle invariably left a little bobble of disturbance on the surface of the cream or potion. Impossible for an unsuspecting layman to detect but glaringly obvious to the trained eye, particularly in an unused pot of cream or gel. The police-woman gave him some plastic gloves and Jacot unscrewed a pot of some kind of make-up remover. It was half-used but the bobble was there. Same detail in another pot.

Just to be sure, he wanted to check the lavatory cistern.

Search teams always checked the lavatory cistern. It was felt to be an excellent hiding place for guns or drugs. But there was one catch to taking the lid off a cistern – because it was so rarely done as part of the everyday cleaning of a bathroom there was usually dust beneath the rim which would then fall onto the water below. A really on the ball team would have known this and flushed it away. But Jacot would need one of the forensic team to help. Bradshaw by this time had arrived. He explained the procedure to the chief inspector who quickly instructed one of his Scenes of Crimes Officers. First she checked the cistern for fingerprints of which there were none, itself suspicious. Then she carefully but vigorously applied a small hand hoover to the underside of the cistern rim. Finally she set up a powerful fluorescent light in the room and lifted the lid off as carefully as she could. There was a thin barely discernible coating of dust on the surface of the water. With the fluorescent light you couldn't miss it.

Jacot was in a quandary. What he needed was not a Provincial Police Scenes of Crime team, however skilled, but a specialist search team from the intelligence services or The Special Reconnaissance Regiment. Lady Nevinson could have one despatched in minutes but could they be trusted? The army people almost certainly, but it would mean going through a couple of layers at least of leaky military bureaucracy. As for the intelligence people, they would ultimately be loyal to their own bosses and to them alone. If it was not in their interest to uncover evidence of the presence of another intelligence agency then they would find nothing, officially at least.

The innocent and unworldly Charlotte Pirbright, her head

full of romantic visions of her hero "Captain S", had really belonged to another age. There was something trusting, enthusiastic and optimistic about her that would have suited Edwardian England. With those looks she would have married well and been free to pursue a private academic career. No doubt about that, thought Jacot. Poor child, she simply had no idea what she had got involved with once Verney began to share with her snippets of highly classified intelligence. Men and women could be murdered, tortured or worse "disappeared" for certain kinds of information. She would have known that. How could anyone not know in the years of the "911 Wars", as one historian was already calling them.

She had one fundamental naiveté, had made one crucial mistake. She didn't realise that the compromises even the good guys have to make in the intelligence world – the world the other side of the green baize door as Lady Nevinson liked to call it – could build up over time into something much more than a ruthless but proportionate operational pragmatism. Ruthlessness builds on and feeds off ruthlessness. Each time the intelligence cycle turned full circle it was spun with more energy and cruelty – to keep ahead of the other side. The process was the same in all countries. Those who considered themselves the guardians of freedom and democracy, and those who revelled in their reputations as brutal and feared secret policemen used the same time-honoured process: Direction – Collection – Processing – Analysis – Dissemination. And for both types the ultimate destination usually ended up the same: everyone an enemy, everyone a target – even Charlotte. Jacot pretty much had the picture now. He knew at last who he was up against.

It was a small comfort that even in her innocence she had outwitted their opponents by carrying the memory stick on her person. The orders appeared to have been kill the girl and search her rooms for what they wanted, or wanted back. No one seems to have planned for the fact that what they wanted, or at least a copy of it, was actually on her person. She had pulled off the oldest intelligence trick in the book, hiding a high value item in plain sight. Jacot was re-assured that his opponents might not be quite as good as they thought they were. They made mistakes under pressure or out of over-confidence.

Both these were factors in the basic error Jacot himself was about to make. He walked down the staircase into the court and took out his scarlet Cabinet Office iPhone. He punched an 11 figure code into the handset and waited a few seconds. The Magenta facility was enabled. It was the first time Jacot had used it. But he had to be absolutely sure that no one could hear what he was saying.

He rang Lady Nevinson's special number. When she replied he asked her a short question – just eight words in all. She replied with the single word 'Yes' and broke the connexion.

Jacot was right to trust the Magenta facility. It was unbreakable. No outside agency could decipher written or voice messages in Magenta. He did not fully understand the technology behind it except that it had been a joint Franco-British venture. But not being able to understand a conversation is a very different matter from not knowing that the conversation is taking place at all. In a darkened room at an airbase not far from Cambridge a young signals operator alerted the officer supervising his shift – an individual in Cambridge and an individual in London were having a short conversation using a heavily encoded signal that their best analysts and most powerful computers could not decipher. The officer made a special entry under the 'Unusual Occurrences' paragraph of his daily report and despatched it up the chain of command, taking care to give it a higher classification than was normal.

Back in her office overlooking Downing Street Lady Nevinson initially felt a wave of satisfaction that Jacot appeared at last to be coming to some solid conclusions about the murder of General Verney. And it was murder. She was also pleased at the existence of the Magenta facility. She had long felt uncomfortable about the so-called secure communications in Downing Street. Given that often we seemed capable of listening in to the most sensitive communications of other countries she could never quite believe that some of them weren't able to do the same to us. But she knew that no one could break Magenta.

If the Verney case was unfolding as she thought it might, she was going to be thankful for absolutely secure communications with the people she needed to speak to. She might have to issue some very austere and uncompromising instructions – bleak even. Illegal even. Worse, the instructions might have to contravene some of the basic ground rules of British intelligence work. And then a terrible feeling of foreboding overtook her. Who guards the guardians? *Quis custodiet ipsos custodies?* The phrase went round and round inside her head like the scrap of a pop tune or a jingle that just won't go away. It was Juvenal she remembered from her undergraduate days and he used the phrase about trying to keep randy Roman wives faithful. If only it were about that today she thought. It was a simple question and it never went away. Suddenly she felt alone. What if Jacot was wrong? In a way she hoped he was.

XX

*The Scott-Wilson Austral Studies Institute, Cambridge
— Director's Office*

The Scott-Wilson Austral Studies Institute had been founded with the excess money from the various popular appeals to help the relatives of those who died with Scott. Scott's last written words had been after all 'For God's sake look after our people' and those in authority certainly had done so. Jacot had an appointment with its director, another Cambridge professor, a Professor Stapley. Apparently, he had something of interest — he had certainly sounded excited on the telephone. Jacot left the warm fire in his rooms reluctantly and set off for his meeting.

It was an icy night. A sharp wind from the east cut across Cambridge making it feel even colder — a good night to be abroad on Antarctic business. Jacot walked briskly towards the Institute, about half a mile from St James'. Looking up as he walked through the gate a few minutes later he saw the institute's motto carved into the wall and illuminated by spotlights. *Quaesivit Arcana Poli Videt Dei* — translated it meant: "He sought the secret of the Pole but found the hidden face of God." Part Edwardian sentimentalizing, part moving tribute to Captain Scott, it was certainly not the feeling Scott himself experienced at the Pole. His journal entry for Wednesday, January 17th 1912 the day they reached the Pole was bleaker altogether:

"Great God! This is an awful place and terrible enough for us to have labored to it without the reward of priority."

If anything, Scott found the power of humanity and comradeship in his Antarctic travels and the wonder of the natural world rather than any sense or glimpse of an Almighty. It is not at all clear who Scott's "Great God" was. To be frank it was more likely some kind of oath than an address to any deity. Scott was a great man undoubtedly, but not a Christian in the conventional sense.

Professor Stapley ushered Jacot into his office. On the back wall was a huge oil painting of the moment that Captain Oates staggered from the tent to his death. The tent looked tiny and insignificant against the immense white background of an Antarctic storm, but the artist had somehow managed to portray an identifiable human being – Oates's handsome features were clearly there, half-hidden by his reindeer skin hood. His mother never forgave Captain Scott whom she, unfashionably then, blamed for the disaster.

Professor Stapley shook Jacot by the hand and ushered him to a chair by the side of his desk. 'Thank you for coming. Terrible business about young Charlotte Pirbright. Awful and here in the institute too. I hope the authorities find the culprit. I understand that you are sort of attached to the investigation. Hush, hush and all that because of Verney. Dreadful. She was a sweet girl. Awful. Do you have any idea who could have done such a cruel thing? First let me give you a glass of whisky. It's a raw and grim night even for polar scientists. Whyte and Mackay – it's the modern version of the stuff Shackleton took with him in 1909.'

Stapley drank his whisky in one gulp and poured another.

He looked pretty shaken up, poor man. Jacot looked him straight in the eye and said 'I have a theory, yes. But if we are going to get to the bottom of this I need to know more about her research. There might be something about what they were looking into that could have contributed to both Verney's, and now Charlotte Pirbright's, deaths.'

'I think I can help', said Stapley drinking his whisky. 'In general terms they were looking into the navigational instruments used by both Amundsen and Scott – the techniques, metallurgical properties, records and so on with a view to pronouncing on their accuracy. I have had a look at the documents recovered from the memory stick you gave me. They are extraordinarily interesting. I may have worked out what it was in their research that was so startling – but I can't prove it and it's only a theory. If I am right, then I can see quite clearly why they went to some lengths to protect the information. They had stumbled upon one of the most stunning secrets or misunderstandings about Antarctic exploration. It was dynamite and would have made any book they had written a global bestseller. The historical importance of such a revelation would have led to fame and fortune.'

'Would someone murder for it?' asked Jacot.

'That's more difficult', replied Stapley. 'But let me take you through my theory. So Colonel Jacot, what do you know about Scott's last expedition?'

'Quite a lot, I think. Anyone who has travelled South feels the pull of the Antarctic and the heroic age of its first explorers. If you are a patriotic Englishman, Captain Scott is the logical man to look into. In any case, English boys born before the iron curtain of political correctness descended over our past would be familiar with aspects of the Scott epic – just about every preparatory school in the sixties and seventies had a dormitory or a house named after Scott. My particular institution certainly had one. Plus a Wellington, a Nelson, a Wolfe and a Havelock. I was in Wolfe I remember and rather proud of it. Most of us had seen the 1948 film with John Mills in the lead role. Not my idea of Scott at all – too tortured, too wooden. And casting James Robertson Justice as poor old Petty Officer Evans was a piece of vandalism.'

'But the music was extraordinary, and the photography too', said Stapley.

'Yes, but watching it again as an adult I can see that there was no effort made to understand Scott. His character is at the heart of the tragedy and we come away from the film none the wiser. It wasn't a heroic portrayal but there were no other signposts about what sort of a man he was. Most unsatisfactory. In some ways the enigma remains. You know as well as I do that despite private criticism at the time Captain Oates, whose last moments grace the back wall of your office, in particular, seemed to have fallen out with him. His letters to his mother were most uncomplimentary. Nevertheless, despite the torrent of aggressive revisionism since the 1960s it remains true that many of the heavyweights on the last expedition were absolutely devoted to him, including Wilson and Bowers who perished alongside their leader. But anyway.'

Professor Stapley smiled. 'What do you know about Amundsen, the man who actually made it to the Pole first?'

'Not much at all. Except that rather tense scene in the film when Scott receives the telegram: "Going South – Amundsen". I rather agreed with Scott's comrades that it was a bit ungentlemanly but to be honest I can't remember why.'

'Amundsen was originally heading for the North Pole. But just before he mounted his expedition news came through that an American, Robert Peary, had bagged it supposedly on April 6, 1909. But the news only got to the outside world after Scott had set off. So Amundsen turned South. But guess what? We now know that Peary had got nowhere near the Pole and was in fact a fraud. No one in his polar party except himself was trained in navigation and he couldn't possibly have made it to the pole in the time he said.'

'Oh well, there you go then. No doubt he went on to a lucrative second career in politics.'

Stapley smiled. 'The point about the Peary scandal is that it is very easy to claim that you have been at the Pole but difficult to prove. Equally, it's quite difficult to disprove unless in your account you commit some egregious error as Peary did about timings and distance.'

Jacot said, 'Are you suggesting that Amundsen made it all up? After all Scott does arrive at the same spot some weeks later. There are photographs of Amundsen's tent there and Scott picks up a letter for the King of Norway from Amundsen.'

'No, not at all. By any account and any standard Amundsen was a fine man, a great man. But Verney and Pirbright were definitely onto something. The mysterious figures you recovered from Dr Pirbright's body after her death. I have an explanation. It's a bit like a crossword and a bit like deciphering an incomplete ancient text – Linear B stuff.'

Stapley unfolded a map of the Antarctic on his desk showing the routes taken by Amundsen and Scott to the Pole.

By its side he put a print out of some figures from the Verney-Pirbright paper. 'It all looks easy and obvious now but in fact until the advent of GPS navigating at high latitudes close to the poles was enormously difficult. Even now GPS is not always reliable – the satellites are too low on the horizon very often to be of much use. It is an additional aid rather than a reliable means. Sensible explorers still use sextant and compass and chronometer. Even then it's not easy.

'There have always been immense problems. Long periods of overcast skies make solar observations difficult to obtain. It's daylight throughout the summer of course which makes it difficult to see the stars. Abnormal refraction may cause or introduce unknown errors into the sights. To top it all off the weather is often horrendous, even in summer, making it difficult to see the horizon. As if that were not enough the magnetic compass is not reliable in all parts of the Antarctic because of the proximity of the magnetic Pole in addition to all kinds of weird localized magnetic anomalies. And all this stuff relies on accurate time.

'There was one additional problem for the Antarctic explorers which did not trouble those at the North Pole, bogus or otherwise. That was ascertaining height. The North Pole is at sea level, obviously give-or-take an iceberg or two. But the South Pole sits on top of a flat and windswept plateau at 9,306 feet. It's one of the reasons that getting there was such a nightmare. The second half of the trek takes place at high altitude, or what would be considered high altitude skiing in Europe. It can be difficult to get a horizon.

'The first set of figures on the paper are temperature readings. Some in Centigrade and some in Fahrenheit but without the degree signs. Their original source were the records made at the time by individuals on both Amundsen and Scott's Polar parties. We believe them to be accurate. In other words we have no reason to suspect that anyone on either expedition would have wished to exaggerate or minimize them. We also believe that for the time the thermometers both expeditions used were reasonably accurate. They are probably accurate measurements on the days they were taken. But we cannot know for sure that they are accurate. We have no real way of checking them.'

Jacot sipped his whisky. 'Why would anyone murder for temperature readings?'

'Quite, but hang on, I haven't finished. A lot of research has been done on some aspects of this recently – some of it here at the Scott-Wilson Institute. To cut a long story short, Amundsen and Scott essentially experienced different weather conditions. Amundsen manages to get to the Pole a month before Scott and, guess what, that month was milder than what Scott's people had to endure and much better than what Scott had to put up with on his return journey. We know from the diaries that Captain Oates dies on probably on Friday March 16, 1912, during a terrible blizzard, and that the temperatures are much lower than they expected. It really was "The Coldest March". Now the crux of this is that these different temperatures had different effects on the kit and instruments that the two expeditions were carrying. The cold is, of course, what does for Scott and his companions in the end.

'What the Verney-Pirbright research was showing is that the temperature made the navigation instruments work in different ways – some were more accurate than others. In particular, that Scott's instruments were in general reading true but Amundsen's may not have been. It would appear that both sets of instruments had been specially machined and designed against the cold but because Amundsen experienced comparatively warmer weather his readings were less reliable. The kit worked best at the extremes. This is what Verney and Pirbright seem to have been onto.'

'So what?' Jacot checked himself. It was the question army officers were trained to ask from the moment they entered Sandhurst but it sounded wrong. 'Sorry, Professor I didn't mean it to come out quite like that.'

Stapley was amused. 'Don't worry, the military and the scientific minds work in similar grooves, I suspect. Do you know who I mean by Elizabeth Hawley?'

'She's ringing a bell somewhere – an American lady who settled in Kathmandu.'

'Well done. There is a long section in the paper about her work verifying the ascents of Everest. Very interesting, crucial even, that her name appears in the file. She is an American journalist. She began at least as a journalist. But now she is the sole authority who certifies ascents in the High Himalaya. No certification from her and you didn't get to the summit. Basically, she looks at the photos and interviews the people involved and then decides whether they made it, or not. Usually uncontroversial but there is one nasty case where a South Korean woman climber who swears blind she made it to the top of K2 I think it was, has had her attempt marked as disputed because the photographs didn't add up quite. Verney and Pirbright reckoned they were onto something on similar lines with Amundsen and Scott.'

'That's why I asked you about your knowledge of Amundsen? Do you know how they took the measurements that told them they were at the Pole? It's all in the chapter of Amundsen's book – "At the Pole" and it's much more Heath-Robinsonish than you might think.'

'So what does it mean?'

'Well, in essence, if the figures are right, and they are incomplete, it is extremely important. In fact it would be a startling discovery. A hundred years after the Pole was conquered…'

'In plain English.'

'It means in plain English that Amundsen missed the Pole. Scott's famous phrase: "Great God! This is an awful place and terrible enough for us to have laboured to it without the reward of priority", was wrong. Actually, Amundsen may not have had priority at all. And from the figures it wasn't a small miss – maybe by up to thirty or so miles. He certainly got closer than Shackleton did in 1909. Most people accept that he was within a hundred miles of his goal when he had to turn back. But the really astonishing thing about Verney and Pirbright's theory was that if you accept their reasoning Scott did make it.

'Look at this map.' Stapley turned to the map on his desk. 'Amundsen and Scott are on different routes. Look. They are coming at the Pole from slightly different angles. If Amundsen's instruments are off a little – don't worry about the maths for now – it would have been easy for them to miss by thirty miles. And you can see how Scott then inadvertently almost crosses the Pole itself on both the outward and return journeys.'

'But not enough to murder for.'

'No! It's an extraordinary tale. No doubt about it. And if they were right it makes Scott's expedition all the more tragic. They did, in a sense, win against Amundsen – or they might have won. If Scott had known that he got much closer to the Pole than Amundsen he and his party might have started the fatal return journey in better heart. One of the strongest men in the party, Petty Officer Evans, went to pieces quite quickly. Soon after they turn for home Scott begins to comment in his diary that Evans is run down and prone to frostbite. He dies on Saturday February 17. There is a distressing entry in Scott's diary about the state he was in but no real clinical data as to why he died. Dr Wilson was unsure too. The scene is slightly glossed over in the 1947 film *Scott of the Antarctic* where James Robertson Justice played Evans. There has been lots of controversy since about why he died. Unfortunately it has played into the English obsession with class. Of the five men who formed Scott's polar party four were officers or could be considered officers. Scott was in the Royal Navy. His faithful companion Wilson was a doctor of medicine. Bowers was an officer in the Royal Indian Marine, the embryonic Indian Navy. Captain Oates was famously a captain in a glamorous cavalry regiment, The Royal Inniskilling Dragoon Guards. Only Evans was from the lower deck – the only non-commissioned officer. In some eyes this made him more likely to crack. His simple mind found it hard to occupy itself during the endless trudging over the Antarctic sastrugi.'

Jacot interrupted 'I know it was a different world and I know the Guards regiments are hardly typical but in my experience the senior non-commissioned officers are the toughest of the lot. If we were like the Israeli Army, without obsessions about where you went to school or insisting that every officer has a degree then they would be in charge. I am not convinced.'

'Quite, Colonel. I am without military experience but I tend to agree. The most convincing theory about poor old Evans is probably that disappointment at not being first to the Pole broke his heart. There is some evidence that he was planning to run a pub and that he had planned his whole future on being one of the first men to the South Pole. Tragic, indeed. It's as if you thought you were going to be Armstrong and Aldrin and you ended up being Pete Conrad and Alan Bean.'

'Who?'

'Exactly. The third and fourth men on the moon four months later.'

'Oh, yes. Absolutely right. What about the rest of the data?' asked Jacot.

'It's corrupted and in a different format. It seems to be about oil but I doubt it's connected with the expedition. Could be though. Paraffin oil consumption rates and leakage of supplies at various depots was one of the things that did for poor old Scott and his companions. In fact there is a rather good scene in the film if you remember. Some of the text is in Spanish. Most odd.'

It was a bleak story, and suddenly Jacot felt immensely sad. England had been spared much of the madness of the 20th and other centuries. Yes, we had sent a generation to die in the trenches. Yes, we had been blitzed. Yes, we had lost an empire. But somehow we seemed to still be in control at home. Masters of our fate at least on these overcrowded and foggy islands. For how much longer?

His more immediate concern were two unsolved murders. He was up against something, a force or a group of people or perhaps even a single individual who were capable of acting with extreme ruthlessness and cruelty. It was beginning to dawn on him who they might be. He was frightened not because he was alone – he had the backing of Lady Nevinson at least, and her formidable will and network of connections. The French as well, he supposed. But the really frightening aspect was that he was fighting a force that appeared to be deeply embedded in nearly all aspects of official life.

His optimism soon returned. Not because he thought the task ahead was going to be easy but because it seemed probable, no possible only, that a great national disappointment was about to be reversed. If Scott had been first at the Pole after all? Well there was something to cheer the heart of every English schoolboy.

XXI

Chapel of St James' College, Cambridge

Jacot was sitting two rows back from the high altar. He could hear the heavy shoes of the college porters as they carried Charlotte Pirbright's coffin slowly down the aisle. At a wedding the congregation craned their necks to look round for a glimpse of the bride and her dress. At a funeral, particularly a young person's funeral, the congregation more often stared straight ahead. All members of the college and university attending were wearing their gowns – black for the most part but interspersed with the dark blue of Trinity and Caius.

The chapel of St James' College, Cambridge was a good place for a funeral – in theory at least. Although Jacot wondered what comfort Charlotte's family and friends would derive from the astonishing architecture and the glorious music.

Jacot looked up. Three great Christian symbols recurred throughout the chapel. First, of course, the crucifix or variations of it as you would expect. Second, and more unusually at least in the British Isles, the Cross of St James. In heraldic terms "a cross flory fitchy" except with the lower part fashioned as the blade of a sword – to remind worshippers of the role played in the Reconquista of Spain from the Moors by the noble and military order of Santiago.

Some of the more "right-on" dons a few years back had objected to what they saw as symbols of ethnic cleansing. It was certainly one way to look at the re-Christianization of Spain thought Jacot. Like the maddest Victorians whom they so affected to despise, the trendy dons wanted to cover up the evidence of attitudes that they did not approve of. The Victorians with their unhealthy attitudes to sex wanted to paint out the naked breasts and the fleshy female bottoms that so disturbed them, and an attempt had been made in the late 19th century to 'bowdlerise' the chapel. But the High Church and worldly dons of St James' at the time would have none of it and the glorious putti and generously endowed angels had survived unscathed. Modern prudishness was different. Its highly developed and over-refined sense of offence felt that severed Moorish heads carved in stone, even ones no longer colourfully painted as they would have been when the college was founded, might give offence to those who were not Christian. It had been a longer, more vicious and closer battle this time round. The still very High Church dons had seemed less confident in their cause but at the last minute had stood firm, not sadly in the service of history, accuracy or truth but because they regarded the group of younger dons mounting the campaign as not quite gentlemen. It wasn't their atheism or political correctness but the way they dressed that offended their elder brethren.

The third symbol which occurred throughout the chapel in various sizes and forms was the scallop shell – the personal symbol of St James, son of Zebedee, disciple of Jesus Christ and the first Christian martyr. In wood on the roof of the chapel, in stone on the supporting columns, in wood once again on the pews and imprinted on the front of the prayer books. Always and everywhere in this chapel, gilded. It gave the impression that the chapel was filled with stars.

Charlotte Pirbright's parents took their seats accompanied by her younger brother. They were not tearful yet, but their faces had the tell-tale tautness of grief barely under control. The overwhelming primal fear of every parent, losing a child, had happened to them. They looked in their late fifties, almost the prime of life in the modern world, but too late to really shake off tragedy and regain some sweetness in life, if indeed any parent in a similar situation ever did. There might be nights when their lost daughter would re-appear in their dreams. The family would be re-united briefly but waking would bring reality.

Jacot needed a drink. Actually another drink. He had knocked back a large slug of vodka in some fresh orange juice just before the funeral. Maybe he was on the edge. His hands hurt badly. By one of those seemingly malevolent tricks of fate alcohol lifted his spirits and soothed most of the aches and pains in his body but never his hands. Something in the burning process or the skin-grafting process had made them immune to the deadening effects of alcohol.

Jacot looked round the chapel. It was almost a partial re-run of the dinner the night before General Verney had died. The Americans were there and a sprinkling of other spooks. Most of the fellows of the college. Pretty much the entire staff of SWASI. A large group of friends and friends of the family. And most of the college servants, including Jones 74 who was acting as a pall bearer. Jacot could see him sitting off to the left of the altar looking very upset. He had clearly been fond of the young don.

They stood to sing "Onward Christian Soldiers" which

should make everyone feel a little better thought Jacot. He certainly enjoyed belting out the comforting words. But the music could not remove his overwhelming sense not of sadness, or grief or even sympathy, but of danger.

At the reception afterwards in the Fellows' Combination Room where tea and sandwiches were served Jacot was introduced by the Master to Charlotte's father. Jacot expressed his condolences and explained, in confidence, his role in the investigation. Charlotte's father even bravely managed a brief smile 'Yes the Colonel with the burned hands. She mentioned you.' Jacot had an urgent rendezvous with Monica Zaden who would be arriving in Cambridge shortly, so he made his excuses and left. They had agreed to meet in a pizza restaurant near King's.

XXII

King's Parade, Cambridge

From his seat in the Pizza parlour Jacot could see her walking along King's Parade. He could tell she had not been to Cambridge before. She was smiling. Parts of the university city had that effect on outsiders. Seeing King's Chapel and the Senate House for the first time with the hint of the river and "The Backs" behind was like walking in St Mark's Square for the first time. It was impossible not to be impressed and cheered by the achievements, aesthetic sense and standards of those who had gone before. Monica swayed deliciously on her long legs.

'There's no code in the text. Nothing to decrypt as far as we can tell.' She shrugged one of those peculiar French shrugs. An acceptance of the way things were or the limitations of the way things could be. Englishmen kept a stiff upper lip – Monica had quizzed him on what exactly the phrase meant. Welshmen grinned with resignation. Frenchmen and women shrugged.

'There is a lot of data in the file, but of a routine navigational and metallurgical nature. We are not qualified to pronounce on its accuracy although we have had the arithmetic and angles checked by the mathematicians and scientists at the *Institut Polaire Francais* and they seem to add up. As far as they go anyway. The lone metallurgist on the staff is beside himself with excitement. Don't worry they won't reveal the details of the paper to anyone. We don't think there are any strange messages embedded in the text. It would appear that your Captain Scott's fate may have been crueller even than he believed at the time.'

'Oh well, it was worth a shot.' Jacot took a mouthful of his spicy pizza. 'I have to say though even if there is no code embedded in the paper its conclusions are extraordinary. You wouldn't understand the impact as a Frenchwoman, but if what Verney and Pirbright wrote stands up to inspection it means that Scott not Amundsen reached the South Pole first. Imagine if it turned out that after all the French had won the Battle of Waterloo.'

'My history books at school always suggested that we did. Quite why the Emperor then had to go into exile and spend the rest of his life on an obscure English rock in the South Atlantic was never explained.' Monica ate a slice of her pizza and then held a forkful of her salad in the air creating a sense of expectation. She used the fork to emphasise what she was saying.

'There is just one more thing. After the main text, which is uncorrupted, there are a few random words. Again we have no idea what they mean and there is no further text beneath them. Something about basins and oils and a date, 24 May 2015. Some other stuff too which you might want to mull over. Very odd. It's as if General Verney was keeping his household accounts on the file. But they are separate from what went before. It looks as though they were a part of a bigger file which has now disappeared. We are not sure, cannot be sure, but there are apparently ways of working it out and tell tale signs according to our signals people. Whatever was in the file was encoded originally – a strongly protected code with a twist. *C'est un fichier cadavre.*'

'What exactly does that mean?'

She ate the salad on her fork and smiled again. 'Well obviously in English it means a corpse computer file. I know, I know, your French is up to that. You got there before me Dan. A corpse computer file is one that dies when it is moved or hacked into. There are lots of different types of varying sophistication. Some die suddenly when they are moved others merely start to degrade or decompose when they are moved from their home location. There you are.'

'Hang on. Hang on Monica. That's all very well, but what sort of people use these files or understand how they work?'

'Anyone who can afford to pay for some clever computer types. Anyone who has data that they are so keen to protect that if it does get stolen or decrypted it self-destructs. Some criminals use them to store data so that if the stuff is found by the authorities it can't be used as evidence – financial records or records of drug shipments are often guarded in this way. The FBI would not have been able to put Al Capone on trial for tax evasion, or is it avoidance, it always confused me in the vocabulary tests, if his financial records had spontaneously combusted once the Feds got their hands on them.

'I must admit our people are puzzled. The uncoded information is dynamite for the Antarctic studies people. The coded stuff seems really low-grade.' She shrugged again. 'There's more to tell. I think we need another glass of wine first. Then why don't we go for a walk on the famous "Backs"? My briefers waxed lyrical about them but I have yet to see them.' She fixed her eyes on his. The look wasn't entirely professional. 'No one will be able to listen in.'

She had been well-trained, briefing rapidly and in a way that Jacot could understand quickly. One of their people had had a quick look round Charlotte Pirbright's rooms, courtesy of the now ever-reliable Chief Inspector Bradshaw. Yes, they had been searched by a team probably with an intelligence background. More importantly, the toxicology tests had come back from Strasbourg. Inconclusive. The samples were not good.

She did not look that disappointed thought Jacot. Her eyes were glistening with excitement.

'But about an hour ago I received an email from a DCRI man in Papeete.'

'As you know Gilles Navarre sent one of the swabs out there. Again it's not a good sample but our man in Papeete had a long conversation with one of the lab technicians at the Government Laboratories. Again the sample quality was not great but the lab guy has had a lot of experience with food poisoning and dodgy fish in the South Pacific, and there is definitely a tiny, tiny amount of Saxitoxin in the sample. It's possible that there may have been cross-contamination but he's fairly sure. I got our man to check the label on the swab – it's from Verney's nose.'

Once Monica had briefed Jacot further they left the restaurant and walked through King's College crossing the Cam by the college bridge. Monica didn't talk much initially. She was too occupied admiring the view. Once in the cover of the trees they talked for a further five or so minutes. Monica made some notes in a small notebook. Jacot seemed keen to make sure that she had got various details right and read over her notes at the end of their brief conversation. Then he took both of her hands in his. She stroked the top of one of his silk gloves and then they both laughed, kissed each other and parted. Monica walked quickly away in the direction of the station. Jacot started on his way back to St James' but turned and watched her until she was out of his sight.

XXIII

North Carolina State University Library,
Chapel Hill, North Carolina

A blue van with Georgia plates parked outside the library of the North Carolina State University at Chapel Hill. A very plain young woman with very thick spectacles got out of the van and went inside. She showed her student identification to a welcoming lady at the desk– she wasn't studying at the Chapel Hill Campus but she was a fully accredited student of the State University of North Carolina. She wanted to have a look at back copies of the student newspaper from the 1970s. Informed that they were now all stored on microfiche she looked surprised and confused. But the librarian showed her to the microfiche room and gave her a short lesson in working the microfiche machine before returning to her post at the desk out front. The very plain girl then spent nearly half an hour looking at images through the viewer – without her glasses on. She worked quickly and methodically. The short lesson she had just received must have been good – or maybe she knew what she was doing all along. There was no one else in the room but annoyingly for other users of the library they could hear the very loud music being streamed through to her iPod earphones, which also seemed to make a rather odd humming noise. Just as a couple of them were about to make a complaint to the librarian the plain and unremarkable girl with no make up and thick spectacles got up from her desk and returned the spool of microfiche she had been using to the desk. She had a funny accent – Cajun maybe.

A week later the library was evacuated early one evening, just after dark, as all the fire alarms went off at once. The local firemen and the police were nonplussed as no sign of any fire was discovered. At least there had been no damage, although the library had been empty for nearly an hour.

*

The offices of the News Observer,
McDowell Street, Raleigh, North Carolina

A few days later at the offices of the *News Observer,* the newspaper serving the academic towns of Chapel Hill, Raleigh and Durham, reporters had a frustrating morning after the pressroom experienced multiple computer failures. The whole news operation was paralysed. Experienced reporters could do little other than look out of the window. When they got really fed up they ventured out to the coffee shop on the other side of McDowell Street, passing a dusty brown van with Arkansas plates – not unusual in the state – annoyingly parked just outside their offices. After hours of investigation the in-house computer geeks could not fix the problem. And then suddenly everything was all right again. No one could work it out. One bright spark suggested there may have been a virus in the newspapers digitized historical records recently converted from microfiche at great expense.

XXIV

Jacot entered Lady Nevinson's office. She was not alone.

'Daniel, meet Richard Ingoldsby from the Security Service. I don't think you have met before. He is the head of counter-espionage.'

Jacot shook hands with a man of medium height and bland features, plainly dressed. He would have been instantly forgettable, as indeed he was meant to be, except for the grey eyes which had a chess player's or a preacher's intensity – looking at you now in the present, but mainly concerned with looking far ahead – many moves ahead or ahead to a different world. Counter-espionage was one of the purest forms of intelligence work requiring a number of talents and attributes that were rarely found in combination. As a result many of its best practitioners came across as slightly odd.

Lady Nevinson said, 'Don't worry Daniel, he is one of the few people we can trust. He is Magenta indoctrinated. Indeed it was Richard who first realised how deeply penetrated we were by our friends across the Atlantic. And now give us both what you have.'

'Yes, well I am sorry Lady Nevinson about the recent drama.' Jacot looked a little sheepish.

'Colonel Jacot telephoned me from the Falklands, Richard, whence I had dispatched him on a tour of inspection. He reckoned he had the answer to the sudden death of General Verney. It was a dramatic night. I telephoned the Chief Constable of the Cambridge Police who kindly arrested Jacot's chief suspect, a onetime Colour Sergeant in the Celtic Guards, and currently Fellows' Butler at St James' College, Cambridge. In the way of these things it now appears that it wasn't the butler after all – your ex chief suspect in pursuit of whom you set off a major emergency. Yes, yes Jacot you were on your merry way back from Chile as special branch and various other men in mackintoshes rushed through the streets of Cambridge to arrest this Fellows' Butler, in itself an old-fashioned term worthy of a Cluedo board, who may or may not have had a grudge against Verney about something that happened in the Falklands War thirty years ago. The Master of St James' has taken some placating. Keeping it from the press has been difficult. And this morning the prime minister had one of his slightly cocky looks. May not have been connected, of course. And basically you have no other suspects. Maybe he did die of natural causes.' She looked at the ceiling. 'Please God let it be that. It would be the easiest solution.'

She didn't look angry. Jacot breathed a sigh of relief. Turning to Ingoldsby he said, 'Lady Nevinson is, as always, right.' A little humility and a little flattery went a long way. 'It wasn't Colour Sergeant John Jones after all. I have known him for a long time. He had a good motive dating back to the death of his brother in the Falklands War, for which he blamed Verney. Long story but not just now I think.' He took a deep breath. 'I don't know how to put this but it looks as though Verney was working for the Americans.'

'In a way Jacot we are all working for the Americans', said Ingoldsby drily.

'No I don't mean involuntarily. Or helping them a little bit more than you should. Or getting your patriotic feelings for your own country mixed up with those for the American dream. I mean working for the Americans, spying for the Americans, giving them secret information and intelligence splattered with "UK Eyes Only London Only Prime Minister's Eyes Only". Apparently on a regular basis. And possibly, initially at least, against his will.'

Nevinson said, 'For God's sake how and why?'

'Well I should have thought of it myself. I was down there thirty years ago and involved in the same incident – the destruction of the Royal Fleet Auxiliary, *Oliver Cromwell*, in a missile attack by the Argentine air force. I am sure you know the story reasonably well. Troops loaded onto a ship. Disagreement about where the ship was meant to be going. Troops don't get off ship. For reasons which I am still not sure of the ship cannot communicate with any other ships nearby, so the dispute about where the ship is meant to be going cannot be resolved. Ship is hit by an Exocet missile. And so on. The circumstances have remained disputed and controversial ever since. But there is an aspect never covered in the official accounts that is probably relevant here. It is so long ago I had forgotten. Something based some difficult rumours which most of us thought were a kind of conspiracy theory to explain a balls up which was at the end of the day just a balls up. Murphy's Law stretched its poisonous teeth deep into the South Atlantic and sunk them deep into us.

'It was a funny time. When we landed in the Falklands we

found chaos. Worse, we found East Falkland in possession of a group of military units that simply did not want us to be there. I don't mean the Argentines either. I mean the first wave of British troops who had landed some ten days before us. They could not understand why we were needed. As things turned out they may well have been right. Other than the counter-attack by the Argentine naval air force in the aftermath of the initial landings, which was fierce and pressed home bravely, the Argies put up little real resistance. Particularly after H Jones and his paratroopers chased them out of Goose Green. That was probably the pivotal action of the war and it happened while we were still en route on the stately QE2. It was an odd feeling. We had expected to be welcomed as brothers in arms with open arms.

'Anyway, it was not to be. As a result there was little organization and less help. Only competition to get away from the landing beaches and towards Port Stanley as quickly as we could. The people in charge of us decided that the quickest way of doing this was to walk, as many others had. Unfortunately it ended in disaster. We failed to get ourselves over a mountain down south – well a hill actually. We were trying to avoid being taken round towards Port Stanley by ship. It was dangerous. Much simpler to walk most of the way. Problem was we had too much ammunition and the vehicles carrying our eight mortar tubes and their ammunition – a ragbag of military and farming vehicles – broke down. So the whole thing got called off amidst considerable shambles. As a result we were taken around by ship – and the ship Jones, his brother Bryn and yours truly got onto was the *RFA Oliver Cromwell*. The rest is history and, as you know, why nearly thirty years later I still have to cut around the bazaar in gloves.'

Nevinson said, 'Go on and I think you need some whisky.'

'It had always seemed to me a cock up. I have very strong views about the countdown to disaster and what actually happened on the ship. If you are ever involved in a big military disaster involving death and destruction on a fairly large scale you will find that most men, and it was only men in those days, try to do their duty within the constraints of where they find themselves and the strengths and weaknesses of their own characters. A few men are extremely brave. And a few decide to run away. That has always been the great arithmetic of military behavior. It has always fascinated me ever since. I remember the confused days leading up to the disaster but they were in the background of our own literally burning experiences on the day.

'Jones' anger is based partly on what happened to him on the ship – mainly not being able to reach his dying younger brother. But partly, and more curiously, on something that he said happened that rain soaked night as we struggled up and then down the hills above the landing beaches. Jones is of the view that a group of officers of unspecified identity, but definitely including Verney, agreed to call the move off because they didn't think it was a good idea. Jones overheard Verney, then a young captain, apparently talking on an unofficial radio net saying:

"Just make it look as though they have broken down".

'I heard an amateur recording of the unofficial radio traffic from that night when I was down there last week including, after two hours or so of happy listening, a young Captain Verney saying those now infamous words. I think he was talking about the ragtag and bobtail vehicles that were trying to lug the mortar tubes and ammunition over the hill. It was a nightmare night and to be fair to Verney and any other officers, even possibly some of our own who may have been involved, the whole thing seemed pretty "Back of a fag packet" as we used to say. Poorly planned and spur of the moment.' Jacot took a large sip of his whisky. 'It was an absolute nightmare night all right. Remember June is the Austral winter. I have never seen rain like it – as if it was coming off the sea straight from the Antarctic. The whole affair did not last long – less than an hour in my memory – before we returned to our trenches. In a way Verney and the others were probably doing us a favour. Trouble is that one of the events that triggered our move by sea was this aborted march. Equally nightmarish, we ended up on three different ships. Some of us made it around OK but the group I was with was eventually embarked on *Oliver Cromwell*. Verney, as I say, may have been doing us a favour, but by pretending that the transport had broken down he was in direct defiance of the orders issued for the move. If at the time anyone had discovered he would have been court-martialled. Half a century before, he would have been shot.'

There was absolute silence in the room. Nevinson stared at Jacot. 'You didn't mention anything about this when we talked on the train.'

'Some things are just too difficult. I am sure you now understand why. In the confusion of the night march Jones, who was crouching on the hill nearby, may well have been the only other person to hear it in the flesh as it were. Although obviously those other officers, whoever they were and I think

I know, must have been listening in. Afterwards, after all the dying and then the recriminations, he knew what it meant but said nothing. No one would have listened anyway. Contrary to what it looked like at one point, Jones did not then harbor a terrible grudge for thirty years or so about his dead brother – killing Verney when quite by chance he comes to stay at the college and quite by chance Jones recognizes the key words after all these years. In the moments after he realized who Verney was perhaps he hated him, briefly. But ultimately Jones is not a killer and the anger he felt was a railing against Fate rather than any human agent. No. Jones had moved on and except on the anniversary of the bombing or at Christmas thinks little of his younger brother.

'But it all came back the night of the feast before the lecture. Jones isn't sure, but he thinks he heard the words at dinner. It took a few seconds, but then that awful night in the South Atlantic half a lifetime before came back to him. The candlelight dinner helped – it was in the Combination Room which is lit only by candles in sconces. As he was saying the fateful words thirty years ago, with Jones half-looking on, Verney had lit a cigarette – the candlelight at the dinner framed his face in exactly the same way and Jones recognized him. Not the voice but the face. Jones wasn't sure who had said the words. The hubbub of the dinner was too loud and Jones had been moving away. He thought the Master might have said them. Later that night, once the dinner was over, Jones went up to Verney's room possibly to confront him, he admits. But he swears blind that he had not gone to harm him. While he is there he hears the words again, distinctly this time, as part of an argument coming from Verney's room – "Just make it look as though they have broken down" – in an American accent.'

Even as the Exocet had struck the *Oliver Cromwell* it had taken Jacot a couple of seconds to realize what was going on. Even as you are being blown up it's hard to believe. Lady Nevinson appeared to be in the same confused, disbelieving state as Jacot thirty years before at this bombshell revelation.

She poured two glasses of whisky. Handing one to a grateful Ingoldsby she said slowly to Jacot, 'What on earth are you suggesting?'

Jacot continued, 'Well there are lots of Americans in Cambridge. But Jones said it was the American gentleman who came for the lecture.'

'Who was?'

'Dixwell.'

'So what if Verney sent a message, long ago, calling off what sounds like a fairly hare-brained scheme Jacot?'

'Well Lady Nevinson, it's a bit like the *Titanic*. No single decision caused it to founder just as no single decision consigned us to an inferno on the *Oliver Cromwell*. It was a chain of causation in both cases. It does not excuse some very dodgy decisions and procedures on *Titanic* or *Cromwell* or anyone who behaved badly during or after the disasters. The moral responsibility for all those dead and wounded men, and my hands come to think of it, hardly lies with Verney. It was a war in any case. But if he and some others conspired to have their commanding officer's orders disobeyed, and it ended in the death and destruction it did, that's different. He may not have felt any guilt and in a way I can quite see why. His act of disobedience, dishonesty even, is quite early in the chain of events – about equivalent to one of the officers on *Titanic* not being able to find the key to the locker that held the binoculars when they joined the ship at Southampton. It wouldn't keep a man of normal sympathetic feeling awake at night over the years. But if at some point someone found out, then he would have been vulnerable. If the Americans had been taping British communications in the way my friend William Say had been. And if later they put two and two together about this long forgotten signals intercept as Verney began his rapid climb of the greasy pole then who knows?'

'For God's sake.' Ingoldsby looked pale and was swallowing repeatedly. 'So what you are saying is that the most senior military intelligence official in the country was in the pay of, or under the control of, Langley.'

'Under the control most likely. And at that level it always helps to get good reports from the Americans. At least it's not the prime minister this time.' Jacot smirked but got no sympathetic response. He continued, 'The Americans helped us in the Falklands… eventually. With equipment and intelligence. NSA would have been monitoring communications in the area. Most people are aware that despite the various treaties their bases in Antarctica are listening as well as scientific stations. They could well have had ships at sea just outside the Exclusion Zone around the islands. Whatever they say, they were well in with the Argentine junta. Hard to conjure up now but as long as you were anti-communist few questions were asked about much else. Maybe they had an NSA installation in Argentina. Who knows how they found out? But however they did it, the most senior CIA official in the UK certainly knew about Verney's little *faux pas* at a big dinner in Cambridge thirty years later.'

Ingoldsby was suddenly animated. 'But why would the Americans need anything on Verney. He was everything the Americans wanted. He even dressed as an American, with generals' stars rather than what our chaps usually wear. He was slavishly, comically, institutionally pro-American. Straight out of central casting. One of the type who appeared to revel in the Special Relationship and its core military belief that the whole point of the British Army is to act as junior partner to the Americans. Forget the petty humiliations. Forget what we once were. Forget that we might have our own interests. As long as we suck up to Uncle Sam we'll have wars to fight and careers to pursue.'

'Yes thank you Ingoldsby', said Nevinson. 'Daniel and I and most of the country as far as I can see share your well-expressed views. But you have a good point. There was a wobble with the new prime minister a few weeks ago on Afghanistan but it passed. There was apparently a terrible scene. I think he has realized that with one stroke of the pen he could get us out of the whole thing. I think a few glasses of whisky had been taken and he was seriously considering it. Luckily or rather unluckily to people of our kidney the grown ups were summoned in short order to administer the smelling salts. Interestingly, one of the people brought into to administer to the PM's late emerging doubts was Verney. As you say he was a true believer.'

Jacot asked, 'How do you know all this? It's a very small circle around him.'

Nevinson looked at Ingoldsby. 'We have someone, a Magenta someone.'

Jacot was astounded but brought himself under control. 'Maybe Verney had changed his mind.'

Ingoldsby nodded. 'I think that was what was going on. We had begun to pick it up from other sources. Verney wanted to get us out of Afghanistan in double quick time and seemed to be having qualms of conscience about the next impending Americano-British war. It may have partly been an inter-service thing. The Navy smarting from their exclusion from Afghanistan and the loss of their carriers are lobbying hard to get involved against Iran – if it comes to that.'

There was absolute silence again in the room.

Jacot rolled his eyes. 'OK so what do we do? Go to the PM?'

Ingoldsby looked extremely nervous and licked his lips. 'Forget it. He wouldn't believe us. And we only know because we have the cheek to be spying on his inner circle.'

'I see what you mean'.

Ingoldsby wasn't entirely convinced. 'I have to say I remain puzzled.' He looked at Lady Nevinson. 'Would it be all right if I brief the good colonel on one or two little details?'

She nodded.

'Listen Colonel, I think you should know that we had been looking into General Verney for some time. I cannot go into the details but he came to our attention some months ago in a routine check. It may surprise you in these difficult times that we have any energy left in the Security Service that is not devoted to pursuing Islamist extremists. But since the Cambridge Spies we have always taken our own internal security very seriously. It is well known now that Mrs Thatcher insisted on unmasking the unfortunate Anthony Blunt as the so-called Fourth Man when she came to power in 1979. What no one knows is that, as part of the process, we at MI5 received what was in effect a huge corporate bollocking. Blunt had been one of our officers – he slipped through the vetting net during the difficult early war years. I had only just joined at the time but one old boy, then at the top of the service, who had an interview with the good lady at the time on the subject of Blunt said it was one of the roughest experiences of his life.' Ingoldsby smiled. 'He refuses to go to the new film with Meryl Streep in case the nightmares return.' She made it clear that there were to be no more vetting cock-ups, ever. So since then we have always put a lot of effort into making sure that the people on our side, remain on side. To be honest it hasn't been that difficult now that no one cares about sexual orientation or stuff like that. We no longer have to ask new recruits or even generals in charge of intelligence that awkward question "Have any of your girlfriends, shall we say, not been girls at all?"'

They all laughed. The tension was receding.

'Anyway, as a result we do random checks on people. Bit like the police sticking up road-blocks for breath-testing. They are usually authorized by Lady Nevinson. We did one on Verney. It wasn't quite random. There had been a little detail which surprised us. Turned out to be a false alarm. I can assure you Verney wasn't spying for the Americans or anyone else. I am even more sure than you might think. Given the closeness of our gallant troops in the field to the Americans we have long had a little programme in place to make sure that they did not exert too much influence on impressionable young officers. Indeed, as part of Magenta, Verney's Aide-de-camp until three months ago was a young and very bright Intelligence Corps captain, who worked for us.

'It's one thing for the CIA to blackmail a senior British official. My guess is that this kind of thing may have been even more prevalent in the Cold War – lots of people with left wing connections at university and so on that could have proved to be career impediments. But to go from an old habit of common or garden intelligence blackmail to murder is a different thing altogether.'

Nevinson nodded. 'I agree. Why kill? It does not quite ring true of the Americans. Of course they tried many times to kill Castro, who got his revenge fairly quickly. And they have bumped off other inconvenient leaders by all accounts. But a British general? Well done Jacot, anyway. We are clearly getting closer.'

'One more thing for you Ingoldsby', said Jacot. 'Jones said Dixwell was arguing so hard with Verney that he had an asthma attack. He distinctly heard the sound of an inhaler being pressed. Could you find out if Dixwell is an asthmatic? Today, if possible. I think it may be crucial.'

XXV

The desk sergeant quickly slid both his copy of the Evening Standard and a small half-eaten Scotch egg under a file on his counter. There wasn't time to straighten his tie. The Commander of the Metropolitan Police's Special Branch swept past in uniform accompanied by a man of medium height and bland features wearing a light brown covert coat. They went immediately upstairs to the Superintendent's office.

Half an hour or so later two uniformed and two plain-clothes men came into the police station. By this time the desk sergeant was immaculate and his counter contained only one highly sharpened pencil and his occurrences ledger, open at a new page and laid absolutely straight on top of the counter.

'Where have you lads suddenly emerged from if I may ask?'

'Suspected break in, Harley Street. Some punter phoned in. But we had a look around and nothing to report.'

'I better enter it into the ledger and give it a code number.'

'Go ahead mate. We are off to the canteen.'

But only three of the men went downstairs to the canteen. The fourth went upstairs to the Superintendent's office.

By the time the time the commander of special branch and his nondescript friend left the station the desk sergeant had come to the end of his shift.

XXVI

Set C5 Pilgrims' Court,
St James' College, Cambridge

Jacot "sported his oak". They still did things the old way around here. 74 had set out a half bottle of sherry – Manzanilla, ice cold as he liked it. He sat down in a faded but comfortable leather armchair and looked out of the sash windows at the River Cam and the Bridge of Sorrows, which connected the two halves of the college. It was a picture post-card view of Cambridge – reproduced in a thousand travel brochures – and greatly re-assuring. Cambridge and its way of looking at the world stood for something. Life was in some ways rational and civilised and that would prevail. That the image of this rationality was so well loved made it more powerful. Even Hitler had held his hand against the great university town – other than a lone Heinkel bomber in the summer of 1940 trying to attack the railway station the town had escaped largely unscathed. It was a satisfying piece of trivia that calmed and fortified Jacot. He leaned back and took a long pull at a glass of the ice-cold sherry. Putting the glass down he slowly peeled off his black silk gloves. The burned flesh was still angry and sometimes painful even after all these years. The only healthy skin was a small patch beneath where his watch had been. The flash from the exploding missile had incinerated his army watchstrap but for a split second before it fell away the body of the watch shielded his skin underneath. He was left with a perfect circle of unburned skin. He cupped both hands around the ice cold and refilled glass – as soothing as Flamazine, the gooey paste used to smother severe burns in the 1970s and 80s. He drank more sherry. It was the hour before dinner and the court was quiet – just a few footfalls. On his own staircase only the creaking of ancient timbers. Even baby Odo sleeping next door was quiet – connected by a baby alarm to his mother Hildegard who was almost certainly in the library less than a hundred feet away. Jacot had chatted to her on the staircase. She would hurry back if the child cried but usually little Odo slept through the night. Jacot was puzzled. He wasn't sure but something did not quite add up.

Would the Americans really have sought to murder Verney? He switched on his iPod and through the high tech speakers came the sublime sound of the first movement of Mozart's Flute and harp concerto – pitch perfect, he could have been listening to it in a concert hall. Joyful, lively and serene all at the same time. Music sometimes helped him to think clearly – as did small quantities of alcohol. He wasn't looking at it the right way. Relaxing the mind would give him a recharged perspective. Jacot dozed.

'Confirm target is in the room.'

'Confirmed.'

'Confirm outer cordon in place'

'Confirmed. Moving through.'

'Await my command. Out'

Jacot woke with a start. His body tensed. He could hear voices – military voices. He was still half asleep. He relaxed. Of course, it was the baby alarm picking up the dialogue from a film. Two men talking to each other – with strange accents. Jacot smiled – just like the dialogue in *Munich* – a film he had much enjoyed. Things were downloaded in so many ways these days it was hardly surprising that a baby alarm occasionally picked them up. One of the voices had been gravelly like Richard Burton's. Maybe it was *Where Eagles Dare* playing on someone's computer. Good choice thought Jacot. Burton and Eastwood were great. Somehow, the film combined a great nostalgia for the Second World War with pleasant memories of skiing holidays while young. It was, according to some sources at least, the prime minister's favourite film. That was probably why one afternoon Lady Nevinson had asked, rather sheepishly for her, if he could lend her the DVD. Another glass of Manzanilla would go down well.

There were footsteps on the staircase. It wasn't the girl from the next floor. Subconsciously his mind and ears had become accustomed to Hildegard's footsteps. He could even tell whether she was carrying Odo or not. These footsteps were men. The only people in a Cambridge college who climbed staircases like that were the rugby hearties or the dining club types as they sneaked up on an unsuspecting victim on one of their rampages. Burly blokes treading carefully and lightly in order not to be heard. The early evening intake of sherry had dulled his wits.

The fight instinct took over. His body was screaming out for a weapon – he could almost feel the comforting weight of a 9 Millimetre pistol in his hand. His hands worked by instinct – the right thumb as if to take the safety catch off and the left hand into the pocket to check for the spare magazine clip. He would need both magazines to have a chance against them.

But there was nothing – he was unarmed. Panic kills. Jacot moved quietly into the small bathroom at the back. The mullioned window was difficult to push open but Jacot was outside within seconds. It wasn't great standing on a narrow ledge eighty feet above the Cam but it was better than being inside. It was too high to jump. Even if he could somehow get back to ground level somewhere in the college and summon help it would not solve his problem. This was not a casual operation – it was an ambush. Whoever it was who was after him would have "cut offs" in place – men in the street at both ends of the college. Once they had flushed him out they would cut him down. He wouldn't even be safe in the police station from men like this. Special forces of some kind – probably retired and working on the international circuit. Taking out a difficult Brit in a Cambridge college was a breeze compared to Afghanistan or the West Bank.

He was expected at dinner. It would not be long before 74 despatched someone to check up but that was not going to help now. And they would come after him when they realised he was no longer in the rooms. They probably thought he was hiding there. Should he try to take them on as they came through the window after him? It was tempting but with at least two and possibly more in the team it would be wiser to run for it. The music stopped. They knew he wasn't there.

Jacot had scrambled round the mullioned window and was perched on top of its overhang. On the wall twenty feet away he could see the reflection of a torch dancing on the wall. They were coming through the window. Where to go? There was no obvious route for escape. No drainpipes or anything that immediately looked useful. He could go down but they would be able to shoot him easily. He had to go up. They could kill him up here and that would be that. They would not even have to shoot him. Just throw him off the roof. But up looked the better bet. He had scanned the roof outline of the college many times over the years delighting in its quirks and crenellations, but his concern had always been aesthetics rather than escape.

A pair of buttresses ran from the top of the roof to the top of the chapel roof a further thirty feet or so high. If he could get onto the chapel roof he would be safe. His own little Fort Zinderneuf that he could defend against all comers. But he would have to 'chimney' in mountaineering slang – force his back against one side of the buttress and his feet against the other and shimmy up. It would be difficult. And, oh God, he didn't have his gloves on. He went for it. One foot and one hand on the facing buttress. Back and the other hand pressed behind him. Each shimmy lifted him about eighteen inches. His hands were agony on the rough limestone – his scarred flesh felt thin and dry as he jammed his hands into any gaps or crevices he could find. He could not look down but could hear the window being opened. They would assume he had gone downwards.

Jacot's back was on fire but he was at the ledge leading onto the chapel roof. Something thudded next to his head and he heard the hiss of a silenced bullet. He heaved himself up and was over. Safe, for now at least. But he wasn't going to be safe in Cambridge for long. These days it wasn't all guns and bullets. He had to be careful they did not kill him some other way. He could see most of Cambridge from the roof of the chapel.

They would be waiting but they could not wait long in college – not this time. Their orders would be specific – kill the target and don't get caught. Above all, don't hurt anyone else. But still time to get out. He looked around. There was a door to a small tower at the southwest corner but it was locked. Just as well – they would have the exits from the chapel covered. He could stay and attract attention but best to get out and get far away.

Peering through the pierced Gothic parapet he took stock of the situation. His opponents were well concealed but with luck only expecting the obvious. If he could get off the chapel roof and across the river he would be safe.

In reality his predicament was nowhere near as serious as his opponents supposed. The courts and chapels of Cambridge colleges were easier to climb than they looked. In the 1930s it had been a popular undergraduate pastime. In those days most of the colleges were locked at ten o'clock. The great front doors bolted as in medieval days against the dangers of the night. The academic communities turned in on themselves. College porters patrolled the obvious and easy points of access. The women's colleges were secured even earlier. Any undergraduate out and about late at night had to have leave from his tutor and wear a college gown. They were easily spotted by the bulldogs and proctors who formed the university police – porters from the colleges and young often athletic dons who patrolled the streets of Cambridge keeping order. But human nature being what it was, there were always young men in pursuit of conviviality or female companionship who were reluctant to be locked in at night. They climbed in and out of the colleges undetected. Some of the more daring sort then developed these skills not for the pursuit of pleasure but for the thrill of climbing itself. There are no hills worth climbing nearby so what better way to keep in trim for the Alpine season than climbing the sheer faces and looming over-hangs of the university's own buildings. Most routes had been covered over the years and Jacot was comforted by the thought that there must be more than one way of the St James' Chapel roof.

Indeed there was: a workable route off the chapel, onto the roof of the library and then down onto the Bridge of Sorrows and then away. It was a sheer drop of some sixty feet onto the library roof. But horizontal bands of stone in the corner of the buttress would make it possible. A very chunky looking lightning conductor clamped periodically to the wall every few feet would make it easier. It was going to hurt his hands but it could be done.

Ninety seconds later without mishap he dropped lightly onto the library roof – unseen thanks to the medieval passion for screens and tracery which concealed him from the ground. But God his hands hurt and by now they were bleeding. He kept low and crawled the final few feet to where the library roof overlooked the bridge. He could see that in order to get onto the roof of the bridge he was going to have to jump for his life. But by then he would no longer be far above the town and if he slipped the worst that would be involved would be a dunking rather than death. The drop was twenty feet but just doable if he gripped the edge of the guttering and let himself down full length. He would have to push off with all his strength to avoid two large stone gargoyles obstructing his descent. He made it just and without any injury. A twisted ankle at this stage would be disastrous. He would lie low on the roof for some minutes – enough to make the opposition nervous. And then come to earth where they wouldn't expect him. It took only a short crouching run across the top of the bridge and a quick scramble down a nicely grooved buttress on the other side and he was once again at ground level.

He was fit for his very late forties. Nothing dramatic like running marathons but long brisk walks in the Dorset countryside at the weekends. Some jogging and a lot of press-ups during the week. And every year, without fail – skiing in Switzerland – preferably in the shadow of the Eiger.

He had slipped his iPhone into his pocket before bugging out. It was off. But you could in certain circumstances be followed even if the phone was off. Jacot could not be sure. In any case if the people who were trying to kill him were who he thought they were then they had access to all kinds of electronic surveillance equipment. There might be a van somewhere in Cambridge at this very moment listening out for him. And even if he managed to slip through the electronic net his opponents might have voice recognition software – if he spoke on a mobile phone or even a landline anywhere within a few miles of Cambridge the system would alarm and very quickly they could get a fix on him and that would be that. He dropped the iPhone gently into a hedge. There was only one thing for it – get out of Cambridge and then call for help. He ran all the way across "The Backs", slowing down only when he reached the Madingley Road. He wrapped his right hand which was oozing blood in a handkerchief, dusted himself down and took a deep breath. Sheltering in the shadowy lee of the hedge he looked carefully around checking to see that he was not being followed. There was plenty of traffic and a few people. It looked as though he had made it.

Actually he was feeling rather pleased with himself. He had outwitted, outclimbed and outrun a group of professional ex-special forces hit-men. Two had come into his rooms. There were probably at least four more in support. Not bad for a day's work. A few minutes later he hailed a taxi and within half an hour found himself in Ely. Celia Nevinson had given him an emergency number which he rang from a call box. It rang and rang and made some very odd noises but eventually someone picked up.

'Hello. Hello.'

'Daniel, are you OK?'

Jacot was amazed – the voice at the end of the line was Monica's.

'Dan don't explain. We have just found out. Where are you?'

'Ely, outside the cathedral.'

'Stay there. We are close by. Don't use a mobile phone. Not even your special one. Keep out of sight. Give us half an hour. We will be in a dark blue Mercedes with diplomatic plates.'

Jacot slipped into the cathedral. He was on the run and his initial exhilaration was giving way to fear. But entering one of England's greatest cathedrals was still a comforting experience and its recesses would provide a safe place to hide, at least for a short period. Unfortunately it was lighter inside than he remembered. There were no shadowy spaces or vast tombs in the nave that he could shelter behind. The Lady Chapel to his left was a blaze of light and too exposed – Cromwell's men had destroyed the stained glass in this their boss' home town. He was fairly sure his opponents had not followed him here but he still wanted to hide. Suddenly he was in the Choir. Slipping into the back row of the choir stalls, Jacot lay down on the floor. He couldn't be seen. The presence of others gave some safety as well. Shame there was no stained glass – it would have made it darker. Even the people he was up against would not want to kill him in broad daylight – or that's what he hoped.

It was a long half an hour but at last it was time to move. He took a circuitous route leaving the cathedral through a small door on the south side that led to the old monastic buildings. Meandering his way unchallenged through these he got himself into a position from which he could observe the West front. Sure enough there was a dark blue Mercedes parked a few feet away. Monica was in the back. The driver got out and walked slowly towards Jacot. A second man got out of the car and stood by the passenger door. Neither man was wearing dark glasses or an earpiece but it was clear the type of men they were.

'Bonjour Mon Colonel.' The tall Frenchman took Jacot's arm gently. Looking round all the time, he guided Jacot to the car and handed him firmly in. They drove slowly off north picking up speed once they left the town.

'Monica! Nice of you to give me a lift.'

'Daniel, give me your jacket. I need to check it. And let's look at your shoes. No mobile phone?'

'No', replied Jacot.

She gave him his jacket back. She looked closely at each of the heels on his shoes. 'No worries Mon Colonel, I think you are clean.' She then noticed his hands – the thin, taut grafted skin was bruised and bleeding. 'Look at your hands. For God's sake what have you been doing?'

Jacot laughed. 'Well, Monica, I had to leave pretty quickly and not exactly by the front door.'

'They look very painful, I will sort them out as soon as we get to the house.'

The car was going very fast by now and the flat north Cambridgeshire countryside sped past. Jacot was relieved. He looked at the backs of the heads of the men in front. Their hair was cut extremely short with a square neck. They could only be French. To be specific they could only be French soldiers or French Rugby players. They were speaking to each other in broadly accented French, but not the broad twang of the south. Something different perhaps from the mountains. He had met ski guides who spoke the same way. Anyway, whoever they were or wherever they were from, he was relieved to be with them. The pair or possibly group of men who had tried to kill him in Cambridge knew what they were doing. It was the strangest feeling of all – being rescued in your own country by a group of foreigners.

Monica cut into his thoughts, 'Daniel you must be wondering why it is us who have come to your rescue.'

'Well, I was rather. I assumed you were in London. Last time we met I thought you had just got off the train at Cambridge Station.'

She laughed. 'No, one of the back up team dropped me somewhere quiet and out of the way and I walked into the centre of Cambridge. For the first time. It was glorious.'

'I know. I was watching you from the Pizza restaurant. But I still assumed you had come from the station. Lady Nevinson made it clear that I could have a quick get out of jail card if I needed one but I assumed the whole thing would be British – some retired spooks or some SAS men working in private security – that sort of thing. Not the French Foreign Legion.'

Monica exchanged a few words with one of the men in front. 'They are not Legionnaires but Chasseurs Alpins. Mountain troops. Back last year from a tour in Afghanistan. Some of them volunteered for special duties and have ended up in the UK.'

'I am not sure I understand. French soldiers wandering around England?' He had seen some of the hardware barely concealed under the front seat. 'Armed French soldiers wandering around England? It hasn't happened for a thousand years or so.'

'It's a long story. The DCRI has safe houses in certain parts of England. The ones in East Anglia are used to rest and brief any agents we have in London or the Midlands. It's convenient for both areas. Most of our people are involved with keeping track of Islamist extremists. You seem to have a lot and you have not always been so good at keeping tabs on them. Remember the jibe of "Londonistan" – it originally came from us. Anyway, the houses also act as bases for immediate back-up – immediate reaction force in the British Army jargon, I think. Obviously, such intelligence installations are not declared to your government and if any of our people were to run into trouble then we would have to rescue them on our own. We could not expect your intelligence services to become involved and we would not wish to place an additional burden on your police forces. Lady Nevinson understands our system. Something alarmed Madame La Baronesse a few days ago and you were added to our list. It's no problem.'

Jacot did not know what to say. He mumbled something on the lines of these arrangements being most irregular.

Monica said, 'Before you get English and angry Lady Nevinson will be here this evening. It's a Friday if you have forgotten. She will explain what has been going on I hope. Let's just get you to a safe place, sort out your hands maybe give you a drink and then I will explain what I know so far. Lady Nevinson can do the rest. And then we all need to have a serious think about what we are going to do next. We'll be there in half an hour. Now you have got your breath back let me update you on the little plan we cooked up in the pizza restaurant.'

The car turned down a muddy lane which seemed to go on forever. At the end was a nondescript and rather dirty looking farmhouse. Only the windows were clean. They got out and walked towards the house.

XXVII

Jacot felt a depression of spirits. The prospect of being holed up in such a place was unappealing, even with alcohol and the company of the lissom Monica. But once through the peeling but stout front door the inside could not have been more different from his expectations. It was decorated like a modernised French farm-house in pastel shades. French hunting scenes hung on the wall and the furniture looked comfortable. The kitchen was a revelation – the latest equipment and a vast array of the most expensive pots and pans were piled neatly and high on smart fitted wooden shelves.

'Don't be surprised Daniel. You have a tradition of victory and discomfort. We were defeated in 1940 and humiliated. Those that fought on in France had to hide for much of the war. So we understand what it is to hide. In modern times at least we try to do it in comfort.'

She poured him a large glass of brandy and placed a medical kit on the table. He downed it in one. And then took a couple of painkillers. His hands were hurting seriously now. It was an intense pain made worse by the remembered pain of the past.

Taking his hands gently, she smiled. 'You've managed to scrape off small pieces from your various grafts. I can sort them out here but it is going to need some stitches and it will hurt. Let the brandy and the pills take effect first.'

It was excruciating but Monica worked quickly and the hands were not badly damaged. After a further glass of brandy Jacot lay down on the kitchen sofa and slept. When his eyes opened Monica was still sitting at the table.

'You have slept a while.'

'Well it's only the third time in my life that anyone has tried to kill me', replied Jacot laughing. Looking out of the window he could tell he was in England. And from the short car journey of the night before, admittedly at high speed, he knew he was still near Cambridge. But inside everything looked and smelled French. An Englishman just after his failed assassination would tuck into a proper breakfast – best thing in the British Army (apart from the people of course) thought Jacot. But when under the protection of French Intelligence it looked as though it would be coffee and croissants.

Monica poured the coffee and put a plate in front of him.

'Where are we?'

The door into the kitchen opened and out came an extremely tall Frenchman wearing a long mackintosh and carrying a weapon. He smiled at Jacot but said nothing and placed his FAMAS rifle on the sideboard. He took a cup of coffee and disappeared into the rest of the house taking his weapon with him. Jacot noticed the safety catch was on, meaning that the rifle was loaded and made ready with a round in the chamber. It looked as though they were expecting trouble. Jacot was amazed but relieved. They were being guarded by French soldiers – not in uniform but military nevertheless.

He was still in his bath when he heard a car pull up to the

front door. It must be Lady Nevinson. He hurriedly got dressed and went down the stairs into the sitting room. The fire was blazing. Both Monica and Celia Nevinson were smartly but informally dressed. They both smelt wonderful the way women do after a long lazy bath and the application of various expensive and seductive scents. A young man came in with a tray of glasses and a bottle of champagne.

'I didn't think we had anything to celebrate', said Jacot half in jest.

'We don't, Colonel, yet. But things are not so bad that we cannot have a civilized dinner on a Friday evening while we plot our next move and while I brief you both on our last moves in which you have both been involved.'

It was never a good sign when Celia Nevinson addressed him by his rank. But she smiled and asked Monica to put some music on. 'Preferably happy and preferably Mozart. It relaxes the good colonel.'

It wasn't just the women who smelt good. There was something that smelled quite impressive happening in the kitchen as well. And then the wonderful sound of Mozart filled the room. It was "Soave sia il vento" – a duet from *Cosi Fan Tutte*. Appropriate for a safe house thought Jacot. They were, after all, in hiding because things were not quite what they seemed.

Monica introduced the young man as Alphonse. 'He is a chef at the embassy in London and from time to time helps us with our work. Sometimes he is just a very good chef, at others he is just pretending to be a chef. As you might expect his speciality is North African cuisine.' The young man poured the champagne cheerfully and went back to the kitchen.

Trust the French to have a chef in their safe house.

Actually the young man seemed to be a hybrid – a kind of chef-spook combination, useful in the dingy North African suburbs of Paris. But thank God he was here. If he had been hiding out with the British it would be warm sugary tea and corned beef sandwiches, or endless curries and Coronation Street and even then the expenses would not be admissible.

Celia Nevinson stood up in a swirl of silk and cashmere and sat on the fire seat. 'I think I had better update you both on what has been going on – particularly you Jacot, since you came very close to being murdered last night. But also you Monica. We are hugely grateful that you have been able to help us out at short notice. To be honest it was something of a desperate throw. I have been both appalled and pleasantly surprised at the extent of your intelligence set up here. But that's for another time. We have been watching various things all day since the attempted murder and we are not sure who was behind it – but we do know the men who came to Cambridge last night. Six Bosnian Serbs who used to be involved with Arkan, the Bosnian Serb war criminal and ethnic cleanser. They were former Special Forces types who, when not running prostitutes and drugs, undertook occasional assassinations. They were good but not that good, thank God. They had come to our notice a few months ago – as you probably know there are some Serb families that take a dim view of Tony Blair for his part in the bombing of Belgrade in 1998 but we do not know yet who was paying the bill. I hope we will find out today.'

'Perhaps we should try to find the Serbs and get the information from them?' suggested Jacot.

Nevinson looked away and said quietly 'I am afraid our

Serb assassins won't be able to help us and they won't be able to take their case to the European Court of Human Rights either. They were victims in a way, but there are limits to what we will tolerate. They can't have been surprised when we came for them – not that they would have realized until too late. By the way', she continued 'only a very few people know what happened in Cambridge last night. I called the Master of St James' College this morning to say that you Jacot had been called suddenly to London. I fluttered my eyelashes or whatever the telephone equivalent is and he was happy enough. Another peerage I will have to lobby for I expect.'

The hairs on Jacot's neck stood up. He had long suspected it to be the case but this was the first time he had actually seen it. There it was in front of him, the iron fist of British Intelligence encased not in velvet but in cashmere and silk. It did not kill often – not in this country anyway. But it would if it had to. Given that Lady Nevinson had serious doubts about the loyalty and reliability of some elements of our intelligence agencies it seemed unlikely that she would have turned to them to dispose of a half dozen troublesome Serb assassins. He wondered who she had used for the killings. It would have been a decision taken by her alone without any political authorisation. How could there have been any? Strange, wonderful and mysterious things were discussed in the tastefully lit recesses of Downing Street, but not murder.

It was strangely reassuring in a world of so much equivocation and regulation. This handsome, beautifully dressed woman in her early sixties was answering every day the age-old question "Who Guards the Guardians?" It was almost a whiff of the 18th century. Individuals could act decisively in defence of the national interest or just plain common sense and everyone pretty much agreed what those interests were. We used to hang pirates then. Now we give them asylum. In the last minutes of their lives perhaps the six Serbs thought they would be arrested and given a cup of tea. Their bodies would never be found. It was partly good security house-keeping, partly a warning to others. The British State still had fangs.

Jacot knew better than to ask any more about the men, but felt another question was appropriate. 'Any idea who commissioned the hit?'

Her pale blue eyes met his. 'Who do you think?' There was anger in them – a blazing anger. But there was also fear. 'I will have proof soon. And once we have it we will act. For now let's enjoy being with our French allies in the most comfortable safe house I have ever seen.'

Dinner was magnificent. The French had clearly made an effort to produce food which they felt their English allies would enjoy. It's what the spooks at the Rue de Nélaton thought would go down well and they were right. The starter was inevitably a prawn cocktail; a little joke, no doubt, by Gilles Navarre. But with just a hint of garlic in the dressing. The brown bread and butter was perfect, thinly cut in a way Jacot could never manage in his flat. Quite how the physics of cutting bread translucently thin worked Jacot wasn't sure. The only places that seemed to achieve the required thinness were the best London Clubs. The wine was a Chablis, flinty dry and ice cold. French spooks had a lot in common with the fellows of St James' College, Cambridge. The main course was a Lamb Tagine meltingly, sweetly tender served with couscous and a salad accompanied by the DCRI's excellent house red Burgundy.

Once again they were in front of the fire. Monica was regaling them with accounts of her time as an undercover agent in the northern Paris suburb of Saint Denis, burial place of French kings from Louis Capet to poor old Louis XVI. But amid the gothic splendours it was almost as if the battle of Poitiers had never been won. Much of the banlieue had now been taken over by Muslim fundamentalists.

In the corner of the room was a small steel briefcase containing a blue telephone. Nevinson glanced at it from time to time during dinner. The conversation was jolly enough but the dinner party had the slightly forced jollity of a family waiting for exam results they expected to be bad.

In the end, much to Jacot's surprise, the blue phone purred rather than rang. Nevinson started at the noise.

'Madame la Baronesse', said Monica. 'I am sure it's for you.'

Nevinson walked slowly, almost reluctantly, over to the phone and picked it up.

'Hallo Gilles', was all she said. And then she listened. It wasn't like a social conversation. It was pure business. Everyone knew in the room what kind of information was being passed. There were no "are you sures" or "is this definite?" All she said at the end was thank you and then she put the phone down. She was a beautiful woman and lucky to have a slightly olive skin. But as she walked back to the table she was sheet white. She moved slowly, sat down at the table, took a long slow sip of her wine and turned to Jacot. She smiled and said very softly 'I'm afraid Colonel that it was an American hit. Probably not officially sanctioned. The operatives, I think they call them, were Serbs, but the money was courtesy of some sort of secret offshore fund. It is clear who was behind this but needless to say there won't be any finger-prints so we can prove it. Proving it probably wouldn't help in any case.'

'For sure?'

'For sure.'

'How do we know?'

'Most of the six lost their families in Kosovo – murdered by Albanian militants. Usually it was the other way round, but not always. So they were victims too. The world forgot that the Serbs were ethnically cleansed as well. They came to the attention of the Americans and were recruited by their Black Ops people to help out in Afghanistan. Mountain men with a strong grudge against Muslims. Ideal fodder for the CIA Black Ops people.

'Some loose talk about Tony Blair brought them to our attention. The money and the man-hours spent on that man's security would bring tears to your eyes Jacot. It was odd though that we could not get anything about them from their Afghan days. GCHQ drew a blank. We didn't think they were that serious about Blair – it's the kind of thing Serbian militia men say after too much slivovitz. All the children in Kosovo are called Toniblair. All the hard men in Serbia want to imitate Lee Harvey Oswald.'

'Not just Serbian militia men Lady Nevinson.'

She laughed. 'It does cause NSA and GCHQ a few problems. So many people seem to hate the man it's hard to tell the wood from the trees. But the guys after you were the real thing and capable of killing both Blair and you.'

How flattering thought Jacot – to share an assassin with the great man himself.

'Anyway, after last night I asked the French to check up on the men. They had been trained at some point in America. In exchange for disposing of you Jacot they were promised new identities and US citizenship for themselves and some additional family members. Life, liberty and the pursuit of happiness as you might say. And on a mobile phone found on one of the men guess what?'

'Don't tell me. The suspense is too much. Dixwell's number.'

'Well we thought it likely. So we rang it. Our friend answered and will be meeting us here tomorrow. He was I think surprised and very rude.'

'No cut-outs. No false trails. Just a plain vanilla telephone number?'

'Yes, Jacot. I can see why. There is no need for caution or secrecy. Why bother with it if you are in a country where you believe you can behave with impunity? And if they had got you that would have been it. Our Serbian militiamen would have been spirited out of the country to new lives on a trailer park out west. And even now there doesn't look as though we can do much to John Dixwell the Third.'

'I thought it was the Fourth.'

'Yes you may be right. "Whatever" as our American allies say.'

'What are we going to do Jacot? Go to the police? Tell the Security Service that the CIA killed Verney and that we have uncovered a CIA plot to kill some Cabinet Office people – who by the way are spying for the French. Tell the prime minister? I reckon friend Dixwell thinks he can get away with it.'

'Why don't we just kill Dixwell when he comes tomorrow

morning? Our French chums have a lot of firepower upstairs.'

'Come off it Jacot. We would be signing our own death warrants and you know it. Let's get a good night's sleep and enjoy the hospitality of our French allies.'

XXVIII

Ford's Theatre,
511 Tenth Street, NW, Washington DC

In the middle of a rainstorm a white van with District of Columbia plates drew up outside Ford's Theatre in Washington. The driver sat for nearly an hour reading a newspaper and smoking cigarettes. But he wasn't waiting for the theatre to open. He had no interest in drama and his van barely attracted a second glance. Passers by on the pavement, if they noticed that sort of thing, might have found the smell of the cigarettes stronger and rougher than those most Americans were used to. The van's specially reinforced suspension meant that it did not look heavily laden, even though there were four men in the back and at least a hundredweight of sophisticated electronic equipment. The heavy sound-proofing meant that it sounded like an ordinary, empty van. Just as there was no sound coming from the van a different kind of insulation, more usually found in stealth bombers, ensured that the equipment in the back did not produce an electronic signature of any kind. You had to be careful in Washington. Security was tight for the President and other senior figures in the American political, military and intelligence hierarchy. A van or an apartment that emanated strange electronic signals would soon find itself raided by the FBI, or worse.

Ford's Theatre is more usually on the tourist rather than

the intelligence itinerary. It was infamously where President Lincoln was shot at 10.15 pm on the evening of April 14 1865 while watching a performance of *Our American Cousin* – just five days after the surrender of General Robert E Lee at Appomattox and the end of the American Civil War. By a strange and lucky quirk of fate General Ulysses S Grant and his wife had refused the invitation at the last minute. But the street had not been chosen by the men in the van for its historical connotations. It had another more important quality. From much of it you could see a small nondescript federal government building at the end of the street, or to put it another way, lots of very convenient parking places in the street had line of sight onto the records annexe of the Federal Bureau of Investigation whose headquarters in the J Edgar Hoover Building is in the same part of the city. Line of sight was what the computer technicians and cryptologists in the back of the van needed to accomplish their task. They didn't need to steal anything or destroy anything or insert a virus into the strongly protected FBI computer system. All they had to do was insert two lines of text into a file on a background check carried out on a federal employee a long time ago.

The FBI's background files into those American men and women who came forward to join their intelligence services were well protected. They were an intelligence gold-mine and those responsible for protecting them knew it. The American system was similar to the British system of positive and later enhanced vetting, introduced in the UK after the Cambridge Spies saga of the 1950s. If you came forward to join any of the United States' non-military intelligence agencies then the FBI was responsible for a detailed background check. The checks and the documents that went with them were regarded as definitive, way exceeding the evidential standards required in a federal court of law.

The original plan had been to activate a sleeper agent within the records establishment who would make the necessary amendments to the file. But the FBI's security had proved too tough to break in this way. The file could be accessed without too much difficulty – their agent was after all a senior FBI official, but it proved impossible to accomplish the task without leaving a record that the amendment was recent. For the plan to succeed it had to look as if the two key lines of text had been in the electronic document since it was computerised in the late 1980s. As far as they knew the original paper documents had been destroyed. They would have to trust their luck on that. They had then considered trying to hack into the system. Again it was more difficult than it looked. Newspapers on both sides of the Atlantic often ran articles about students hacking into American defence and intelligence computer systems. But it was much more difficult to get in and out of a system without being detected than many thought.

The insoluble technical issue for a hacker was that there appeared to be an air barrier between certain parts of the system and the outside world. In other words there was no electronic connection that could be exploited. Much the same technical problems had been discovered by the Israelis as they planned to attack the computers controlling Iran's nuclear programme in early 2008 by introducing the so-called Stuxnet virus – a simple enough piece of code which played havoc with the centrifuges processing uranium by turning them on and off at random – it was as if a naughty child with a sugar high was in control of the master switch. The Israeli solution had been elegant and simple. Ensure that Iran's nuclear scientists were bombarded at international conferences by all kinds of electronic freebies including memory sticks of the most stylish and expensive kind. The most sensitive parts of the system were almost impossible to hack into. The Israelis were correct in thinking that it would only be a matter of time before someone, somewhere or a member of someone, somewhere's family inserted one into a lap-top that would later become connected to the Iranian nuclear Intranet. You cannot build a nuclear bomb without sending emails.

It was going to be difficult but with luck they would pull it off. They would still need to activate their sleeper but in a much less risky role. The windows of the building were protected from electronic intrusion by a special copper film on the inside. An electrical charge run through the copper molecules embedded in the glass made each pane behave as if it were a sheet of metal – even though, of course, it was still possible to see through the glass. The glass was also strengthened so that it did not vibrate in response to sound waves. In other words if you directed a powerful microphone at the glass it was impossible to hear what was being said inside. The system was about as good as it could be. Variations of it protected the White House and other sensitive installations.

It had one weakness. Once a month the FBI tested its back-up power generators. As an organisation that relied on a bountiful electricity supply to power its computer analysis and country-wide communications, it could not risk being caught in the kind of power cuts that from time to time afflicted parts of the United States, particularly in winter. Sensibly and properly, the Agency had bought a series of powerful petrol-run electricity generators stored in the basement of the building, hooked up ready instantly to take over the power load in the event of an interruption. Or almost instantly. And it was the almost instantly that had given the men in the van outside Ford's Theatre their break. For perhaps a hundredth of a second at most the electric current through the copper molecules in the glass was interrupted as the mains current died and the generators switched in. The minute interruption did not even make a computer screen flicker. But it was enough.

Like the highly efficient organisation it is, the FBI tested these procedures every month or so. The precise dates and times of the test were highly classified. But if someone knew when it was going to happen they could get a tiny packet of information through the temporarily ineffective shield in a burst transmission and into the hard-drive of a computer, provided someone was standing near the window with a specialised modem. If the little packet of information had been prepared properly then it would find its way to the correct file and nestle there as if it had been there all along without leaving any footprints in the electronic snow. An attempt to hack into the system through the internet and it would alarm in short order. But the FBI security people had never envisaged an 'outside job' or at least the men and women in the van hoped they hadn't.

The DCRI's only agent within the FBI had been relieved that the instruction from Paris had been so undemanding. During the run-up to the First Gulf War she had been far busier and that comfortable expatriate retirement to a Provençal farmhouse seemed that much further away.

The date and time of the monthly generator test was dutifully transmitted to Paris via a dead letter drop outside the Smithsonian Institute. The instructions she picked up a week later were simple: stand near a switched on computer – not her own – close to a window carrying a tiny modem as the generator test took place. To her horror French technicians had originally planned to conceal the modem in a cigarette lighter, unaware that no one in the modern day FBI smoked at work or would even dare to admit smoking at home. In the end they secreted the gadget in a lipstick which was easy enough to slip into a pocket.

Ironically, Ford's Theatre was a suitable backdrop for this very high tech operation which was all about revenge. President Lincoln had been killed there by John Wilkes Booth in revenge for the fate of the Confederacy in the recently finished Civil War. The United States authorities in their turn would wreak a terrible revenge on Booth and his fellow plotters for their crime. Five of them in all were hanged within a couple of months. The doctor who had set the leg Booth had broken leaping from the presidential box onto the stage to make his escape received a life sentence. The unfortunate stage-hand at the theatre who had, possibly innocently, held Booth's horse out the back during the assassination received six years hard labour. According to his testimony at his trial he was held in prison hooded and manacled throughout.

The sophisticated electronic operation taking place in the street in front of the theatre 147 years later had more in common with the fate of Booth and his fellow plotters than the assassination of a president. It was an official operation by a state designed to take out a senior official of another state.

It was designed as both revenge and a warning to others. A great deal of discussion had taken place in offices far far away on a different continent as to how it should be done. Some had recommended violence. Many had been tempted by the idea of an assassination. But in the end cooler heads had prevailed.

No violence would be involved. There would be no gunpowder or blood just high pulse electronic signals lasting nanoseconds – intended not to kill but to destroy a reputation, a career and a livelihood permanently.

XXIX

DCRI Safe House
– secret location outside Ely

Dixwell and his sidekicks arrived just after twelve. Maybe they thought they had been invited to lunch. He started up as soon as he was through the front door. 'Jesus you Limeys are so far up your own ass. Just who do you guys think you f…..g are?' The college tie and the preppy suit were still there but the thin veneer of East Coast civilization had fallen away. The America of the Constitution and powdered wigs was gone. This was the America of Guantanamo Bay and the internment of its Japanese citizens in the Second World War, with just a touch of Hurricane Katrina added. Aggressive. Sure of its own judgments. Determined to impose its will come what may. But underneath not as sure of itself as it pretended. And luckily, not always competent.

Lady Nevinson glared at him. It was powerful stuff. Even Dixwell looked a little shifty. Jacot laughed inwardly. The big time CIA baron was intimidated by this powerful Englishwoman.

'You killed them both didn't you, General Verney and that poor young girl, Pirbright?' Nevinson spoke slowly, not with fury but disdain and contempt. 'And we know how you did it.'

Dixwell looked genuinely surprised.

Lady Nevinson continued, 'Some dubious poison which I can't pronounce concealed in a Ventolin inhaler. Perhaps you had been given the antidote beforehand or maybe when you got into the embassy car. Anyway, our toxicology people tell me that a minute amount of the poison if breathed in would cause a ghastly sort of living death within a few minutes to be followed by death itself an hour or so later. It was a cruel way to kill a man Dixwell.'

Dixwell's eyes glistened. It was almost as if he was drunk. He wound his body up to give his reply as if he had rehearsed it many times. He probably had in front of his shaving mirror. Jacot knew what to expect. Men like Dixwell had been living their lives as if in a film since just after 911. And predictably, it started – a rehashed version of Jack Nicholson's speech in *A Few Good Men* but with more swearing and less convincingly delivered.

'So f…..g what. People who get in the way get whacked. We are fighting for civilization. Jeez don't you f…..g people see that? Are you completely mad? General Verney had lost his bottle, lost his guts, lost his will for the fight. Do you think we were just going to stand around while he tried to get your troops out of Afghanistan early? Or worse, much worse, go soft on the Iranians. That's the next conflict. It's going to happen. It has to happen. We just couldn't afford the likes of f…..g Verney. We gave him a chance with that little radio blast from his past. But he wouldn't take it, the a…..e.'

Nevinson sat up straight, the essence of English hauteur. 'Please stop swearing Mr. Dixwell. It's not necessary and not customary here, at least not in front of women. I very much doubt it was allowed when you were growing up in the States.'

Jacot and Zaden exchanged glances. If it hadn't been for the Neanderthal CIA muscle in the room they would have been enjoying themselves.

Dixwell continued, still in Jack Nicholson tribute mode. 'I am going back to Washington on promotion. And there is nothing you or your crappy little country can do about it. And there's nothing the crappy f…..g French can do either. And nothing your ludicrous colonel friend with the burned hands can do.' He turned on Jacot. 'Who the f…k do you think you are with those black gloves – the Count of Monte Cristo? A Falklands War wound? Take my advice, next time get off the ship earlier. Except there won't be a next time because they are going back to the Argentines where they belong. Dial M for Malvinas.' Dixwell clearly enjoyed this unrehearsed joke.

The muscle laughed, shoulders heaving, like Hollywood gangsters.

'As for the young lady. She just got in the way. That's life. Remember two and a half thousand innocent souls were murdered on 911. Sometimes you just have to walk on the dark side.'

Jacot let lady Nevinson do all the talking. He watched the exchange from the centre of the room. Quiet, but never taking his eyes off Dixwell's chunky hands or the hands of his henchmen. How ironic that a violent confrontation with the CIA might turn on who was quicker on the draw. Jacot would certainly be able to kill Dixwell and maybe one of the goons. But it was going to be tight. Monica was armed – or rather he hoped she had her MPA-15 pistol with her. But Nevinson wasn't. On balance, Jacot was hoping to avoid a gun battle. At best in this enclosed space it would be a score draw. Which meant that if anything did kick off just about everyone would get killed or wounded.'

Jacot stepped slowly forward and picked up an iPad in scarlet Cabinet Office livery from a side table. 'Dixwell, I think you should understand that you are not in as strong a position as you think.' Jacot shuffled some photographs on the iPad. 'Look at these. Can't see the inspector general of the CIA being too amused. Or Mrs. Dixwell either.'

Dixwell made to grab the iPad. Jacot took a step back, hearing at the same time the dull metallic click of safety catches being eased on Famas high velocity rifles. The goons' hands moved in their pockets.

Jacot said 'Easy Dixwell. Easy. Here it is. Slowly now.'

Dixwell looked at the photographs. He sneered. 'So what, Monte Cristo? OK, I was humping some dame – big deal!'

Jacot looked him straight in the eye keeping one hand on the Browning 9 Millimetre pistol in his pocket. 'It tells me two things Dixwell. One, you are not as good as you think you are. The head of the CIA station in London caught in a honey trap. Sloppy Dixwell, very sloppy.'

Dixwell glared and chewed his gum manically. The look wasn't hatred or contempt but pity and incomprehension. The truth of it was that he was far, far gone.

'Langley couldn't care less. These things happen. Mrs. Dixwell might not be so amused. But hell maybe it's time I was moving on. You know it's weird living in London. All the senior people here seem to be still married to their first wives. Not so much in Washington. Even the generals ditch their West Point sweethearts and move onto something more upmarket when they hit the big time. Same in the Agency.'

Jacot held his gaze and said, 'The other thing it tells me Dixwell is that you have allowed yourself to be corrupted.

What have young prostitutes got to do with the war on terror? Why does working hard for your country allow you to behave like that?'

'It's not against the law. What are you, a f.....g revivalist preacher?'

'As if you cared. Actually, Dixwell in this case it is against the law. She looks nearly twenty but I can assure you when you met her she was just under eighteen.'

'Come off it Jacot, the age of consent is sixteen. Less in the Southern states I come from.' He grinned unpleasantly.

'Normally it is. They are fairly tolerant of these matters. But professionals have to be eighteen. The Code Napoleon gets the vapours about that. The photos were taken in Paris. The girl in question is French. You were on French soil subject to their laws. And without diplomatic immunity – you are accredited to the court of St James not the French Republic. If you are not careful Dixwell we could hand you over to the French authorities. Imagine the scandal.' Jacot looked around the room. 'In fact we could hand you over to them now and they could no doubt render you to some remote farm-house on the other side of the Channel.' It wasn't much but it seemed to put Dixwell off his balance.

Dixwell looked angrier than before. He was clearly a man who was used to pushing or rather bulldozing difficulties out of the way. Another sign of corruption. The best intelligence officers found ways round obstacles or tried to turn them to their advantage. Guile was the cardinal virtue of the spy, not anger. But America had been angry since 911 and Dixwell simply reflected both the popular and official mood. The muscles in his face were moving, almost rippling with rage.

'You put those photos on the street or send them to Langley and you are a dead man Jacot, mark my f…..g words. In fact I'm tempted to shoot you now.'

Dixwell was bluffing. Jacot knew it. Dixwell knew it. Even the goons appeared to understand it. No one went for their guns.

He glared round the room. 'I'm out of this Mickey Mouse country tonight. Don't even bother checking your airports. You don't seriously think we ever bother with the official system. Not that it would be a problem I understand. If a Jumbo Jet in Al Qaeda colours landed at Heathrow stuffed full of suicide bombers you'd probably let it through and put them up for the night in a hotel. Good bye, National Security Adviser. You know what I would do if I had your job – get a f…..g grip of your borders. Good bye Monte Cristo. Don't forget to check under your car every day for the rest of your life and take care crossing the road with that lady-friend of yours.'

With that he was gone – the goons in hot pursuit.

'What time is it in Jerusalem?' asked Jacot.

Nevinson glared at Jacot.

'Well, you could have done something. Why didn't you help me?'

'To be honest I was concentrating on working out how to get my gun out. It's been a while since I used a pistol and my hands got chewed up in the hair-raising escape from the Serbs. Monica is also carrying but CIA muscle can be very quick on the draw. And like the Russian Mafia, and their own Mafia they pack a lot of firepower. I am sure we would have managed though.'

Monica laughed, and produced a machine pistol which had been leaning on the far side of the fire screen and her pistol from a shoulder holster. 'They weren't going to kill us. In any case they would have clocked our guards outside. They didn't come for a shoot out. They heavies were only carrying side-arms for self protection.' She removed the magazine and made it safe.

Jacot felt just a little embarrassed as he made his Browning 9mm pistol safe and put it on top of the mantelpiece above the fire. While the Americans had been there the fire had blazed, as if drawing energy and sustenance from the confrontation. But now it was burning weakly and Jacot threw two more logs gently onto it from the basket.

Celia Nevinson flopped into an armchair with a glass of wine. She looked exhausted. 'It's so humiliating. He was right in some ways. We are powerless in our own country and completely powerless when we come up against the Americans. They are a law unto themselves. He was right as well about our borders. My guess is if we are not more on the ball we will end up losing the Falklands.'

Jacot laughed, 'He was right about getting off the *Oliver Cromwell*. So many people have been kind enough to point that out over the years.'

'Jacot why are you laughing? He's going back to Washington scot free.'

'Not quite. What time is it in Jerusalem?'

'What do you mean what time is it in Jerusalem? You keep saying that. It's like a Jewish wedding – next year in Jerusalem. Who cares? Pull yourself together Jacot.'

Jacot, who normally went red when Lady Nevinson ticked

him off, looked unperturbed. 'What are they, four hours ahead at this time of year? So it's early evening.'

Lady Nevinson looked puzzled. He walked to the windowsill and picked up an iPad.

'Lady Nevinson look at this.'

'Jacot please. This is no time for guardsmen's parlour games.'

'Read the headline.'

Nevinson reluctantly took the iPad and scrolled down the front page. 'Of what interest to me is an unofficial Israeli Defense Force website.' She looked up at Jacot.

'It's semi-official actually, and the entries are moderated by the IDF press people. Read the headline on the first article.'

A moment later she laughed. It was a young and girlish laugh. Attractive and amused. There was nothing gloating about the sound but the facial expression was less innocent, menace, relief and resentment were all there.

'How did you do it Jacot?'

'Well actually it's mainly down to Monica. We thought hard about how to permanently damage or terminate the career of a US official who appears otherwise untouchable in a plausible way. Once we were starting to realize what had happened to Verney we got some people to look into Dixwell's life. See if there was anything irregular. Girlfriends. Unpaid taxes. What you might call an Al Capone or indirect approach. The Feds could never pin the Valentine's Day Massacre on him. They never had the proof, and even if they had getting witnesses to testify would have been hard work – if not impossible. Capone was a law unto himself for a long time.

'Too many people like that in the modern world, including

some intelligence services corrupted by the whole war on terror thing. Very often that means that some of the individuals involved get carried away in other ways. But not Dixwell. We found just the one slip, in Paris of all places. He was there in April 2010 for the big meeting with General McChrystal. Remember that one – too much beer and McChrystal's staff getting too mucko chummo with a *Rolling Stone* magazine reporter. Well Dixwell was in town as well. Turned out that he was quite a mate of McChrystal's. All kinds of Special Forces types and Black Ops people were in town, their guard was down. Monica you should tell the story.'

She smiled. 'They were all staying at the Hotel Westminster near the Opera and drinking heavily in Kitty O'Shea's pub nearby. It is popular with certain types of American tourist. They were delayed in Paris by the volcanic ash spewing out of Iceland. We did not originally intend to have a look at what was going on but we got a telephone call from the concierge. The mask may have slipped a little just now, but what you see is what you get. Devoted family man. Good college. Staunch Roman Catholic. There appears to have been just one slip in Paris. And he was right, we doubt Langley would care much about a drunken and lascivious weekend in Paris in the company of the US Special Forces. The only thing completely out of control was his patriotism.'

'And his manners', added Nevinson.

Monica said something unintelligible in French. But the gist was clear. 'So in the end, helped by our best signals people, we decided to go after his reputation. It was electronically quite difficult I understand. What we did was tamper with the records of some newspapers in North Carolina where Dixwell had been a student. That wasn't too bad. But to make it stick we had to make an after-the-fact entry into Dixwell's background checks when he joined CIA. The files are held in impressively secure conditions by the FBI in Washington, who actually did most of the checking. Dixwell's bosses will be downloading them as we speak. The doctored photographs of a young Dixwell collecting money for the PLO on the campus of the University of North Carolina are one thing. They are a very skilled job, but backed up by a confidential personnel file from the late 1970s confirming that Dixwell had collected money for the PLO – then they are dynamite.'

They all sat down for an excellent lunch. Like many involved in the intelligence world they were good at compartmentalizing their lives. All thoughts of murder, blackmail and looming crises in the Middle East and the South Atlantic were put behind them. Alphonse produced another excellent meal. He and the Chasseur Alpins joined Monica and her English guests. The group talked of skiing and food and children. Lady Nevinson was at her most vivacious and charming. Both the soldiers had families back in the Haut Savoie. Their stint in the UK meant extra money and possibly promotion. So although they missed their families they thought the separation was worth it.

XXX

They sat in silence for some miles and then Lady Nevinson said, 'I must write to the commanding officer of those young soldiers. They have done us a great service. Let's see if we can't get them promoted to Chef Caporal or whatever the next step is for them.'

'That would be a fine gesture. Probably best to go through the Military Attaché in Paris. I'll have a word with him when we get back', replied Jacot. He paused. Better get it over with. 'I am afraid, Lady Nevinson, that it's worse than we thought.'

'I know Jacot. Dixwell was lying about why he killed Verney and then Pirbright. It had nothing to do with Afghanistan or Iran. Although he was happy to let us think that.'

'I was hoping you shared my suspicions.'

'That's why I never mentioned poor Charlotte Pirbright's memory stick.'

'Quite, Lady Nevinson. I am not sure the French quite understand. They worked out that the second half of the data was a so-called cadaver cipher. But I'm not sure they worked out what it meant. At least Monica could not see the significance when the French signals people had a look at the data on the stick.'

'I have my own ideas but what's your assessment?'

'Well I have had a look at a slightly fuller text now. A bit more has come to light after some more technical work by the French. To be honest it looks to me like some kind of forward contract – an agreement to sell oil at 40 dollars a barrel after a certain date – the 24th May 2015. The first half of the document was in English and the second half Spanish.'

'24th May, I wonder what the significance is? For some reason from my dim and distant past I'm fairly sure it was Queen Victoria's birthday.'

'It's National Day in Argentina. The anniversary of throwing off the Spanish yoke.'

'What's the price of oil these days?'

'100 dollars plus a barrel. Whoever negotiated the contract has got quite a discount.'

'Would you say it would be worth killing a British general to conceal such a contract?'

'I think it depends who the contract is between', said Jacot. 'Argentina, obviously. The other party remains obscure but certainly an English-speaking country shall we say? Both parties assume that all the oil in the Falkland islands will be under Argentine control by that date. I would go further. Perhaps the English-speaking party to the contract intends to help the Argentines gain control of the Falklands in exchange for many years of lovely cheap oil.'

Lady Nevinson changed the subject. 'I understand that there is some good news on that memory stick. Scott's ill-fated expedition may have got to the Pole first if the Verney-Pirbright research eventually stands up.' She smiled. 'In these grim times that is heartening news. Good old Captain Scott.'

Lady Nevinson dropped Jacot in Montagu Square. 'Get some sleep. MI5 are still outside your door but watch your security. I will expect you in the office tomorrow. I know it's a Sunday but we need to think this through.'

XXXI

National Security Adviser's Office,
10 Downing Street, Whitehall, London SW1

The door was slightly ajar and Lady Nevinson was on the phone. Jacot waited. 'Come in Colonel, come in. I can tell you are out there.' She pointed to the coffee and went back to her phone call. 'My dear Air Chief Marshal,' she continued, 'I am not telling you how to run your marvellous service, to which we owe our very existence as an independent country after all. I am just suggesting that you might need to modify your plans to reinforce the Falklands.' She took a sip of her coffee and listened to the Air Chief Marshal's booming voice. 'Well, I'm fairly sure it's the question the PM will ask you next week and the more prepared you are the more pleased the PM will be.' She winked at Jacot. 'No, I very much doubt that the next Chief of Defence Staff will be a soldier. Afghanistan is coming to an end. And remember how the PM revels in detail, so the number of tankers required and so forth will be important... Yes, yes not from Ascension Island but from the French bases at Dakar or Libreville... until the airport at St Helena is up and running. Good-bye Air Chief Marshal.

'I think we probably worked out what the hell was going on in the car last night Jacot. But I have had a bit more background information this morning', said Nevinson.

'From our people in Buenos Aires?'

'Curiously, no. From our people in the City who understand the oil markets. The protective web we have thrown the Falkland Islands is pretty effective. Actually, I wouldn't even call it a web. Any suspicious activity about those islands and the information soon wends its merry way to London without us even having to ask. Anyway, I hope you are feeling better and the hands are hurting less.'

'Yes, thank you. Forgive me for picking up fag-ends but I listened into your conversation with, I assume, the Chief of the Air Staff.'

'Yes. Sweet man. And yes I read your report on the Falklands. Ascension Island is the weakest link. It's a British colony but pretty much run as far as I can see by the US Air Force and NASA. So we are putting into place a Plan B at least until the new airport on St Helena is ready in the next few years. So you don't have to worry about it while you are on leave.'

'Leave, Lady Nevinson?'

'Yes a month's leave. You were technically on leave when this whole Verney saga began. In fact a month's leave in France. You will be safer there for now. Here is an emergency number for you to call at the embassy just in case. And a month's pay and diplomatic allowances for a colonel attached to the Paris Embassy, including a lavish entertainment allowance.' She passed Jacot a thick pile of 100 Euro notes. There's a British diplomatic passport as well – in a different name.'

'When do you want me back?'

'I'm not sure. Report to the embassy a month from tomorrow for orders. Don't use a cash machine or a mobile phone in the meantime. And take your gun.'

'What about the French authorities?'

'They won't be a problem. I understand from Gilles that an agent of the DCRI has already been allocated to look after you for the duration.'

Jacot said good-bye and made for the door. As he was closing it Lady Nevinson looked up and said, 'Give her my regards.'